Eyes in the Fire

Eyes in the Fire

Deborah Grabien

St. Martin's Press
New York

Quality Printing and Binding by:
Orange Graphics
P.O. Box 791
Orange, VA 22960 U.S.A.

To Nicholas, who doesn't laugh at the mixture of
women and power.

The author wishes to take this opportunity to achieve a few small
necessities.

Firstly, a grateful thank-you to the inhabitants of the charming town
of Okehampton; although I have taken some liberties with your
topography, this tinkering has been done for the purposes of
entertainment. This must serve as my excuse, since the town itself
requires no alteration to improve it.

Secondly, to point out that any similarities in people or situation to
anyone living or dead is not merely coincidental; it's improbable.

And, lastly, a passing sigh for the memory of a soft wet day, eating a bag
lunch at Okehampton Castle and waving farewell to Dartmoor, which
fixes itself so indelibly in the memory, when the meal was done.

Chapter 1

A light rain was falling on the M4, misting the road signs and slicking the asphalt. It was unseasonably chilly for August. Many of the cars heading into the country for the bank holiday weekend had their heaters going full blast; more than one driver, swearing under his breath, was forced to take his attention from the road in order to wipe steam from his windscreen.

One of these automobiles, a new Jaguar, faithfully kept the glowing promise of its advertisers: its heater was quiet and efficient and its glass showed clear beneath the gentle breath of its defogging system.

Julian Dunne had barely a thought for his superb car. It had cost him almost as much as his *pied à terre* in London, and he tended to regard it in much the same way. The car, like the small flat in Sloane Gardens, was elegant and functional; he had actively desired neither while acquiring both. The flat kept him housed during the four nights each week when he must stay in town and run his business; the car carried him out of London each Friday afternoon and back again on Monday morning. At the moment, it was bearing him home to the one place on earth, to the only things on earth, that he actually cared about.

The countryside around him was lovely, beautiful and fresh and above all so very green — surely nowhere on earth could be so green as this. The grey horizon, and massed clouds looked soft and unearthly. Julian smiled to himself, looking with love at the endless, uncompromising vista that swept away to the south -west.

'England's green and pleasant land,' he said aloud and, still smiling, turned the Jaguar on to the road that led through the town of Okehampton, past the ruins of Okehampton Castle, and then to the south and home.

The house called Four Shields sat perched on a small tor. It was surrounded by some twelve acres of gentle rolling hills, and the twelve acres were surrounded by a high stone wall. The grounds had an air of spacious privacy echoed harmoniously inside the house itself.

Four Shields had not gained its name from any actual shields. A small Georgian manor house, it had been commissioned by a Scotsman, one Duncan MacBride, made wealthy by the seaports of the south coast. The story was that Mrs MacBride had been barren since her marriage but no sooner had they moved into the serenity of their new home than she proceeded to produce four children, exquisite girls each more lovely than the last, in just under four years. Hence the original name of the house: not Four Shields but Four Chiels.

Sometime towards the end of Victoria's reign, the house changed hands and the name with it. Four Shields it became, down to the addition of a hideous Victorian window of stained glass that hung in the hall, depicting four fanciful crests. The Dunnes had lived there now for ten years. Their friends assumed that the glass remained because Victoriana was back in fashion whereas in fact the family had thought it far too funny to remove. For the rest it was a pleasing and placid house, in a beautiful and secluded setting.

Julian turned his car into the stables, now converted to a garage which would comfortably hold six vehicles. The Range Rover, his personal mechanical conqueror of the muddy wastes of Dartmoor, was in its proper place at the back. A green Volvo wagon, wet and slightly plastered with leaves, stood a bit too close to the wall; Marian had been out, and had come back by way of the country lanes with their low-hanging trees.

He lifted his briefcase from the Jaguar's back seat and went quickly through the partially covered passage that ran between garage and house. The front door, approached by steep stone stairs, was used mainly by guests, rarely by the family. He let himself in by the side door.

'Hello,' said a low voice behind him.

Marian Dunne, in her middle forties now, looked younger. This was due neither to artifice nor effort; she was simply one of those tall, strong-boned country Celts who never look their true age but can be taken for anything between twenty and eighty. Her hair, the short blue-black helmet inherited by her daughter, showed a few random streaks of grey but her face was smooth as a girl's, her eyes a deep and canny blue. She had a formidable store of intelligence and showed it unobtrusively.

'Here, darling, give me that coat. Don't stand there dripping.' Her voice matched her appearance; it was deep and slow, an accurate reflection of her contemplative nature. She was partly Welsh and partly Cornish, and embodied the best of both of those idiosyncratic cultures.

He handed her the Burberry, which in fact was fairly dry, and kissed her brow. 'Here you are. Are we alone, or do we expect Gemma this weekend?'

'Don't know. She called me yesterday to say she would try to make it down. Apparently there's a concert on, or some such thing. You know London.'

'To my cost,' he sighed, and followed her into the spacious family room, its high beamed ceiling making it look even larger than it was. 'I think I want a drink.'

'I'm sure you do. Gin and tonic?'

'Perfect.' He took the glass from her and took an appreciative swallow. 'Lovely weather,' he said, no hint of irony in his voice. 'I shall get a few days of tramping the moors in total privacy if this keeps up. What does the BBC have to say about it?'

She measured out a finger of gin for herself. 'Rain, rain and more rain. Might ease up on Sunday, might not — you know the

3

weather service. Puts a strain on the church picnic in Dowbridge, though. I spent an hour listening to Mrs. Rolling complain.'

Julian sank, grinning, into his favourite chair, and kicked his shoes off. 'To hell with the church picnic,' he said. 'I'll take being cut off from the tourists and the trippers over a pot of Jean Horn's lethal potato salad and marmite sandwiches any day.' He raised his glass in a mock toast. 'Long may it pour. What are we eating, by the way, and when?'

'Lancashire hotpot. It should be ready in about half an hour, maybe less.' She hesitated. 'Julian . . .'

'Mmmm?'

'I think I ought to tell you . . . I've had the Area Gas people from Dowbridge in.'

He raised an eyebrow at her. 'Have you now?'

Marian seemed nervous, which was highly unusual for her. 'It was very odd. Yesterday, right in the middle of the afternoon, I suddenly smelled smoke.'

Julian listened attentively. Fire is a great peril to those who do not choose to live in the city with every amenity close at hand; the fire brigade nearest to Four Shields was in Dowbridge, some fifteen miles away. Should a fire break out, the house stood a good chance of being completely destroyed before the brigade ever got there. 'Smoke? Did you find the cause?'

'No.' The monosyllable was curt even for Marian, who was habitually economical with words.

Julian stared at her. 'Come on, out with it. What is all this?'

She got to her feet. 'You'll think I'm crazy. I was in the kitchen, having a cup of tea and reading, when all of a sudden my eyes began to water. Smoke, and lots of it.' She hesitated. 'I got up and looked, of course.'

Inexplicably, he had begun to feel anxious. 'And . . . ?'

Her voice was low and troubled as she continued: 'Julian, it was the oddest thing. My eyes were stinging — they were really watering with it. I got up and started trying to fan it out of my eyes.' She took a deep breath. 'But I couldn't *see* any smoke.'

4

He said nothing, simply stared at her. It wasn't like Marian to be fanciful.

'I looked in the oven, I searched the entire house, I even went out in the garage to make sure one of the cars wasn't leaking petrol — but there was nothing. And Julian, all this time there was no visible sign of smoke in the air. I couldn't *see* anything out of the ordinary.'

'I don't understand any of this,' he said, bewildered. 'What do you mean, you couldn't *see* anything?'

'I couldn't see any reason why my eyes were running, absolutely bloodshot. I had to go and wash them out. With that much in the air, I should have been able to see it. But the air was clear, except for the smell.'

'A gas leak,' he said immediately, and to his surprise Marian shook her head.

'No. I told you, I had the Area Gas people in. They went up and down — not to mention under — with every meter they had. They told me that everything was normal; no leaks in sight. And there was another thing . . .'

She bit the words off. Julian was by now seriously perturbed; Marian was not imaginative, nor was she a woman to get upset about trifles.

'Julian, none of the Gas Board men could smell anything. None of them were affected by it at all. No one had watering eyes, none of them were coughing. Only me.'

She moved jerkily back to the bar and poured herself out a second drink. He saw that her hand was not quite steady and spoke calmly and quietly.

'That is odd. There must be a perfectly rational explanation for it, though I can't think of one offhand. It only happened the once, you say? And if the gas people found no leaks then there are none — they'd simply love to charge us to fix something. I suppose they could have been mistaken, but it seems rather unlikely. Could you be developing an allergy to something?'

In the act of draining her glass she looked up, surprised.

5

'Darling, I've never been allergic to anything in my life. Pollen, do you mean? Hay fever?'

'Well, I suppose its possible,' he said dubiously. 'I can't think of anything else to account for it, unless the house is haunted, or possessed, or something like that.'

She grinned at him suddenly. 'I think I'd find it easier to believe in a sudden allergy.' She paused, looking for the right words. Then: 'Thank you for not suggesting that I'm losing my mind or something.'

'Now why in heaven would I suggest that? You're the sanest woman in the world.'

'And the least imaginative? I wouldn't have been surprised if you had suggested it. After the gas people left, and I could still faintly smell the smoke, I began to wonder if I was hallucinating. The looks they were throwing at me . . .'

'Well,' he said soothingly, 'we'll keep our eyes — and noses — open, shall we? Maybe I'll be here the next time it happens and we can track it down to its source. Who knows, maybe we've got a nice Georgian ghost on the premises. Gemma would love that.'

'She would, wouldn't she?' Their daughter, now twenty-two was an insatiable reader of ghost stories, an avid user of the Ouija board and an expert on all things that went bump in the night. While she dearly loved Four Shields, the lack of anything remotely abnormal in its history was an enduring disappointment to her. 'If she does make it down, you can tell her about it. I'm sure Gemma will have some ideas.'

'University graduates,' said her mother drily, 'are invariably full of ideas. I believe I smell the ghost of a Lancashire hotpot. Are you ready for dinner?'

The Range Rover, following a thin curve of road that would have been invisible to an uneducated eye and impassable for nearly any other vehicle, nosed into the eddying mist and vanished from view.

It was Saturday morning. Sometime during the night the temperature had changed considerably, and with the warmer air came some relief from the rain. The great expanse that was

6

Dartmoor looked unearthly in its cloak of ground fog; patches of light green, clear as a warning bell in the clear sun, melded dangerously into their surrounding and more solid patches of solid ground, providing potentially lethal traps. Even as Julian drove through sunlight, a gust of rain moved across the horizon to the south in a melding of weather that is one of Dartmoor's idiosyncrasies. The hot sun had already dried many of the higher spots, even as the low fog kept the ground damp. Here and there, a bird came flashing out of the mist, the beating of its wings loud and eerie in the heavy air.

He knew virtually every inch of this astonishing terrain. As a young recruit in the army he had been assigned to help the local police in Okehampton, and then, to his own delight, to patrol Dartmoor itself. He had come to know the moor as well as any man could during that time; he had studied its varied and sometimes unusual life, learned which shades of green were safe to traverse and which were not. One day he had been trying to rescue a lamb which had unaccountably walked straight into a patch of bog — animals are not usually prone to doing this — and a young woman, dark and beautiful, had suddenly materialised as if from the rocks or the bog itself, and come to his aid. To city-bred Julian, she had the look of a gypsy; in fact, the colouring of the black Celt had given people before him the same notion. She seemed to him an embodiment of the moor itself — dark, cool, and mysterious.

Now, more than twenty years later, it was he who roamed the moor while Marian stayed closer to home. Dartmoor, with its wild and alien beauty, its stark contours, was the greatest source of serenity in his life.

The moor, at just past seven on that Saturday morning, seemed as remote from the world of man as the moon. No human voice marred its perfect peacefulness. Julian stopped the Range Rover and got out, listening to the living silence.

He stood, as so often before, by the standing stone in the broad field to the south of Four Shields. This was known simply as the Longstone and had been there even before the days when

7

the druids had sacrificed to their gods. Beyond the Longstone was a small mound of earth known as Beacon Tor. From its summit, one caught the sharp contrasts between valley and hillock, the mysterious and ever present mist moving against a background of sun.

Behind him, silent for the moment, was the Okehampton Artillery Range, inaccessible to the public by virtue of its natural protective surrounding of dangerous bogland. A mile or so away a curling edge of stone shadowed the horizon. This was the line of huts that formed a Bronze or Iron Age village, one of the many that dotted Dartmoor from end to end.

Julian climbed to the top of the tor, embracing the warm air and the desolate view. The air smelled crisp and full of loam, but there was another smell on it which was less innocent.

After a few moments he identified it, first with incredulity and then with alarm. Smoke — sharp and unmistakable — wafted and eddied on the August breeze.

So dense was the odour, and so pungent, that he looked back immediately at the Range Rover. It was just possible that his pampered and expensive vehicle had suddenly developed a drastic problem, but his first glance disproved that theory. There was no smoke coming from that direction.

Julian bit back the anger that misuse of the moor always roused in him. So, some idiot had decided to be adventurous and had camped in the area, had they? No doubt they had left their litter strewn behind them, he thought savagely, and forgot to extinguish the remains of their campfire.

Sunlight was trying to break through the morning mist. It dazzled him, making his eyes water. The smoke too was getting stronger. He drew breath and the sharp acrid bite of fumes caught in his throat, stifling and choking him.

In the empty field below him the Longstone stood silent, shrouded in its banks of eddying mist. There was nothing out of the ordinary there, and yet the smoke seemed closer by the moment ...

He found it, quite suddenly, by the simple expedient of

8

shielding his eyes with one hand. For a moment, he stood staring. There was smoke on the horizon, though surely too far away to be stinging his eyes like this?

Training dies hard and in his army days, when he was not a successful securities consultant in London, he had been trained to watch for fires. He scrambled down the side of Beacon Tor, to the lower ground where the earth was still damp, then jumped into the car and headed in the direction of the stone huts.

The Range Rover, engine purring, took very little time to cover the distance. Julian passed White Hall, noticing Tawsand Beacon from the corner of his eye. A snipe, disturbed by the noise from the great tyres, burst shrieking from its cover and flew low and away, disappearing behind a cairn. As he turned the corner that led to the hillside village, he saw a fresh drift of blue smoke waft lazily into the sky directly above his head. Tight-lipped, he killed the engine and, not bothering to lock the Range Rover behind him, strode purposefully over the hilly terrain into the direct centre of the ancient circle.

Smoke, thin and fresh, spiralled upward to blend with the clouds. Julian coughed, fanning it away with his hands. He knelt down, hoping to trace its source, but instead saw the smoke dissipate by the second. There was no trace of a fire, and soon none of smoke.

The village was empty. There was no fire, no litter, no sign of life. Silence settled around him.

Julian, oblivious to the pain in his knees as they pressed into the dry pebbled earth, stayed kneeling and watchful for a long time. He extended his hands, palms downward and began to probe the loose surface of the ground, mechanically turning over pebbles and cool clay. At the northern edge of the settlement, a spring burbled; from directly above him came the liquid trill of a skylark. Stray shafts of sunlight fell on him, warming and comforting. He sat silent, surrounded by stone and air, and tried to think.

There had been no campers, no fires. Yet there had been smoke, pungent and potent, making his eyes water from a

9

distance of a mile. He lifted his head, vision straining into the morning sky. The air was clean and vivid now, everything sharply limned. The smoke had gone.

The memory of his arrival home the previous day came to him suddenly: Marian, searching the house for something burning, going so far as to call in experts. They had found nothing, had not even been affected by whatever had drifted through the house as it had drifted this morning across the moor, in bitter wreaths and plumes . . .

His knees began to ache. Julian sat properly, crossing his ankles. He could not have put a name to the confusion in his mind. He knew only that he was unwilling to get to his feet, to go back to his car, to do anything other than sit where he was, growing drowsy and inert, and wait . . .

Peaceful and unreal, the morning dew in around him. Still he stayed, his mind and body falling gradually but inexorably into the quiet pulse of the moor around him. After a while his eyes grew heavy and he slept and, sleeping, dreamed.

Chapter 2

Lunica was at the stream again.

Cryth, who was a man not easily angered, felt irritation slowly mount within him that she should find the water so alluring, alluring enough to forget her chores within walls so that she could go and run her fingers through the dance of its wetness. He bit back his irritation, knowing it would be both unprofitable and unworthy for a priest of Leucetius, a young man born into high favour among the Dumnonii, to lose his temper with a mere woman.

Besides, it was difficult to be angry at Lunica; she was young and pleasing, and though not allowed by the elders to aspire to high caste in the worship of the gods, it was a common and open secret, known by all but the elders, that she had knowledge of things not usually found in a young girl.

Behind him, the child stirred and, sighing, fell deep once more. He glanced back over his shoulder at it, a boy, fat and healthy and serene. He himself found the child an endless source of fascination. He spent hours watching it: the clutch of its fat and dimpled fingers as they reached, striving, toward anything bright or shining, the way its eyes would virtually disappear into its oak and poppy cheeks when it was held or tickled.

He turned his face to the door of the hut and frowned once more. Women, not men, were supposed to find babies fascinating, yet Lunica's attitude toward Cel was one of detached interest. See how she had left him, and all so that she might get her hands wet . . .

Cryth thought for a moment longer and abruptly made up his mind. Pausing only to assure himself that the child would come to no harm, he went quickly out of doors and joined Lunica at the village stream.

At first, she paid no heed to him, all her attention concentrated on what she was doing. She was holding her hands in the water, turning them slowly this way and that, watching with an odd intensity the fall of droplets from her skin to the rocks below. As he came up behind her and stood waiting, he heard her murmuring under her breath. He could not make out the words.

After a while, she looked up and saw him. Lunica had a very discerning eye for one so young. She saw at a glance that she had somehow angered him, and at once her face fell into a smile of welcome and pleasure that disarmed him. She had power over him, and they both knew this. Though her charm was not a conscious thing, nor a weapon offensively used, she could not help but be aware that it had often saved her a scolding or a cuffing or perhaps worse. Even her father, that grim chieftain, had seemed unable to resist it.

Cryth saw the smile and with a certain wry amusement felt the anger fall from him like the drops of water from her fingers. She looked down at her hands and wiped them on her dun robes, shaking her head and smiling ruefully. Against all custom, so sure of him was she, she made first contact with him and linked her arm through his.

'I know — you have no need to say it. Cel is still asleep, I take it, or you would not have left him to find your woman who is so badly behaved. Yes?'

He pinched her arm. 'Yes. And you are badly behaved, or so I am told. As for Cel,' here he tried to infuse some severity into his indulgent tone of voice, 'he is far less trouble than you are, Lun. Why this need for the stream?'

Her voice, when at length she answered him, held a note that he recognised. It was deliberately vague, a warning to him not to probe, that here was a question she would not answer. 'Oh, I don't know. Water pleasures me, I suppose. It is nothing important, and need not worry you.'

His voice became dry. 'I suppose, Lunica, that you are not regretting the priesthood?'

'Whose priesthood, Cryth? Yours or mine?'

Cryth winced. This was plain talking with a vengeance. The druid elders, who directed the spiritual life of the tribe of the Dumnonii, allowed no woman in their vestments. Since it was known that other tribes, the Catuvellauni for example, had women priests and healers, this struck Lun as peculiarly unjust and she did not hesitate to say so.

Usually, however, she was not so foolhardy as to speak her mind where she might be overhead. To do so was to court retribution from the powerful elder priests. An indictment for heresy or sacrilege meant death of an ugly variety, and even Lun's high birth and marriage to the most promising of the young priests of Leucestius would avail her nothing then. Cryth felt a stab of fear and looked over his shoulder. Only old Cryl, hobbling and weak in her wits, was making her way slowly to the stream, ewer in hand. There was no one else about. He glanced down at Lun and found her watching him.

People had been wary of her since she was scarce out of swaddling clothes, and the most obvious reason for this was the pair of eyes now fixed on Cryth. The people of the Dumnonii were small and wiry with dark skin, hair and eyes. 'Brown and red people' other tribes had called them, making gestures of protection against evil. Yet they were a civilised people, at least in their own eyes. They fought valiantly when necessary but preferred to farm, and their religious rites were ordered and logical if somewhat bloody. But the Dumnonii were only human, and the human mind is incurably superstitious. One of their oldest and strongest superstitions concerned the wolf, the devil who haunted the flock, a creature both venerated and feared.

Lunica, small and brown-skinned like her kinsmen, had yellow eyes. They were the eyes of the great beasts that haunted the northern forests, and came down sometimes even to the

13

lowlands to carry off a child or a goat. Her eyes, long-lidded and brightly amber, were like no human eyes seen among them in all their history. Those eyes gave her status, mystery and some protection from the curious, for it was whispered that she was a born witch, and a wise woman that Taranis the thunder-maker or Nodens of the clouds had marked for their own. The elders scoffed in public and wondered among themselves in the sacred grove, and her people gave her a wide berth or courted her favour, depending on their bent. Mostly they accepted her as someone out of the ordinary and let her be.

For Cryth, reared almost from birth as an initiate of the fire god Leucetius, Lunica's wolf gaze was unsettling. He grasped her arm and pulled her into the privacy of their hut, dropping the goat's hide that served to keep the weather out and shutting them in alone together.

She watched him with a small knowing smile, almost as unnerving as her look. Behind them, the child Cel whimpered in his sleep and smiled as his hand closed over the bit of polished bone that was his plaything. Cryth glanced at him, then back at Lunica. His voice was sharp and low.

'By Camulos, Lunica, I think you yearn for death! What have I done that you should speak so, and perhaps draw the ears of the elders to you? Have you run mad, to speak of forbidden things within the hearing of the village? Can you not wait and speak your thoughts only to me?'

Suddenly she seemed tired, and abandoned whatever game she had been playing. 'Not mad, Cryth. I have no wish to anger or sadden you, I ask your pardon if I did so. But you don't understand . . .' Her voice tailed off. She began to move about the hut, gathering the makings of their dinner.

Cryth was insistent. 'No, Lun. I will know what you want to say to me. What is it that I don't understand?'

She had picked up a stone bowl full of barley. Now she set it down sharply, making the grain rattle, and turned to face him. Her face looked pale and drawn.

'Very well. You don't understand that I have knowledge of

things that no male priest could guess at. You know what is said of me, even as it is said of old Asulicca: that I am a witch, and a wise woman. You have seen how they come to me for the plants to heal their ailments, how the foolish young women come to me when their men have gone, and beg me for potions?' Suddenly and shockingly, she spat. 'Faugh! Fools, all of them! I tell you Cryth, I was *born* knowing things that the elders, who worship that very goddess who may someday call me to her service, can only beg for, scattering their entrails in the groves and burning the flesh of the living, grovelling like old women for auguries.' She stopped as abruptly as she had begun and, with a visible shrug, took up the bowl once more, making for the door.

He barred her way. 'Lun, heed me. I know you have power, yet did I allow myself to fear it when I asked your father for you? Tell me what it is you want.'

She regarded him, her head tilted to one side. Around her neck, the copper bands of the married woman shone the same hot colour as her eyes. 'What do I want? It has no meaning for you, Cryth. I want only to worship in peace, in my own way. Is that so very much to ask?'

He spoke slowly, puzzlng it out. 'No. But which god do you speak of — and what is your own way?'

'My own way is quietly and in private. As for the god, that I do not know — yet. But it is not your god, my dear, that much I do know. It is the water and the air that call me, and your fire — the druid's fire — is a sham and a lie.' She sounded exhausted and bitter. 'It is near time for supper, Cryth, and they will call you to the locus when the sun is down. Tonight is virgin moon, had you forgotten?' She ducked her head to leave the hut.

He continued to bar her way, speaking urgently and pleadingly. 'Lun . . .'

'No,' she said. 'Let me go out.'

He stood aside numbly, watching the goatskin fall back into place behind her. From out of doors came the sounds of the

15

village stirring, of the women moving to cook the evening meal, of the men beginning to wake from their afternoon sleep and talk, in low voices, of the next meeting of the tribe at the locus. Behind him, Cel woke with a jerk and began to cry.

Chapter 3

The rain woke him, that and the pain in his hand.

Julian stirred to wakefulness slowly. He did not know how long he had been lying asleep in the settlement but now, all around him, the earth was sodden and running and his hair was plastered against his face. The hot sun had gone and the ground mist had turned to heavy rain, streaking his face and turning the moorland that surrounded him to dangerous mud.

Disoriented, he pulled himself upright, shaking the pins and needles from his cramped muscles. A wave of intolerable dizziness washed over him, forcing him down again. He tried to shake it off, but found himself weak and languid. Good grief, he thought, I fell asleep, in the middle of nowhere. And talk about the power of suggestion. He had been dreaming, something strange and vivid, and very much suited to a man asleep in a two thousand year old tribal settlement. What had it been, now? Something about a woman washing in a steam, and a baby sleeping with one chubby hand clasped round a bone . . .

Thinking of his dream, dissolving now in the way dreams do, Julian realised that he was very thirsty. There was a bottle of beer in the car, he remembered. He did not make the sometimes lethal mistake of taking his environment for granted, and never went out on the moors without taking something to eat and drink in case he was stranded. There was a small jar of pâté, too, and a tin of biscuits. Mouth watering with sudden hunger, he got to his feet, ignoring a second wave of vertigo, and started for the car, rubbing the loam from his hands as he went. The sudden pain in his hand struck him like a hammer blow. He stopped in his tracks, the Range Rover glistening in the driving rain some fifty yards away, and carefully brushed the earth from his palms. For a long time he stood looking down at his hands, oblivious to the driving water that was soaking him to the skin.

His right hand, beneath its surface coating of boggy soil, was blistered and peeling; from under the cracked skin oozed a thin layer of fluid. The pain was intense, hardly bearable. Even working on the Range Rover's engine, he had never sustained a burn like this one.

Shaken and confused, the beer and food lying untouched on the seat beside him, he drove painfully back to Four Shields. He wanted, rather badly, to talk to Marian.

The first thing he saw when he opened the garage door was the twelve-year-old Mini parked at a rakish angle against the back wall. His daughter Gemma had arrived.

She must have been on the watch for either of her parents for she met him halfway between the house and the garage, flinging herself into his arms. He hugged her with his left hand, keeping his right carefully away. She drew back from him, her brows creased.

'Hullo,' she said, 'what's wrong with you?'

He attempted to smile, but the painful twist of his lips alerted her that something was wrong 'Daddy! Have you — no, you haven't been drinking, have you?'

'I have not.' Giddiness and pain sharpered his voice.

Gemma, all her life the centre of her parents' universe, was nevertheless not so spoiled that she could not recognise an unusual situation when she saw one. Nor was she without tact. In a gesture habitual with her, she linked one arm through her father's and moved with him towards the house. 'Mum's not here, I suppose she's off in Dowbridge. You look absolutely beat. Let me get you a drink and some food. Been out on the moor, have you?'

18

He stopped in the doorway and turned to her. The expression on his face took her aback. Her own features, a mobile mixture of her parents', stilled into alarm and watchfulness. He put his good hand on her shoulder.

'Gem,' he said quietly, 'something very strange just happened to me. I think I could do worse than to talk to you about it. First, do me a favour, will you, and get me some cheese and a beer? I'll be in the sitting room after I've taken care of this hand.'

'What about your hand?' She looked down and flinched; even the light brush against her shoulder had started it oozing. She looked sickened. 'God, that's awful — you'd better do something with it quickly. Mum's got some antiseptic stuff and a few bandages left over from the time I gashed my arm. They're up in your bathroom. You go do that, and I'll get your lunch.'

Halfway up the stairs, he stopped and called down to her. 'Gemma?'

She stopped in the kitchen doorway. 'Yes?'

'If your mother comes in while I'm ...' He hesitated, not sure exactly what he wanted to say. She finished for him. 'I'll keep her down here, don't worry. When you've cleaned up, could you deal with stilton and brown bread?'

'Definitely.' He resumed his progress up the stairs. From the bathroom he could hear Gemma rattling crockery below. The sound was reassuring.

When he came downstairs again, she was curled up in her favourite position: cross-legged in the heavy Victorian rocking chair by the hearth. She had lit a fire and laid out lunch. Now, silently, she watched him deal with the bread, cheese and pickles she had set out for him. She refrained from commenting or even watching as he opened his third bottle of beer. When he had finished and lit a cigarette, she straightened her skinny body in the chair to face him squarely.

'Now,' she said, 'you wanted to talk to me. I assume it's got to do with that masterpiece on your hand?'

19

Julian glanced down at the clumsy bandage and grinned involuntarily. The combined effects of his own fireside, a good meal and his daughter's company were making him feel much more like himself. 'It does look as though I've hurt myself while under the influence, I suppose. And yes, it has to do with the burn, but not only that. Look, Gemma . . .'

'Well?' She found herself holding her breath. Something in her father's manner spoke of a tension that was out of the ordinary for him.

'Are you still a member of that Cambridge society — what is it, Soap? The one that deals with spiritualism?'

They stared at each other silently for a moment, then Gemma said, 'Well, well, well,' and exhaled noisily. 'Yes, I am. Maybe you'd better tell me about it.'

'I intend to.' He shifted to a more comfortable position, and lit a second cigarette from the butt of his first. 'Of course, I may be making a great deal out of nothing at all — I don't mind telling you, I'm way out of my depth here. But something odd happened to me today, and something similar and just as odd happened to your mother yesterday, and frankly, darling, I really don't know who to ask about it, or even what questions I ought to be asking. Do you see?'

'Tell Madame Gemma, she who sees all,' she teased him. 'Seriously, Daddy, I've never known you so fussed before. I'm dying to hear about it all.'

He told her.

Her reaction summed up with the beautiful clarity and simplicity of youth his own feelings. 'Bloody hell. Now, that *is* weird.'

'Yes, a good word for it.' He smiled fondly at her. 'You known what a horrid materialist I am; if it wasn't for this burn I'd be very much inclined to drop the whole thing. You just can't imagine how silly I feel. But as it is . . .'

'You can't just let it drop. No indeed, you can't.' She got up and began to pace about the room. Over her shoulder she said, 'I'll tell you what strikes me about it, and feel free to disagree if you think I'm not making sense. One: whatever happened, it's

20

nothing to do with the house. I'm more inclined to think you've stumbled on an ancient burial mound or something. That sort of thing's well-documented: spirits or grave guardians upset over desecration, you known the sort of thing.'

Julian reminded himself that he had asked her opinion. It was up to him to keep an open mind now. He said temperately, 'I don't think any of the villages on the north end of the moor have remained unresearched. The few that contained evidence of any sort of burial have been excavated long ago, and not by me. So with all due respect to your angry grave guardians, darling, I don't think that's the answer. What else have you got?'

'Well, it happened to both of you. That would seem to indicate that it isn't just you, or just Mum, who's sensitive to whatever it is.'

He lit yet another cigarette. 'And?'

'I've done a lot of reading about this type of thing, and never,' she jabbed a finger in his direction, 'never once have I come across a single instance of a spirit causing physical harm to anyone.'

She had, at last, succeeded in surprising him. He spoke sharply. 'Meaning?'

'That ghosts are incorporeal, and nothing incorporeal is supposed to be able to cause physical damage. All the documented cases show that any damage that occurs stems from the fearful reaction of the humans involved.'

Something was stirring in the depths of his memory. 'In that case, what about poltergeists? I seem to recall . . .'

'Good for you,' she said enthusiastically, pleased to see him opening his mind to the non-rational explanation. 'But poltergeists aren't ghosts or spirits, Daddy, they're simply undirected energy. They move things, throw things around, by way of telekinesis. Mind over matter.'

He looked at his bandage. 'But I got burned by a non-existent fire.'

'Yes, you did. So it probably wasn't a ghost, or a poltergeist.'

He sat thinking silently for a while. Something had burned

21

him; something had sent phantom smoke into his eyes and into his home. And something had sent him drowsing in the morning so that he had fallen asleep in a place uninhabited for centuries, and dreamed ...

Gemma's voice was timid. 'Daddy?'

He looked up, surprised. 'What?' Something about her expression unnerved him. 'What is it, darling? You look scared.'

'Your face, just now,' she said slowly. 'You looked ... different. Peculiar.'

He crooked an eyebrow at her. 'Did I, darling? In what way?'

'Your eyes — they went black and glazed looking. For a moment it was almost as if ...' Her voice trailed away as her eyes, narrowed and worried, traced the well-known features that had been briefly, and frighteningly, obliterated by something else.

'It was nothing, darling. Exhaustion, probably. I had a very tricky week dealing with a pompous Arab consortium, and I was up with the lark this morning.' And, indeed, Julian was very tired. He thought longingly of his bed upstairs, and felt the food and drink prompting him gently towards a long nap. Then, sharp and unexpected, came another thought: the image of grass, of bracken bearing no footprints but his own, of stone huts black in the morning rain. He got up, willing the picture away, and yawned hugely.

'Christ, I'm sleepy. I think I'll have a nap. Thanks for listening to your nutty old man, Gemma, and for making my lunch. You take a walk, or maybe watch the box for a while, why don't you. Leave the washing up for me, don't worry about my hand.'

She watched him move slowly up the stairs and disappear in the direction of his bedroom. She could not put a name to the urge that made her clean up as quickly as she could and then go and sit in the quiet of her little red car, going nowhere, thinking strange dislocated thoughts. She sat with her hands clenched in her lap in the quiet of the garage. After a long time she realised that she was frightened.

Marian Dunne woke into soft blackness and the silence of a country night.

She lay breathing softly and evenly, listening for the sound that had woken her. It was like travelling twenty years back in time. Had that sharp thin cry that was almost a wail meant that Gemma had woken with baby thirst, or dropped a beloved stuffed toy over the side of her cot again?

Then she woke completely and realised that Gemma, sleeping down the hall, was now a young woman. The house was solidly silent. The night air from the slightly opened window fanned her face in passing, and left her cheeks cool. Beside her, Julian slept deeply, the burned hand dangling over the side of the bed, healing as he slept.

Her ears seemed preternaturally sharp, tuned to the sounds of the summer night. In the distance some creature called plaintively into the enveloping darkness, a dog fox or one of the birds that swept across the moor in mist or moon, looking for the small warm creatures that crept cautiously through the gorse, in fear of their life . . .

Marian lay still a while, trying to recapture sleep, but the cry of the distant animal had brought her completely awake. She knew that if she tossed restlessly in bed she would wake Julian; he had an uncanny ability to know on any layer of consciousness if she was sleepless. Moving quietly, she got out of bed, wrapping her thick cotton robe around her. In the dim wash of moonlight, close-cropped black hair silhouetting her face, she looked like an ancient statue.

From the depths of the goosedown cover, Julian muttered something. It was a word, a name perhaps, but too muffled for her to recognise. He turned over and settled deeper into his pillows, breathing like a child. Walking very softly, mindful of Gemma asleep at the end of the hall, she went downstairs.

Marian was not a woman for small talk or superfluous words. Indeed, she rarely spoke unless she had something to say. The pure Celtic blood that had bred unadulterated and, in the end, had shaped her over the course of a millennium had given her a serenity that verged on secrecy. She had deep reserves of energy but no real enthusiasms, only passions. One of the greatest of these was for the gracious airy haven of Four Shields.

She loved the house, at any time, in the way Julian loved the moor. Now, the only wakeful presence within its walls, she drew the comforting presence of the light oak walls, the overstuffed chairs, the little things she had accumulated over the course of ten years, around herself like a cloak against the outside world.

She stood looking out at her enclosed acres, shining but muted under the waning light. The ornate hands of the ormulu clock on the mantle showed four o'clock. The moon was down, the knife edge of its curve just touching the horizon. In the upper reaches of the sky, large pale clouds, fantastically shaped, hurried past.

Marian wandered into the kitchen. By the soft glow of the electric oven's luminous dials, she brewed a cup of strong tea and stood with it, staring out at the ending of night. She felt peaceful and serene, had almost forgotten why she had woken. The cry seemed already the figment of a dream, the echo of an owl or a fox out hunting.

She had put her cup in the basin, ready to be washed with the breakfast dishes, when she smelled the smoke. And, with the beginnings of that elusive scent in her nostrils she remembered the cry that had woken her, and the burn on Julian's hand, and for the first time in her life she knew panic.

Yet the promptings of heredity are strong, and panic was an unfamiliar sensation to her. So, even as the complex neural network of ganglia at the base of her spine tightened to the edge of pain, she acted logically and methodically. She flipped the kitchen light on, wincing at the sudden glare, and made certain that she had in fact turned off the hot ring. The kitchen was cold yet smoke without fire stung her eyes and hurt her lungs. The white china cup, a solitary menhir in the kitchen sink, gleamed dully against the gunmetal grey of the stainless steel. Suddenly, appallingly, she remembered Julian's deliberately casual retelling of his experiences on the moors the previous morning. A dream of a baby holding a teacup — no, not a teacup, a bone. A white shining bone . . .

Nausea rose within her. As she gulped it down she swallowed more smoke with it. The smoke had a dreadful taste; it seemed laced with something foul, something noisesome, blood or burnt meat. Yet she saw nothing, even as the taste of it settled bitterly into the put of her stomach.

She had barely managed to reach the sink before her peaceful cup of tea came up, spattering the sink and the white china alike with a reddish substance like blood.

Over head, a door slammed. Clutching the counter with both hands, retching, she wondered dimly if the smoke had reached upstairs and woken the others. She had not been aware of her own terrified cries for help. Then a pair of strong hands took her by the shoulders and pushed her, hard and insistently, through the french doors and out into the garden, where the air was crisp and cold and blessedly clear.

Consciousness, and a voice in her ear that struck her as vaguely familiar; a chill wind across her face, lifting her hair into witchlocks. Marian opened her eyes.

The light was greyish. Night had ebbed away, and even through the lingering residual taste of sickness at the back of her throat Marian could taste the difference in the air. It was clean and fresh, redolent of morning.

'Mum? Mum, can you hear me now?'

Slowly, she turned her head on the wet grass. Gemma, looking absurdly young with a huge patchwork sweater thrown over her pyjamas, sat cross-legged on the grass beside her. Her eyes were huge and frightened. It was Gemma, then, who must have pushed her out of the kitchen . . .

The sound of her own voice in the cool breeze was so sharp that it surprised her. 'Of course I can hear you. Gemma, where's your father?'

Her daughter's face was wet, whether with tears or dew

25

Marian could not tell. She looked as though whatever had happened had at least temporarily robbed her of the capacity to feel surprise. 'Asleep, most likely. He hasn't come down anyway.' She hesitated, but only momentarily. 'Mum, are you feeling better now? Can you tell me what happened?'

'What on earth do you mean, tell you what happened? You were there in the kitchen. You must have seen it, smelled it.' Marian, suddenly becoming aware that she was lying flat on her back in a wet garden, struggled to her feet. Fumbling with the tie to her dressing gown, she caught the look on her daughter's face and abruptly stood still.

'I was asleep,' Gemma said quietly, almost conversationally. 'I heard you cry out. You know how sound carries late at night, loud and very close, but you're never sure if you're dreaming or awake. I thought I'd better check.'

Marian watched her, puzzled. 'Well, I'm very glad you did, darling. I only hope you didn't get half as sick from the smoke as I did.'

Gemma reached out a hand in a curiously tender gesture. Her voice was shaking. 'I don't know what you're talking about. I didn't know what made you sick, not until you told me just now. I didn't see anything, or smell any smoke. I didn't smell anything at all.'

Marian stared at her, unseeing, for several moments. Then she lifted the skirts of her gown in one hand and fled into the house, taking the stairs two at a time, pushing open her bedroom door so hard that it crashed against the wall. She could hear Gemma's stumbling footsteps and panting breath behind her.

His body curled into a tight foetal ball, Julian slept peacefully, the ghost of a smile on his face. The burned hand still dangled over the edge of the bed, fingers lax and loose. As she backed quietly out of the bedroom, Marian caught a hint of that ugly smell, so faint that she might well have imagined it. Then it was gone, and the clean sharp edge of the rising sun touched the bedroom walls with rosy light.

Chapter 4

They had lit the fire in the precise centre of the holy place. The men of the Dumnonii, born and raised in the vast peat marshes of Britain, were experts at stacking the raw fuel. It burned clean and hot, sending up a steady pulse of light into the night sky, casting moving lines of firelight and shadow on the faces that surrounded it and the single stone at the very edge of the circle of light.

There were twenty of them. Most of them, the druid elders, wore robes of coarse stuff in the white of the goddess in whose honour they came to the grove called Nemet. The Father, Bel the High Priest of the goddess of the grove, wore white as well, but his robes were edged in wide bands of gold. As the most powerful of the elders he stood apart, waiting, as was his right and his privilege, to give the signal for the death of the sacrifice.

The others, the sacred five, wore nothing but their own skin, coated head to foot in the dye that came from the herb called woad; their bodies were a dark and disturbing blue, luminescent in the firelight.

Normally, the sacred five would not have been present at this ceremony. The servants of Nemetona knew and respected the fire god and his rites, and those servants of the other, smaller gods paid homage and service to the oldest worship they knew. But the rites were generally kept separate, each cult preserving its mysteries.

Tonight, however, was the fifth virgin moon, the festival of

27

Leucetius. It called for sacrifice to both the goddess and the fire god, and on this one night of the year the two sects combined for the offering. The blue-skinned five, their torsos ornamented with charcoal images, stood in a ring around the fire. On his bare chest Cryth had a crudely drawn triangle with an eye in its middle.

At the edge of the clearing was a basket made of rushes and stiff grass. From within came a frenzied bleating.

Cryth, as oldest of the five, stepped alone to the fire and, chanting the ritual words, cast the herbs he held into its heart. The smoke twisted and soared. Its pulse had a rhythm, a cadence, matched precisely by the four priests who now began to dance and chant, chant and dance, bare feet stamping on the warm ground, arms weaving continually in delicate or violent patterns.

Bel stared mercilessly through the slits in his thick hood, lifted his arms to the fire and then to the sky. Two of the white-robed elders at the edge of the circle came forward. Between them, suspended from a strong pole of iron, was the wicker basket. It moved and lurched as the animal within smelled the fire and the fear in the night air. Had this been a normal night, it would have been taken from the basket, its throat slit with the curled knife, its entrails offered up to the goddess.

This was the festival of fire, however, and the rituals were different. Carefully keeping their white robes from the floating ash, and licking tongues of flame, the elders deposited the basket with the goat inside in the heart of the flames. Cryth cried out, a bestial cry loud with satisfaction, and threw the rest of the highly flammable herbs he held into the heart of the fire.

The goat was maddened with fear and pain, throwing itself against the walls of its flaming prison. But the basket was weighted at its bottom with heavy stones; it swayed and tipped, but did not fall. The bleating became screams that rose to their zenith as the column of fire rose to a soaring pillar which lit the night, as the chanting of the crowd flexed and moved like light falling, like desire itself.

The smoke, heavy with the smell of roasting flesh, settled sickeningly on the robes and hair of the worshippers. The screams and chants died as the men fell first to their knees in the flattened grass and then, spent and sated, on to their stomachs. The only sound, now, was the crackle of peat and blackthorn as the fire sank, and died.

From behind the monolith, a small figure slipped into the darkness. Silent and sure-footed, naked as the night itself, Lun went quickly from the circle, the moon at her back. If they caught her here, she would be in the basket when next the elders craved the sound of screams. Her disgust was so violent that it seemed to consume her. But all was well. They were glutted, the pigs of the fire, limp with the feeding of their bloodlust, and she had got away.

She reached the stream in the darkened settlement without seeing a soul. The men of the ritual were at the holy place and all others were shut, frightened or incurious, within their own walls. She might, once the circle was left behind, have been the only thing alive . . .

In spite of the need for haste, she stood for a few moments, hands lifted to the heavens, the cold water lapping at her ankles. The movement of the water against her bare skin was lovely, so smooth and cool. Then she stepped off the rock and the stream took her, washing the betraying smell of the fire god into the current and away.

Wet and cleansed, she slipped into the hut she shared with Cryth. Cel slept beneath his thick hides. He had not moved in all the time she had been gone. This was not surprising for Lun knew a good deal about which plants give sleep, and she had rubbed some into the bone that he chewed to bring relief for the pain of teeth coming. He would not wake until morning. She had gone safely to spy on her enemies and come safe back again.

Water dripped down her face in cold runnels. Moving in the darkness with the speed of one who knew her surroundings, she found the robe she had been married in. It was dry and soft, a perfect towel for her hair. She rubbed her head vigorously until the thin dark mass was nearly dry. All the time she thought of the fire and the chants, and disgust burned in her.

Was this their power then? Was this their great secret, their holiness? Lun knew nothing of betrayal, she only knew that she could not put a name to what she felt. Sniffing at herself to be certain that the tell-tale odours of her trespass had been washed away, she crept into her bed and, still trying to swallow her horror, feel deeply asleep.

Not dreamlessly, however. In the small hours of the night Lun woke suddenly, lying still for fear of waking Cryth who, cleansed of his blue paint, snored gently beside her. For a long time she lay awake in the dark, trying to make sense of what had come to her as she slept . . .

She had been dreaming of a figure. A woman, from the look of her, but like no woman she had ever seen, taller by far even than Cryth and draped in the robes of a queen or a goddess. She had been surrounded, this figure, by artifacts that must surely have come from the gods, in odd shapes, made of precious metals. She had dreamed that this woman stood taking water from a sacred and unearthly cup of sacrifice, a cup that was as purely white as Cel's teething bone.

Sleeping, Lun had moved from this temple of the unknown to her own village. She had known it for what it was. There was her own hut, and the edge of the stream in the distance. But there was no life here, no smoke came from the huts, no one washed or drank at the stream. Of human life there was nothing. Yet the place was not empty.

A god lay, splendid in his solitude, in deep repose at the centre of the settlement. Dreaming, she yearned toward him. As she watched, the god put a hand out and down and moved it in the gesture Cryth had used, the beautiful violent gesture that invoked the power of Leucetius . . .

Then she was awake in the hour before dawn, staring straight up as though she would pierce the colour of night and make the sun rise. She was not frightened but she felt a deep sense of awe that this god and goddess should come to her in sleep. And she wondered, too, what the visitation could mean, and what it augured for her quest for power.

Beside her Cryth was motionless. His sleep was tense and immobile; his exhaustion was not the kind that comes after a day in the fields or after love but from the thorough draining of all resources, from his deliberate abnegation of himself to the will of the murderous god he served. Lun had learned, deliberately and well, all that she could of Cryth's kind of power; in secret she had studied it. It was not her kind of power. But soon, someday soon, she would have her own power. That much she felt each time she put her hands in the stream, and gave her mind and her heart's eye to its cold potency.

She felt herself relaxing, sinking down into the warm arms of sleep. The gods had come to her tonight after she had gone, in contravention of all tribal rules, to spy where no woman was allowed to go on pain of death. They had shown their approval. She did not know yet which name to put to those awesome figures she had seen, or know how to interpret their wishes for her. But they had come and, coming, had reassured her. She doubted no longer. She had done the right thing.

The last stars of the night dimmed against a grey dawn. Lun did not see them. Relaxed and secure she slept, this time without dreaming.

Cryth slept late into the morning. Usually he was up betimes, before the dew had burned off. On the morning after the rites of Leucetius, however, no one expected a priest to do anything other than rest.

When he did wake it was to a room full of quiet, punctuated by the soft muffled sounds of the settlement going about its daily business. He heard a gurgle, a charming baby laugh. Cel, outside, would be playing with Emunicca who was close to his own age. Her mother Arinicca, chubby and cheerful, would be spinning sheep's wool into frail grey yarn. The smell of cooking drifted in, tantalising him. He pushed the heavy covers off and got up.

31

He saw the change in Lun the moment his eyes met hers. Outwardly she was much as usual, kneeling beside the iron pot, stirring the grain with a heavy spoon to make the mash that was the late morning meal. Behind her on the grass the two babies rolled and tumbled, helplessly giggling. Arinicca, fondly smiling, had paused from her own task to watch them. But Lun . . .

She turned and saw him, and the hand that had been stirring stilled. The pupils of her yellow eyes, dark molten centres, were too wide, almost as if she had been frightened or had eaten some of the plants that gave the waking dreams. But she was not frightened. He could see painfully clearly that whatever had happened, whatever had touched her, was not the touch of fear.

Every line of her body, down to the slender fingers that held the spoon, seemed to be newly drawn. A kind of pride he could not identify showed in her very stance. Their eyes met and locked.

With deep satisfaction she saw the shock, the recognition of something new and different, ripple in his face. Her thin mouth stretched over perfect teeth into a smile that held equal measures of dark sensuality and contempt.

He took a step towards her, and then turned on his heel. As he ran towards the moor, heedless of the gorse that scratched his bare legs, he saw Arinicca look up, startled, and felt rather than heard her questioning remark. As the village disappeared behind him, he felt that Lun's impossible smile went with him.

He did not know where he was going. Instinct rather than knowledge led his footsteps to the scene of the previous night's rituals. He walked around what was left of the fire where a few burned bones, all that remained of the sacrifice, lay scattered. There was nothing here; no power, no knowledge, no answers.

At the edge of the clearing the stone stood, seeming to watch him. He went towards it, touched and circled it.

He stood for a long time staring down at the small footprints in the wet earth. As if her name were emblazoned on the ground itself, the knowledge of her drifted up to him on the morning air.

Fragmented thoughts, panicked and chaotic, chased each other through his mind. She had come here and stood, waiting, watching. She had witnessed the ritual. If the elders came to know of it, they would call it sacrilege. And for those who committed sacrilege the elders kept the ugliest, the most vile and unclean death of all.

He dropped to his knees beside the stone, praying to Leucetius or to any god that might listen. His prayers had no form to them for he was frightened beyond that. Even as he prayed that she might be spared, his hands of their own volition were wiping all signs of her presence away, moving in the patterns of sacrifice.

Chapter 5

For the first time since the day he had seen it, Julian left Four Shields for London with a feeling of relief.

He was wearing driving gloves. The weather, which had suddenly warmed into the ripe and beautiful softness proper to August, did not call for them; one touch of his burned flesh against the steering wheel, however, had sent him hunting through his dresser for some kind of buffer. There was a short week ahead of him but it promised to be a more than ordinarily hectic one, and he did not know how he was going to sign papers and amend draft documents when he could not even close his mangled hand around a pen.

He had left Marian at Four Shields almost unwillingly. Something had happened on Saturday night, he knew. Waking late on Sunday morning he had found Marian drawn and devoid of energy, and Gemma silent and preoccupied. Yet, when he asked them what was wrong, all he got for his pains were reassurances that came too quickly for comfort, and unconvincing denials that did not ring true. The Dowbridge church picnic, held in the hopes that the sun would shine, had seemed to revive both of them. Yet he could not blind himself to the fact that Marian had relaxed when Four Shields disappeared behind them, and tensed when they came home. That something had occurred, something of which both women were determined that he remain unaware, he did not doubt.

Now, driving too fast for perfect safety toward London, he

could almost convince himself that he had imagined the oddness of the weekend, or blown something simple and easily explicable totally out of proportion. But even as the thought came to him, his hand twinged and he knew that he had been touched by something he could not understand.

He parked the car and, taking his briefcase in his left hand, walked toward his elegant office in St. James's. London, that urbane and civilised place, settled around him. Under its muted skies, hearing the coo of its pigeons and the constant blare of traffic, he could not bring himself to believe his daughter's attempted explanation. It was all too ridiculous. Grave guardians . . . What next, voodoo dolls?

Mrs Potter, his middle-aged and frighteningly capable secretary, greeted him with her official smile. It faded as she caught sight of the bulky bandage.

'Goodness, Mr Dunne, whatever have you done to your hand? That looks very nasty.'

'Yes, it's rather a bad burn. I hope it eases off by tomorrow. I'd hate to hold my meeting with those people from the Saudi Consulate unable to shake hands. You know how touchy the Arabs are. Hope you had a pleasant holiday, by the way. Anything happening this morning?'

She followed him into his office. 'Nothing much, Mr Dunne. Sir James rang up with those figures you wanted on the North Sea consortium. I've gone over them and, frankly, I wouldn't touch that option. Much too risky. You've got that conference with Dymock's at eleven tomorrow. I believe they have lunch in mind. Shall I make reservations for you?'

'Yes, please. Make it for twelve-thirty, my usual place. Are we ready for the mail?'

In the city of London, the working week had started.

A few hundred miles away, Gemma Dunne was unwillingly putting her battered handgrip on to the back seat of the Mini. She had to return to London but was unwilling to leave her mother alone at Four Shields. Marian, for some reason Gemma could not understand, seemed almost anxious for her to go.

35

They had argued it out over morning coffee. 'Look, Mum, I don't pretend to know what's going on here — '

'Nor do I, so it seems rather pointless to sit here and worry about it. Darling, your job! I'm sure they'd frown on an extended weekend.'

For the fourth time, Gemma repeated, 'But I'm worried about you. I mean, what if . . .'

Marian's effort to keep from snapping was almost palpable. 'What if, what if! Remember how I used to read you *Sherlock Holmes* when you were younger? Didn't he say that theorising without data is a futile occupation?' She saw that the childhood quip, quoted whenever Gemma's lively imagination had threatened to get out of hand, had failed to bring the accustomed smile to her daughter's face. Sighing inwardly, she said mildly, 'Look, darling, I promise I won't stay in the house much. I'm planning on being out quite a lot. Does that make you feel better?'

'I suppose so.' Gemma sounded reluctant. 'And I really should get back to town. The newspaper's got a special feature on cats coming up, and the cat show at Olympia starts today. My camera's back at the flat, and I'll need to get some film. I wasted my last roll of high speed on the ugliest arrangements I've ever seen at the Chelsea Flower Show. Are you sure you'll be all right?'

'Absolutely positive. Now, are you all right for money? Do you need to take anything back up with you?'

Gemma gave in without further struggle. In truth, she was aware that as the most junior of the photography staff on a major newspaper, she could not afford to take unannounced days off at the beginning of a show she had been detailed to cover. So, swallowing her reluctance, she allowed Marian to shepherd her out to the garage. But as she drove off to London a feeling of panic threatened, at every curve of the road, to take control.

Marian watched the red car disappear over the hump of road that ran in front of Four Shields. Then, pulling on a light cotton jacket, she drove to the Lending Library in Okehampton.

It was small by urban standards. An oddly eclectic selection of books was delightfully displayed in an eighteenth-century house built by a long-dead mayor. Periodically, someone on the town council would raise the question of moving the library to more suitable, more modern accommodation, and the remainder of the council would cheerfully vote, en masse, against the proposal. The librarian, Roger Dawkins, was the latest in a long line of Dawkins of Okehampton to leave the nest, train as teachers or librarians in one prestigious school or another, and return like homing pigeons to the West Country.

Dawkins was under thirty, exuberantly cheerful and painfully thin, combining a love of hiking and ornithology with his family's traditional passion for books. His position as Okehampton's librarian afforded him the best of both worlds. Marian and Julian had often bumped into him in some windy, obscure corner of Dartmoor, peering at snipe or grouse through the tiny and costly binoculars that he wore constantly around his neck. He had acted as elder brother and adviser to Gemma during her teens, and occasionally graced the Dunne's dinner table as a guest. In the small, close community, the two families were close friends.

Late on a Tuesday morning, the library was nearly empty. Roger Dawkins greeted Marian cheerfully.

'Good morning to you. Did you enjoy your long weekend? I saw you and Gemma at the picnic yesterday.'

The last words had a questioning tone. Marian answered the unspoken query. 'Yes; Julian was rather tired, and decided to stay away.' An idea, sudden but logical, came to her. 'Roger, you're often out on the moor, aren't you? Watching birds and things?'

He grinned lopsidedly looking behind his thick glasses about fourteen years old. 'Birds and things. Yes, a fair bit.'

'Well, have you been out there recently?'

He was growing interested. 'About a week ago. I get out most weekends, but my sister — you remember Eliza? — went into labour on Wednesday, which meant I had to go to Truro. Family ties and all that. I've got a new nephew.' He looked quizzical. 'Why do you ask?'

She glanced down at her thin brown hands, folded quietly on the gleaming mahogany of the counter top. 'I wondered . . . this may sound a bit strange, but have you come across any, well, small fires or anything? Recently, I mean.'

She had caught his attention completely now. 'Campfires or ghost fires?'

Her head jerked with surprise. 'Ghost fires? What do you mean?'

He shook his head reprovingly. 'And you a Celt, born in the blood. Shame on you. Ghost fires are unexplained lights or actual fires found in unexpected places, away from human dwellings.' His hands moved, in a large expressive curve. 'Pixie lights. Is that what you mean?'

'No, not quite. Not even fire, really. Smoke . . .'

For a moment Roger stood quietly considering her. There was something about her today, a tension that was different and vaguely disquieting. Watching her hands tighten as she awaited his answer, he made up his mind. Taking a bunch of heavy keys from his desk, he locked the library door, flipping a neatly printed notice that read 'Back Shortly' into place as he did so. Then he came back and took her firmly by the arm.

'What you need,' he said amiably, 'is a cup of tea and a heart to heart. Something's obviously up. So come into the kitchen and tell Uncle Roger all about it.'

Twenty minutes later, Marian looked down at her untouched cup of tea and became aware that it had grown cold. Behind his hom rimmed spectacles, Roger's eyes were narrowed in concentration.

'Well,' he said reasonably, 'that has to take the biscuit for being the most peculiar thing I've heard in a long while. What do you think the explanation is?'

She was suddenly thirsty. Pouring herself a fresh cup, she replied, 'I haven't the faintest idea, Roger. That's why I've come to the library. I was hoping I might find something in one of the

38

books you insist on classifying as Local History.' She looked at him squarely. 'Have you any ideas?'

'I might.' He spoke cautiously. 'That is to say, I might if the whole thing had happened out on the moor. But my ideas aren't going to be much help when it comes to Four Shields itself.'

She refilled his cup as well. 'Let me hear your ideas anyway, will you? I'm so utterly at sea, just talking about it is a help.' She sipped her drink and sat back in her seat. 'Were you thinking about ghosts?'

'Not the conventional kind.' Roger stared out across the spacious gardens. 'More like an impression of history.'

'I beg your pardon?'

He brought his gaze back to her face. 'Well, we don't know very much about the people who inhabited those stone villages. We know what they were called . . .'

'The Dubonni.' Marion brought the name out with conscious pride, but Roger shook his head.

'No, they were further east, I think, I'm fairly certain these parts were settled by the Dumnonii. That was the Latin name for them, of course, not what they called themselves; the name Caesar gave them, when he compiled his chronicles of Britain.'

He spoke as though everything he was saying was common knowledge, and Marian's voice held a tinge of irony. 'Of course. Do go on.'

'Well, as I say, Caesar had the inhabitants of the island chronicled, not just in the west but everywhere he found people. So we know the Roman names for them, and we know a few of their customs.'

'Ah, yes. Blue war paint.'

'Woad, yes. Painting themselves blue. Or was that only the later Picts? Never mind, it isn't important. The thing is, we know that all the Celtic and Gallic tribes were polytheistic, and we know a bit about the druids.'

'Druids?' Marian was keeping pace with him but, for the life of her, could not see where this discussion was leading.

'The religious elders. Not very nice, most of them, with their sacred groves and wicker baskets. They burned their sacrifices alive, you know. They used to read omens in the fumes. That's where the expression "holy smoke" comes from.'

'What delightful people.' Marian spoke with an attempt at humour, but something chilly had moved up her spine and down again. She swallowed hard, and finished her tea. 'What about the druids?'

'Well, if I remember my chronicles properly, the tribes all worshipped pretty much the same gods. They gave them localised names, of course, and the rites probably differed slightly from tribe to tribe. The Dumnonii . . .'

'What were they like?'

'Farmers, mainly. They grew barley, it seems. They lived on Dartmoor and in Cornwall. But the druids . . .'

Her spine tautened. Now, they were coming to it. 'Yes, Roger.'

But Roger was maddeningly indirect. 'There are standing stones all over Britain. In Brittany, too. Caesar said that wherever you found standing stones, singly or in circles, you found a centre for religious rites. There are quite a few standing stones on Dartmoor. The Dumnonii had their own druid elders, I suppose. But as I recall, they were very big on the fire god. I don't remember his name.'

For a moment she sat gaping at him, not understanding. Then the sense of his words coalesced in her mind and she stood up, sending the delicate table rocking.

'Are you trying to say,' she said slowly, 'that what happened — that the smoke, and Julian's burned hand . . .'

'That you might have been receiving the physical impression of a religious rite performed two thousand years ago.' He finished her sentence for her. 'Stranger things have happened.'

Her voice was absolutely flat. 'Not to me.' She sat back down again, staring blindly at the table top, moving the spoon in her tea cup in a ceaseless circle. 'Suppose — just suppose — that you're right. That might explain what happened to Julian — the burn, and his dream. But what about Four Shields? We're not on a burial site, or near a standing stone. So how would that explain what happened to me?'

'I don't know. I told you, my idea only really covered what happened out of doors.' He thought for a moment. 'Unless you happen to be particularly sensitive to it. After all, you're pure Celt going a thousand years back, aren't you? No tatty Saxon or upstart Norman in you anywhere?'

'True.' Her eyes, the dark and fathomless eyes of that most secretive of races, stared back at him. For the first time he noticed the thin yellow rings that surrounded her pupils. Strange, he thought, why did I never notice them before? He suddenly remembered Gemma's fascination with spiritualism and asked, 'Did you discuss this with Gemma?'

Marian's expression relaxed. 'Of course. She had a host of different theories. Angry grave guardians, as I recall, was Julian's favourite. Interestingly, she ruled out ghosts.'

He pounced on that. 'Did she? Why?'

'Because she says that ghosts — excluding poltergeists which, according to my daughter, are not ghosts at all — can't do physical harm. Something about being incorporeal.'

'Ah, I see. Julian got burned, was physically harmed. Ergo, whatever burned him could not have been a ghost since they cannot cause harm. Logical, if a bit slick and simplistic.' He smiled fondly. 'That's Gemma all over.'

Marian laughed for the first time in days. 'How true. Roger, my love, thank you for the tea and chat. It has, in the words of whoever said it first, "given me furiously to think". Can you recommend any books that might be helpful? I can't tell you how confused I'm feeling . . .'

An hour later she climbed directly from the Volvo into the Range Rover and deposited a small stack of library books on the seat beside her. Not until she had parked the car on the side of the road hard by Beacon Tor did she realise that Roger Dawkins had never directly answered her question about whether or not he had seen any fires on the moor.

41

Chapter 6

The clatter of the cooking pots and the hiss and scrape of the food slowly heating over the open fires, made a strange background to Lun's thoughts.

The women had gathered, as always, in a circle of chattering life. It was a hot day, thick and sultry with the threat of thunder. The heat from the cooking fires was unbearable for long. As a result, the women would take over for each other, minding each other's pots and babies, when the dizziness grew too great to bear or thirst became overpowering. Only Lun, who of all the women disliked fire the most, had not stirred from her position by the iron pots and the cooking barley.

She was barely aware of the heat, or indeed of the voices and bodies that moved and chattered around her. She had not slept the previous night; she had slept, in fact, hardly at all in the past few days. Yet tiredness alone could not explain her sense of dislocation.

Asulicca, oldest of the women, was watching her; she could feel the thoughtful gaze on her back, hear the fragmented mutter of the unspoken questions in the woman's mind. Yet this experience of hearing and seeing with new senses, terrifying though she had found it at first, was something she was growing accustomed to. Since the night she had gone to watch the false priests, she had been slowly but irrevocably changing.

It was on that night, too, that the gods had come to her. So many things had happened to her since then. She had woken on the morning that followed, after only a few hours' sleep, and had known immediately that Cel wanted her. He was making no sound; a glance showed her that he had not yet woken. But she had heard nonetheless, inside her head, a baby gurgle, the noise he made when he was hurt or frightened. A heartbeat later he had reached his arms out to her in sleep. It had been no dream, this time. The power, latent but enormous, was growing in her. If only . . .

And it was on that morning that Cryth had come out into the village, and she had heard him too. She heard him as he stretched, and yawned; heard the thoughts not of a man but of a stupid herd animal, the grunts and sated stretching of his spirit. She had seen him with new eyes, the eyes the gods had given her, and she had seen a pitiable creature, a servant and a slave of a god who ruled nothing, with no power save the borrowed status that blood and fire lent him.

And he had known. That alone, in all the days that had passed since then, of all the things she had sensed and heard and interpreted since that night, worried her. He had met her eyes and she had not been able to keep the betraying power, the knowledge and contempt, from her face. He had run from the village without a backward look, and she had heard the scream inside him and smiled at it.

Since that time Cryth had treated her differently, in a way even Lun could not understand. It was a mixture of terror and tenderness; he seemed worried to let her out of his sight, and she felt his eyes constantly on her. The love and fear poured from him as powerfully as the scent of an animal; it was all there, for Lun to see and understand.

Once or twice, in the privacy of their hut, he had suddenly taken her and held her painfully tight. Before the eyes of the village Cryth, already considered unusually uxurious in a society where affection was rarely publicly displayed, was even more her husband, more solicitous of her welfare. But at night he mostly pulled himself as far from her as he could lie. And she, who in the late hours lay unsleeping, and watchful, would see the gleam of reflected light that betrayed his waking gaze fixed on her.

Lun knew now what she was waiting for. The gods must return to her. They had come, as they came so rarely to men, and given her a sign. And they would come again to their chosen one. Meanwhile she must learn what she could about the power which was growing and moving in her. There were women similarly blessed who had lived before her, gone now to dust, queens and priestesses. Even old Asulicca, who she knew was now watching her and sensing the difference in her, had been a holy woman in her youth in a place far from here, the servant of a goddess who had not allowed men at her altar.

Yet one of those she had seen was god, not goddess, and this Lun did not understand. She only knew that since that night she could do something that none other could: she could hear the thoughts of her people, smell their fear, see their lusts and suspicions lying on their skin like a pall of sweat. Comprehension came as clear to her as if these feelings and thoughts were painted with woad...

Asulicca had risen from her pots. Lun could hear her, making up her mind, rising to her feet, could feel the ache of the joints swollen and stiff with rheumatics. She head the scurry of feet as the younger women hastily made way for her, felt their mixture of awe and respect. She brought herself as completely back to the present as she could and, hearing the distinctive limping tread and the thump of the ash stick that proved her once again, correct, waited.

When Asulicca had come to within a few steps of her, she got to her feet and turned. Stepping forward, she reached out and took the old woman by the arm. Her yellow eyes were wide and guileless; she smiled charmingly.

'Here, mother, you are tired and stiff. Let me help you. Were you wanting to go to the stream?'

'Indeed.' Asulicca's voice was as dry and dusty as leaves fallen from the tree through lack of rain. She was a very great age and had learned, over her enormous span of years, the value of inscrutability. Her eyes, the black of her tribe, were set so deeply into a galaxy of time lines that only the glittering pupils were visible.

Now she met Lun's gaze. 'I grow hot by the fire. Walk with me, Lunica, down to the water.'

The bright yellow eyes did not waver; at the corner of Lun's mouth a dimply twitched. But her voice held only the courtesy due to Asulicca's age and position, nothing else.

'Of course, old one. Cel will be safe playing with the others. I will be happy to take you.'

They walked down to the stream in silence, Asulicca leaning on her stick with her left hand, Lun's hand under her elbow. Waveringly, her powers not yet fully developed, Lun could yet see behind her to the shifting of eyes that followed their progress. The matriarch's face was impassive; the eyes of the young woman danced. She knew, very nearly, what Asulicca had to say to her.

At the water's edge the old woman sank slowly to the great flat rock used by the women for beating their pots and cleansing their clothing. She looked up at Lun and received a shock. The younger woman's face was demure, her tawny eyes lowered, yet there was no doubt about it: she was laughing as if at some darkly humorous thing that only she could see.

'You wish to ask me something, I think?'

There was no mistaking it, Lun's voice held challenge. She was smiling, and those uncanny eyes — Asulicca fingered the amulet she wore on her wrist — were genuinely amused. Insolence, the old woman thought grimly, but was aware of another response deep inside her. She had power of her own, and she knew power when she met it. It hung around Lun, new and potent, as threatening as the distant rumble of thunder in the heavy air. Well, she thought, I have borne ten priests, and I will not be frightened of this girl. I know more of what she has than she does herself, and I have my years behind me.

She spoke clearly, holding Lun's eyes with her own.

'You knew that I did, then. That is interesting. How did you know, Lun? Did you reason it out?'

45

She was quiet. As the old woman watched, the yellow eyes narrowed to slits, the pupils enlarged, blurring and widening until the thin face seemed swallowed by them. The look, frightening and unnatural, was one Asulicca had seen before, but not on a woman of the Dumnonii, she thought; never on a woman of this tribe. I have seen it, yes, but where? If I were not so old. If only I could remember . . .

Then the look was gone and Lun was smiling down at her. The smile held a terrible confidence. The girl seems so tall, she thought, she stands over me like a goddess or a thunderbolt of Taranis, poised to strike.

'Yes, I am tall for a woman, am I not?'

Asulicca drew in a short sucking breath. Her heart rose, chokingly, into her throat. She knows, Asulicca thought. She knows what I think, and she is amused by it, by me. She is not afraid, or even awed. I guessed at her power, but I never dreamed . . .

Lun sat gracefully beside Asulicca, drawing her bare feet in under her. Her voice was cool and assured.

'You have fear of me, Asulicca. But why? Do you think I would harm you? I have great respect for you, old one. You have lived long, and seen much. And you have done nothing to harm me. So why would I abandon my respect for you?'

But if you thought I could harm you, Asulicca thought, if you believed for one moment . . . the threat was implicit in Lun's words, in the girl's smile. She was dangerous. Yet Asulicca, stiff with age and knowing that death might wait behind every word, was as detached as only those who have lived long and seen much can be. She shrugged.

'No, young one, I have no fear of you. Rather, I fear *for* you.' Her voice took on the edge of command, enforced by her years. 'What has happened to you?'

Lun regarded her thoughtfully, weighing the words. She was but human after all, and she had told no one about the visit of the gods. There were times when she had thought she must confide or die from holding her secret. Asulicca was powerful and respected; even Cryl, simple and useless for the things women were supposed to do, had fallen under her protection. It was due to the respect held by the settlement that the idiot had been allowed to live to be an old woman. Asulicca watched her now with such understanding eyes ...

'Tell me.' The whisper was persuasive. 'To hold glory or pain to oneself is foolish and dangerous. You have nothing to fear from me. Tell me now, Lunica. It will be better if you do.'

'All right, old one. All right. You wish to know and I will tell you.' Lun's uneven dimples widened as she smiled triumphantly. 'The night of virgin moon, the night of the rites of Leucetius, I had visitors.'

'Yes.' It was a statement, not a question. Perhaps the old woman would comprehend after all.

'A goddess, drinking from a cup of sacrifice. And a god, asleep in the heart of the village. They wore robes such as I have never seen. They brought no death but visions. They were gods.'

Asulicca's gaze was now steady and hard. 'Yes, young one. Yes. They came to you in the dark, and they left you with the Eyes.' She spoke softly, more to herself than to Lun. 'I guessed as much.'

'The Eyes? What do you mean, the Eyes? What can you know of this?' Lun's hand closed hard on the old woman's arm, in a biting grip. Asulicca seemed unaware of it.

'I have seen it; years ago, when I was young, I have seen it. But not here, among your people. It was in the old place where I was born, among my own people.'

Lun let go of the old woman's arm. She was remembering something she had heard once and since forgotten. Asulicca was not of the Dumnonii. She had come to the village as a young bride, many years before, from the Catuvellauni.

And Asulicca knew. Lun, for all the power she now held, knew nothing of the nature of it. Yet this old woman, who sat and stared with her flat black eyes, had known what the visiting gods had gifted. Lun closed her eyes and listened to her own breathing. The Eyes, Asulicca knew of them ...

47

But it was to her, to Lun, that the Eyes had been given. Until she knew what the power was, she did not know how to use it. She *would* know. She had the right to know. And Asulicca held the knowledge.

She breathed deeply, drawing on the well of strength she had known was within her since the fire rite, and lifted her eyes to Asulicca's face. Fathomless black orbs met hers and, with a shock that both women felt, yellow and black locked in silent battle. A streak of lightning broke the sky and was swallowed in the crack of thunder.

Asulicca, with the ease of great age, held her mind blank. She thought of sunlight, of small birds on the wing calling over the great marsh. She did not think of the Eyes, or of Lun, or of anything very much. The deep pity she felt for Lun and for Cryth she kept well hidden.

They held each other in this way for a long time. At the settlement, the young women stirred uneasily and the babies, ignoring the thunder, rolled and laughed. Cel, who was playing with Emunicca, rolled sideways and in so doing brushed one arm against the hot cookpots. In a moment all was commotion and comforting.

Down by the stream, Lun lost her battle. Her head jerked as Cel's shriek sounded, a moment before it was actually made, in the back of her head. The lock of eyes was ruptured, the power gone. Asulicca, unsmiling, slowly got to her feet. She had won, but the victory was a joyless one. She turned towards the settlement, Lun falling in step beside her.

'You will not tell me?' Lun's voice was dull and lifeless with misery.

Asulicca did not turn her head. 'No, young one. I shall not, for you will learn it for yourself.' And she moved, slowly and painfully, towards the fires and the voices, the world to which she had grown accustomed.

She said nothing to Lun about her own powers. She had lived long and come here as a stranger, and she had deemed it wisest to keep her own counsel all down the long years. She had known that Lun had been given the Eyes because she herself had long ago been given something even stronger, a vision that travelled even further. And she had seen behind the yellow irises, to the flash and pulse of time, to Lun's past and to the black sword hanging over her future.

As she reached the settlement, with Lun a step behind her, Asulicca realised there were tears on her face. She reached up and swatted them away, saying nothing.

Chapter 7

On Wednesday, two days after the bank holiday ended, the weather broke. In London the sky took on a sapphire hue, casting a pitiless light on the pigeons who huddled, moulting and miserable, on the heads of the lions frozen in their eternal watch over Trafalgar Square. The city was awash with tourists. By night the hard bright sky gave their faces, shining and sweaty above their summer clothes and expensive cameras, a metallic sheen.

In the St. James's office of Dunne Investments Limited, the overhead fans circled endlessly. Julian, his hand pink and shiny with puckered new flesh, managed to end a meeting with three immaculate Japanese businessmen and went so far as to roll up his shirtsleeves. As he leaned back in his chair with yet another in what seemed an endless line of glasses of cold water, the buzzer on his desk sounded.

'Your daughter's on line two, Mr Dunne. Are you free to speak with her?'

'Yes, of course. Thank you, Mrs Potter.' He wiped his sweating face with a handkerchief and picked up his phone, reflecting unfairly that Mrs Potter could hardly be human to sound so cheerful in this intolerable heat. 'Hullo, Gem. I thought you were off at Olympia, taking pictures of the Russian Blues.'

'I am, but even junior navvies for the photojournalistic industry are allowed an hour for lunch so I rather thought I might

50

get you to buy it for me. If you're free, that is.'

Julian grinned. 'I see. Skint again, are you? How much do you need this time?'

She sputtered indignantly. 'I am not skint. I am a hardworking young woman of the progressive eighties and I pay, all by myself, for a one-room flat in a questionable part of town. It's merely that I am not above using my feminine wiles on a rich male to make them pay for my meals now and then. Welcome to the progressive eighties, Daddy.'

'And you can tie your own shoes, too. Atta girl! As it happens, darling, you're in luck. I've just got rid of three excruciatingly well-mannered gentlemen from Honsho who wanted to know everything ever discovered about investing in West Riding chicken farms, and I'd love a shrimp salad and a bottle of beer in more stimulating company. Can you be here in fifteen minutes?'

'Try and keep me away,' she said cheerfully, and rang off. Julian regretfully rolled down his sleeves, emptied his water glass yet again and went out into the heat-glazed street to wait for his daughter.

She arrived on foot a punctual twelve minutes later. In khaki trousers and a loose white shirt, she looked very young and unusually frail; her camera, as expensive and well-cared for as the pedigree felines she had been taking photographs of for the past two days, dangled around her neck. She looked spotless and absurdly cool. Even her black hair looked dry and unruffled. Linking arms with her father, Gemma led him off down Piccadilly.

Her favourite restaurant, on the fringes of Soho, was dimly lit and deliciously cool. Since it catered for local office workers and tourists alike, the air conditioning was kept in perfect working condition. The salad was fresh and crisp, the beer more than drinkable. Julian found that he was enjoying himself.

They had eaten lunch and were halfway through their third beer when Gemma asked casually, 'The hand looks much better. How's it feeling, then?'

He regarded her steadily over his glass. 'Do you know, I'd

51

acutally forgotten all about it. Yes, it is much better, though on Tuesday it hurt to pick up so much as a pencil, much less my phone.'

His daughter's voice grew more elaborately casual. 'Speaking of phones, have you spoken to Mum in the last couple of days?'

'Subtlety,' said Julian dryly, 'is not your forte, my love. I spoke with her last night. She said everything was fine, and how was my hand, and had I sold any stocks?'

Gemma sounded both thoughtful and relieved. 'Well, that does sound just like Mum, doesn't it? Or does it?'

'She sounded preoccupied,' he answered shortly. 'And before you can ask me yet more questions with an even greater degree of elephantine subtlety, I will tell you that I did in fact ask her what was on her mind. She simply said she was working on something and she'd let me know if anything turned up or that she'd see me on Friday whichever happened first.'

Gemma's eyes widened. 'Did she? That's interesting. In fact, coming from Mum, that's very interesting.'

Suddenly Julian's playful mood was gone, replaced by the sense of uneasiness that had haunted him all week. 'I don't see why.'

'Well, working on what? She didn't tell you, did she?'

'No, she didn't. But she's no fool, Gemma. Very likely she's checking over the old parish registers and haunting the Oke-hampton library.' He stopped abruptly, wishing he had not used the word 'haunting'. Gemma seemed to sense his sudden shift of mood for she changed the subject. They spent the rest of the hour pleasantly enough, Gemma discoursing on pedigree cats and her father on the business manners of the Japanese.

She walked back to St. James's with him, on the grounds that Piccadilly was a likelier place to find a taxi than the winding alleyways of Soho. As they stopped on the corner of St. James's and Piccadilly and began to scan the streets for an empty taxi, she turned to him.

'By the way,' she said, 'I shall be down again this weekend.'

'Will you?' Julian was conscious of a faint feeling of surprise.

52

'I thought you were going up to Cambridge for that get-together on Saturday?'

'No, I've decided to give that a miss. To tell you the truth, Daddy, I want to pay a visit to an old friend in our part of the world, and I can't very well hop off to the country in the middle of the week. So I'll see you at dinner on Friday night, if my brakes are still functioning. Oh, there's a taxi and it's empty, wonder of wonders! Daddy, would you . . . ?'

He waved the black cab over. 'Here you go. One taxi. An old friend, Gemma? Who?'

'Roger Dawkins, our lunatic librarian. Thank you for lunch, it was lovely. See you Friday. Olympia, please.'

Julian stood on the dusty pavement, watching the taxi pull out into the crush of Piccadilly traffic and vanish westward. Then he went quickly to his office and tried to call his wife. There was no answer.

Marian, just killing the Volvo's engine in the garage, heard the distant trill of the telephone carrying clearly on the hot air. She sighed, knowing that by the time she got the side door unlocked and reached the phone, it would have stopped, and she would be left holding the receiver, hearing the maddening buzz of disconnection. Better to let it ring. If it was important, whoever it was would call back.

She opened the Volvo's boot and pulled out two large sacks of groceries. It was one of the benenfits, she thought, of having a daughter who lived elsewhere and a husband who spent most of his time in London that she did not have to waste her time pushing a trolley up and down a supermarket's aisles . She could spend an hour or two stocking the larder for herself and then eat lightly all week. The only heavy consumption of food at Four Shields occurred on the weekends, and meals for herself were easy to plan . . .

Inside the house she stowed away tins of soup and plastic bags full of mushrooms and tomatoes, and began to sing under her breath. The kitchen, sunny and spacious, was its usual friendly self. No smoke darkened its air; no sharp pungent smells filled her lungs. This was her home, her kitchen, and when she was done stowing tins and bottles and green growing things she was going to make a cup of strong tea and take her little stack of library books and notepaper out on the lawn.

Since her conversation with Roger Dawkins, she had twice taken the Range Rover and driven out to the moor. Standing in the sunlit beauty of the open space, taking deep lungfuls of the pure clean air, the events of last weekend seemed distant and improbable.

She knew Dartmoor as well as Julian did; her family was Cornish and she had grown up in the west. From Julian's description, she had had no difficulty in pinpointing precisely which settlement had gathered him into itself, to sleep and to dream. She had gone there directly from the library, wary and alert, tensed against the threat of smoke and the terror that accompanied it.

Nothing had happened, nothing at all. She had parked the car and climbed straight to the settlement, standing with her face to the sun. The ground beneath her was dry and covered with pebbles, the green distance dotted with heather and speedwell. There was nothing here that did not belong.

Marian had waited, out in the bright summer day. She had waited a long time for something, anything at all, to happen. She was not really certain what she expected; she only knew that in some mysterious way time, the day and the hour, seemed to be flowing in the direction of something she could sense but not clearly understand.

She had stood alone, her five senses straining towards the impossible. There was no sign of humanity neither close at hand nor in the distance. She might have been alone in the world. From behind her, at first softly then insidiously noticeable, she heard the bubbling stream churning its bed and sharp anchored rocks, splashing bubbles and foam on the great flat rock that for time out of mind had sat where water met land.

She had become aware of a feeling new and strange to her. It was peaceful but mixed with a deep uneasiness that was almost awe. She became highly conscious of the sound of her own breath, of the warmth of the day against her bare arms. Small insects danced and buzzed around her but, although insects generally found Marian irresistible, they kept their distance from her. She might have been invisible.

Time stretched out, an almost tangible thing, hanging between earth and sky. After a long time had passed, Marian had climbed down the hill and driven slowly back to Four Shields. She did not notice how, in her wake, her footprints contracted into seared patches of earth as if touched by fire.

Now, in a comfortable wicker chair, she sat in her own quiet garden and deliberately, with something resembling sensuality, sipped a cup of tea. A mosquito, droning and thirsty, settled on her arm. She swatted it irritably away and, at random, lifted a book from the pile on the little wrought iron table beside her.

The afternoon moved on. She had forgotten her tea, forgotten her sense of peace and quietude. She digested the first book, a short pamphlet on ancient religions, and moved on to the next, a leather-bound volume that Roger most certainly should not have allowed out of the confines of the library building. The sun began its slow descent to the west. She did not notice.

The sun was already over the yardarm when she put a marker at the halfway point of her book. She set it down on the top of the pile and stared blindly at books and garden, at the sky that had gone from liquid gold to a dark and angry vermillion. The sun in its death throes looked huge and ominous; the air had cooled and there was a smell of rain.

She carried her books and her teacup back to the house and latched the storm shutters. Standing in the kitchen she watched the small scurrying clouds whipped by the circling wind. Soon there would be lightning, thunder, all the noisy pageantry of a summer storm.

She wandered from room to room, methodically making sure that the windows were fastened tight against the onslaught of bad weather to come. Then, with the house brightly lit, secure against the night and whatever waited within it, she reached for the telephone.

After twelve rings she dropped the receiver back into its cradle, a tiny furrow of anxiety drawing her thin brows close together. Wednesday was early closing in Okehampton, and the library must have long since shut. The weather had turned and no man born and bred to the vagaries of the West Country weather would ever be fool enough to venture out in a storm of the magnitude of the one which threatened. There was no reason why Roger should not be ensconced by his own hearth, no earthly reason at all . . .

She stood irresolute, looking out of the window. At the meridian of her vision, the alder trees that leaned against the stone gates of Four Shields were whipping themselves into a frenzied dance. She heard the whine of the wind, its gleeful mindless voice howling around the chimney pots. She saw some small animal run across the yard, fur ruffled in the teeth of the wind, and vanish into its burrow.

She tried Roger's number again and stood counting the rings. Seven, eight, nine . . . no answer.

The names she had read echoed in her mind. Leceutius, Herne, Clota, Camulos, Bel. . . fire and light, beasts of field and forest, water, sky. She thought about bodies painted blue, about skulls painted with gold and used for drinking cups. She thought about druids, about living bodies encased in burning baskets, about the ancient concept of sacrifice. She thought of Julian sleeping as though drugged, his seared hand dangling in the morning air, as phantom smoke laced with something rotting and unclean bit into her lungs. She thought of Gemma, voice layered with rationality over a bottomless well of uncomprehending terror, unable to smell or see anything at all. She thought lastly of Roger Dawkins, of his fondness for wandering the moor in all weather, his interest in the story she had told.

She remembered that when Gemma was a baby and therefore at risk, her own sense of peril, real or impending, had been as sharp and real to her as her sight or her hearing. Not since her daughter's childhood had she felt what now took hold of her and filled her mind. She had been worried before, and uneasy. Now that worry was becoming active fear.

The whine of the wind had modulated to a deafening howl as she struggled into her fisherman's oilskins. She fought the wind all the way to the garage, listened to it batter against the walls around her as she added petrol to the Range Rover's depleted tank. As she was struggling to force the garage doors shut against the driving rain, the telephone began to shrill again. The fury of the storm and the cramp of fear that had settled like bad food in the pit of her stomach took all her concentration. She did not hear it ringing.

The lights of Okehampton wavered in her field of vision through the bitter lash of the storm.

Marian, a safe and careful driver, did not much care to be out in bad weather. It was the habitual wetness of her chosen sur- roundings that had decided her in favour of purchasing a Volvo, that secure and weighty automobile. Now, feeling the even heavier Range Rover slide under her as strong gusts of wind slipped beneath its chassis, she was thankful she had had enough sense to take a vehicle designed for precisely the weather con- ditions she was facing now.

She could not have put a name to the feeling that had driven her out of doors in search of Roger Dawkins. Surely there was no reason for this worry. He was a sensible and well-educated young man, an experienced hiker, someone who could be trusted to do nothing silly or dangerous. He had grown up within sight of Beacon Tor and he knew, none better, that in this weather the moor became dotted with boggy pits, bottomless traps in which a man could sink from the light of day as quickly as a stone in lake water . . .

The Range Rover skidded with a scream of its powerful front tyres as a dog, its fur plastered to its skin, shot across the narrow lane and into the bushes. Marian sat for a moment steadying her trembling hands, and wiped sweat from her face. Only three streets and a left turn, she told herself silently, and she would be at Roger's house.

She took the remaining distance at a snail's pace, the car's wheels throwing up miniature tidal waves in their wake. Already the town's drainage system was showing signs of strain. Rainwater with no place to go lapped at the gratings and formed large moving pools with a life of their own. A good inch of water must have fallen since the storm started, she thought vaguely, and in only an hour. And, impossible though it seemed, it was getting worse.

A left turn into Ploughman's Lane, and three houses up on the right. She killed the engine and sat, hands clenched on the leather-covered steering wheel, staring at the blackened windows of Roger Dawkins' cottage.

She stayed parked in Ploughman's Lane as the storm worsened around her. She felt numbed and helpless and, in some odd way, guilty; it was as if by suddenly believing that Roger might be in some kind of danger, she had taken that danger and materialised it, given it substance. After a while it came to her that perhaps he was home but sleeping or doing something at the back of the house. She pulled the heavy oilskins tightly around herself and, wincing from the force of the rain that seemed intent on cutting through fabric and flesh to flay her very bones, stepped out into the street.

The rush of wind lifted her off her feet, slamming her like a leaf against the open door of the Range Rover. She grunted with pain, grabbed at the door and tried to right herself. As she brought herself completely upright she heard a thunderous crack and something whirled through the air directly above her head. It smashed into the side of the Rover, leaving a deep dent in the immaculate blue paintwork. She reached out and picked it up. Supporting herself against the car door, body braced and aching, she examined it.

In her hand was a storm shutter. It was the final, irrefutable proof that Roger Dawkins was not at home, had not been there since morning. She could see precisely where the shutter had come from. Blown with great force by the gale winds, it had snapped free of its heavy hinges to smash itself in the street below. It was the shutter from an open window of the room that must be Roger's bedroom.

Even in August, people did not leave storm shutters dangling loose. If Roger had been home he would have fastened the shutters, as Marian herself had done at the first cold whisper of rain. She dropped the shutter into the street where the swirling torrent took hold of it and carried it like a feather, lodging it firmly between the sewer gratings. She turned the key in the ignition and, shaking with tension, headed the car back down the street.

She did not take the road for Four Shields. Instead, dropping her speed to a minimum and silently blessing the four wheel drive, she turned the car towards Dartmoor.

Roger Dawkins had been thinking.

For two days, while taking care of the library and its patrons at his usual leisurely pace, he had found his mind returning again and again to Marian Dunne's story. The more he considered it, the more interesting he found it.

He had known the Dunnes a good long time, in fact from the very first weeks of their move to Four Shields. He had for a short time borne the title of 'Gemma's young man', with good-humoured indulgence. As they had grown older, however, the boy-girl romance had evolved gently into a platonic friendship based on mutual respect and enjoyment of each other's company. Then the university years had sent them off in different directions, Gemma to Cambridge and Roger to Edinburgh.

Since that time, their professional lives had taken turnings that had seen Gemma ensconced in London, Roger left behind in Okehampton, and they now saw little of each other. The affection between them, however, was still strong. Since Marian's visit he had found his thoughts returning more and more often to Gemma, to her fascination with spiritualism and the occult. She knew a good deal about the sort of thing her mother and father had apparently experienced, and might well have known what she was talking about when suggesting an explanation.

Moreover, Roger knew Marian Dunne. In the days when Gemma and her small group of friends had sat round the fireplace at Four Shields discussing ghosts in fact and folklore, she had listened with her usual placidity. She was the last woman in the world to dramatise the story she had told him. In fact, if he had been asked to sum Gemma's mother up in one word, it would have been 'unimaginative'.

So if Marian said her house had filled with phantom smoke, said that her husband had fallen asleep to dream with frightening clarity of an ancient tribe of settlement dwellers and waken with his hand mysteriously burned, then Roger Dawkins was inclined to believe it. His problem was not the suspension of disbelief; rather, it was to put a clear and logical interpretation on what had happened.

So he turned the matter over in his mind, and spent a fascinating Tuesday night pouring over several old books he had found in the history and folklore stacks, making enigmatic notes on what he found. On Wednesday he packed his notes into his knapsack, locked the library door at one in the afternoon and decided to continue his research in situ.

His elderly Cortina was hardly designed for traversing the rougher edges of Dartmoor. This fact did not worry Roger in the least. He was a tireless and energetic walker and he had taken the precaution of wearing his hiking boots today. With a sense of pleasurable anticipation, he stopped off at a local roadside cafe for a hearty lunch. Then, with his knapsack hitched over his shoulder, he drove the car as far as Beacon Tor. There he pulled it off the road and beagan his walk toward the hillside settlement.

Marian had a gift for imparting information clearly and her description of Julian's adventure had left him in little doubt as to which settlement had been involved. The weather was clear and bright, if a trifle too hot to be perfect for a long walk. He took his time and reached the settlement at just about the same hour as Marian, in her garden to the northwest, was opening the second of her borrowed books and becoming conscious of the first twinges of uneasiness.

The hot sunlight, the lazy and distant drone of the bees and butterflies that danced across this vast and lovely expanse of primordial land, and the pleasure of being abroad in the middle of a workday afternoon, combined to lift Roger's spirits. He began to sing as he approached the settlement and continued lustily in a clear tenor as he climbed the hill, an old folk song about fairies and witches, about love betrayed and revenged. Then he clambered into the settlement and made his way to its centre, and the singing died in his throat.

The footprints led from where he stood, in the vortex of stone huts, to the precise spot where he himself had entered the settlement. They ended at the edge of the hill. Roger followed them, aware of a constriction in his chest that was too nebulous to be called fear; it might have been awe, or simple superstition. He stared at the prints, his breath coming heavy and fast. They were not Marian Dunne's footprints, that was certain. She was a tall woman with feet to match and, with her Celtic blood and country upbringing, would never be fool enough to wander barefoot across this hard pebbled terrain.

These footprints were tiny, almost child-sized. They were the bare impressions of a half-grown child, or a very small woman, who had seemingly fallen from the sky itself to the heart of this abandoned iron age village and walked to its edge, then away into the sky once more. He knelt and touched the perfect imprint of one toe. The edges of the prints, where sole had met ground, had fused in some heat so intense that it could turn pebble to virtual glass. The prints were framed with it; it was as though the creature who made them had trod this ground with feet of fire.

Roger stood looking down as the afternoon drew in around him. He tried to marshall his thoughts, to impart some semblance of order to the chaotic pictures that spiralled through his inner senses. Names of forgotten gods and descriptions of barbaric rites mingled in a horrific brew with the memory of Marian's cool voice. These thoughts reached the rim of sanity only to be swept back into the maelstrom when he focused once again on those perfect and tiny unnatural prints in the dry ground. His breathing did not steady. The layers of sophistication that the twentieth century had imposed upon his kind were stripped away, leaving him raw with the weight of an age-old fear.

The blue sky above him changed slowly to red-gold. Roger, warring against his own weakness, did not notice. He wanted with all his being to turn his back on this place, on the cool stones, the footprints, the shadowy doorways, and flee screaming back to civilisation, to things he knew and could understand. But he was a scholar and a man of his time, and even greater than the primal fear, the sense of danger that spoke with a voice all its own, was the habit of the age. What he saw here and what he felt were unreasonable. He was a child of the age of reason. He could not give in to himself.

He sat crouched for an eternity of time. The first drops of rain took him unawares. So taut were his nerves that at the splash of the first big drops he cried out, dropping his pack behind him to come whirling up, fists bunched against the weather and whatever might ride it. One look at the colour of the sky was enough for him. The rain had begun to fall in earnest, and to wander the moors in a heavy rain was lunacy; if he did not get back to his car, he might have to spend the night here. The thought was enough to spur him to movement. Shaking, his body dripping with sweat, he reached a trembling hand towards his pack.

Inches away from the comforting reality of the heavy nylon, his hand stopped as if struck. The air was growing heavier by the moment and his movements grew more and more difficult. Panic took him in an iron hold, squeezing him mercilessly. He was not alone in the settlement. He was being watched, he could feel it. They were watching him. If he turned to face those dark entrances he would see their eyes.

The thought planted itself in his mind and refused to be

budged. Eyes. There were eyes on him, all-consuming, greedy eyes, reeking of madness and danger. The eyes of the wolf. Hungering, desiring. Bright, wide, yellow eyes . . .

Roger got to his feet, moving like an old man. He was completely unaware of anything his body did, moving as though commanded or automated. He could hear a voice, small and clear, dark with passions he had never encountered. It came from the huts, from the sky, from inside his own skull. It commanded him, directed him, made of him no more than a wooden puppet to do its bidding. He could no more disobey that voice than he could suddenly sprout wings and fly. He was tuned, body and soul, to his own obedience to the unnatural.

He was going to die, he knew it, and yet he could do nothing, absolutely nothing, to help himself. His feet carried him slowly across the humped hill and came to rest on a large flat stone, fixed deep into the bank and jutting out into the flow of the stream. He stood staring down at the moving water that gathered upon brutal rocks some six feet deep, trying, from some forgotten source, to summon a prayer. His lips formed a whisper, a whimper, a desperate shapeless plea for help. It did not come.

The voice was pounding him. Fear of the yellow eyes sucked the marrow from his bones, and all his self-will with it. The sky was a bitter, bloodied scarlet, and his ears could not distinguish any longer between the insidious commands in his head and the whine of the wind.

I don't want to die, he thought. I don't understand. I only know that I don't want to die, I can't die, I won't let it make me, it can't make me die . . .

The useless cycle of words spun ceaselessly in his mind as he slid into the stream, as his mouth opened, as he gave himself up to the relentless pressure and filled his lungs with the brutal crush of moving water. Above his body, as it thrashed and then grew limp in the fast flowing stream, the sky suddenly opened with a thunderous crack of sound and light, and the rains came down.

Chapter 8

Cryth was even more frightened than he had been at the ceremony that had marked his coming to manhood. His body was frozen into a painful crouch, his palms pressed flat against the chilly ground. All around him was darkness and the smell of the unknown. His eyes were blind and useless. Beneath his hands the earth seemed to breath, a steady and knowing susurration of heat.

That he found himself in hell was Lun's doing, and this knowledge frightened him most of all. He could feel his love for her, a total and abject enslavement to what she had been to him, refusing to mutate or die, impossible though it seemed in the face of whatever it was she was slowly becoming.

There was a voice in the velvety blackness with him, the voice of Asulicca, so old and wise. Her voice was huge and hollow as the wind. She was chanting words he could not distinguish in a tune that wafted like the smoke from the fire rites into his brain and out again, leaving an odd sense of inevitability behind them.

He could feel Lun there beside him, crouched with him in the empty place, unafraid and knowing. She seemed to vibrate with the power that had come so disastrously upon her. Though he could not hear or see her, he was intensely aware of her presence for he could smell her. It was not the smell he knew, the touch of cooking mingled with the warmth of the season. This was a musky reek, overpoweringly erotic, and he felt his body acknowledge her even as he choked on the bile of purest fear. For what crouched beside him was only the shell of the Lun he had known and loved, a shell inhabited by something he could not even envision.

She was reaching out to him. In the dense darkness he saw her eyes, the twin points of hot amber. They moved towards him, and then suddenly they were growing with incredible speed into the eyes of some beast from the swamps that had been here since before time began . . .

His own scream, pitiful and deafening, woke him. He sat up, panicked and confused, until the familiar feel of his own straw resting place, the touch of the rough covers and the sound of Cel's rhythmic breath convinced him that he was awake and alive, the nightmare over. In the darkness he ran one shaking hand across his face. It came away dripping with sweat.

Cryth sat up, tensed and listening. He had just realised that the only breathing he could hear was Cel's. He flung out an arm across the other half of the bed and found it empty.

It was only when he tried to rise, and found his legs unsteady beneath him, that he knew what had happened. She had drugged him, and Cel too; the child's breathing was too deep and slow for the normal restless slumber of a baby. He forced himself to his feet, pushing himself across the hut to the hide door. As he pushed it cautiously open, a thin line of moonlight fell in a direct line across the floor, like an accusing finger pointing directly at the empty pallet. It fell across Cel who slept on, unknowing.

His head was spinning. He could feel the drug, whatever it was, working through his system. A heavy dose, he thought savagely. It had been Lun's bad luck that something, the gods perhaps, had brought him a dose of dreams even more powerful than whichever powder she had stirred into his food this night.

He shook his swimming head and moved unsteadily out into the sleeping settlement, bright in the moonlight.

The clearing was empty of life. All around him, the covered doors of the huts looked like thin mouths set against him. The pots had been scoured and left for the morning. Near the door to one hut, that of Mydd who was the finest smith in all the tribes,

65

was a half-finished spear. The arcane carvings on the hilt looked like wounds bleeding darkness in the dim light.

He walked quietly to the centre of the clearing and craned his neck, his eyes scouring the distance for her. The night air moved in a dry dance against his naked body. A movement in the distance caught his eye; Lun, down at the stream. He took a step forward, his mouth clamped into a thin line, and felt his heart stop momentarily as a dry hand closed tight on his shoulder. He turned, biting back a cry, and found himself staring into Asulicca's black eyes.

'Do not go to her,' she said. 'It will do you no good to go to her now, and it might bring you both harm. Do not.'

They stared at each other. Cryth's voice was thick with shock. 'I did not hear you come, old one.'

'I came quietly. I knew you would wake in confusion.'

'She drugged me.' The knowledge knifed him. He turned his head once more as a thin humming sound, flat and uninflected, reached him on the breeze. 'She gave me something, and Cel too, so that we would not wake. How did you know I would wake in spite of her?'

Her voice was casual. 'Because you were dreaming, that I knew, and once you dreamed, you would come out.'

He turned his back on the figure in the distance to stare at Asulicca. 'Yes, I dreamed. How did you know?'

'I gave you the dream.' She sounded both apologetic and reasonable. 'I m sorry it could not be a pleasant one, but I knew you would not wish to wake if the dream was pleasant.' Her tone changed suddenly to one of flat command. 'You will tell no one, young one.'

'No,' he agreed. The situation was too strange for him; it defeated him by its lack of precedent. Old women did not give orders to priests of the high cults. Yet it was impossible, looking into those fathomless black eyes, listening to the voice of an authority so much stronger than his own, to deny her. 'I will say nothing. Now tell me, old one. What do you know of this — this fever of Lun's?'

Her eyes held his, unmoving but comforting. 'Something, young one, something but not nearly enough. She is still Lunica, for now; still Lunica when the sun is high and there are things to distract her. But she will not be Lunica much longer, young one. You must face that.'

Cryth turned cold. 'Not Lun? I cannot understand you. How can she not be herself?'

She reached out and touched his face in a gesture of infinite beauty and tenderness. 'She is waiting, Cryth. She awaits the return of the gods that have claimed her for their own.' She added, very gently, 'I am sorry for you.'

As Asulicca spoke a sharp breeze sprang up, carrying dust on the night air. Overhead, clouds raced across the face of the waning moon. Distant thunder rumbled among the open plains to the south. Cryth almost unknowingly made the two-handed gesture used to placate the great Taranis who pleasured himself with thunder. A few drops of rain fell, loud against the dusty earth. In the distance the thin chanting grew marginally louder.

Asulicca's voice became urgent. 'You can do nothing, young one. Pray to your fire gods, if you will, for the way to save her. Pray that the elders learn nothing, that she has the wisdom and the strength to keep her gift to herself. But I do not think you can help her. I think she is too young, and the taste of power too strong for her. She has been given the Eyes, the Eyes that see inside the souls of men, the gods' way of hearing our very thoughts. Once given such a gift cannot be revoked. It is her own now for as long as she lives.' She turned her head and, as though mesmerised, Cryth's eyes followed.

Lun stood, a straight figure against the clouds. Her hands were held high, palms opened to the night. Her hair streamed loose behind her as the wind rose with unnatural speed. She lifted her voice, arched her body, singing. A thin wisp of steam rose from the water at her feet. Thunder cracked like a whiplash. As Cryth watched, shuddering, a single streak of the fire of heaven shot from the clouds above them and seared the water. Steam billowed in a column straight as Mydd's spear, and Lun was obscured from view.

'There is something in the water with her. She is calling the god,' Asulicca said dully. 'The power grows in her every passing moment. She should be dead now; no one can live in the fires of the god. But see, no harm has come to her, nor will it. This is more than just the Eyes. She has summoned the rain, and called the river to herself. It does her bidding. The gods hear her well.'

Cryth turned his back on the stream, his eyes wide and black. His hands closed on Asulicca's in a crushing grip.

'You say she calls the god to her,' he said fiercely. 'Which god, old one? You will tell me which god has done this to her, to both of us. Camulos? Great Bel? Which?'

'That,' she said softly, 'I do not yet know. But I will know, and soon.' His hands loosened and fell away. They stood in the rain that was driving down now, the young priest and the old woman. Slowly, insidiously, a strange smell crept into the water-logged air. It was similar to the fires of the cult burnings, unclean, disturbing. They heard Lun's voice raised once, in a cry of triumph.

Asulicca touched his shoulder. 'Come,' she said quietly, 'you can do nothing here. Go back inside now. I will watch until she has done.' She pushed him, a gentle but authoritative shove, toward the huts. 'Go.'

He went. Until just before sunrise the world was lashed with rain and Cryth, unsleeping and sad as an old man in his dry hut, spent the hours watching through the hide, cracked open just enough to allow him vision. Lun stayed down by the stream. And Asulicca, turning her back on the stream and what happened there, walked back and forth from the heart of the village to its edge, in a solitary and unceasing vigil. He knew enough to realise that she was praying. And he knew enough, in spite of himself, to guess what might pass between them when, as the rain stopped, the two women met.

In the dead hour of the night, Lun had woken and gone directly to the water's edge.

She came awake like a cat, eyes wide, senses alert. She had mixed the grey powder with Cryth's food and in obedience to its properties he slept on the edge of coma. Cel, too, had chewed happily on his doctored bone. Although the hut was blanketed in night she could see him lying peacefully on his back in the beautiful sleep of babies, mouth open, cheeks flushed. He would not wake until morning but Cryth was not as deep as she would have liked. Despite the darkness she saw him, and smelled the sweat on him; once he shifted as if in pain, and whispered her name. It was enough. She would be safe, for the god would protect her. Cryth might, by some mischance, awaken to find her gone but she did not doubt her hold on him, or her ability to bend his will to her own.

The searing heat of the day had been tempered by a cooling breeze. Disdaining clothing, Lun slid quietly past the hide and strode lightly across the village. Under a huge and gibbous moon the water glimmered, magically patterned, scoring the stream banks with black lines.

She squatted on the washing rock, staring down at the murky depths. There was power here, hovering on the edge of time; she could taste it, acid and undeniable, on the soft summer breeze. The sky was laced with a million points of light. Some were stars and some, she thought, were the eyes of the gods themselves, watching, looking down, approving . . .

She slid like an eel from the rock into the embrace of the stream. The water was deliciously warm, wrapping her legs, as she found a foothold against its current and stood thigh deep, with sensuality and desire.

She had come tonight for a purpose, and to meet the dawn with that purpose unfulfilled was, to Lun, unthinkable sacrilege. She had lost once to old Asulicca who knew what moved on the tail of the winds and the rains. She would not lose this time. She had the power. It was her own, it could not be taken from her. All she needed, the only thing that mattered to her now, was the name of her own god. Once she knew that, she would become the power.

And she knew, in some dim way, that let her only become one with her own strength and no one could touch her. Not Cryth, not Asulicca, not the elders themselves, with their blood-soaked baskets and their black curling knives ...

Her body was hot; it seemed to warm the lapping water around her. She closed her eyes and saw, behind shuttered lids, the image of the goddess as she had been, tall and queenly. She saw the white cup of sacrifice, surely finer than anything human hands could make. And the golden body of the god asleep, eyes fast, hands weaving...

Delicately, feeling the night, she opened her hands to the touch of the sky. 'You summoned me,' she thought, and the words became tangible, first in her own mind and then in the flesh, as she unknowingly began to chant in a low keening. 'You summoned me, great ones. Now I summon you. Give me of yourself, give me, return to me now. Taranis, Brigantia, Nodens, Clota who is the Old Woman of the River ...'

Above her head, small clouds began to form, shot through with light. She did not see them. Neck stretched taut, hair blowing on the breeze, she concentrated on the water and the wavering, indistinct vision that slowly, from the mists of time and space, took shape before her.

He was like nothing she had ever seen before, and yet he was no god. She could not have said how she knew this, but know it she did. Perhaps it was the fear that, over whatever distance separated them, she could smell coming from him. He was young and strangely dressed. He sat in the settlement, hands outstretched towards an indistinct bundle that lay near him. She heard him feel. She heard him think.

He thought no words that she knew. But the sense of them was clear to her; he saw eyes, yellow eyes, her eyes, fixed on him with power and command. And he was afraid. Beyond him was the stream and there, moving, trying to take solid shape and failing, was another figure. The figure of a woman, a figure she knew ...

70

'Goddess,' she thought, and did not hear her own voice burst into a low, thin cry of exultation. 'Goddess, you have given me my power. I will offer to you. I will offer . . .'

He could hear her. Staining the strange garments he wore was the sweat of fear. His very bones seemed racked by the desire to escape the place of offering. 'No,' she thought, 'you do not escape me now. You will go to the goddess. She asks for you and it is for me to offer you. I give you freely . . .'

He rose now, the young stranger, docile to her will. Around the sleeping huts of the Dumnonii thunder cracked. Her hands lifted, commanding, supplicating. The goddess was gone . . . no, she remained, yet faintly, as though watching from another place, another time. She seemed distressed. Lun could see the glow that lit her, a spectral aureole of brilliant light, now sharp, now flickering. Lun's hands opened to their fullest and pushed, out and down, pushed towards the stream in a surge of power that filled her like the terrible taste of blood.

He was gone like a shade. She saw him struggle as the watching woman grew distinct then faded once more. Then the thrashing body was still, one hand clenched in cadaveric spasm on the jutting shelf of the great rock. The goddess had no features now as her long body bent to receive the offering in the water, and Lun could feel nothing. But surely she was pleased. Sacrifice pleasured the gods.

Lun knew the name at last. She who guarded the rivers and waterways; the hag, the crone, who had beauty and ugliness, strength and pity. Clota, mother of water. It could be none other. Clota, who came when man was ready to die, she who washed your bloodstained clothes in the cold water, staining it with red. Clota the protector. Clota, giver of this power, this miraculous wondrous gift . . .

Her hands relaxed. She let her breath out. The sky above her split suddenly in a shearing of light as the streak of lightning she had unwittingly called down struck the water with a sound like death and the stream became a raging flow of running fire.

She stood, untouched and unharmed, in the heart of the

inferno. Legs planted in the water, body tingling, the water boiled and coursed around her, its gentle froth maddened by the bolt of heaven. A huge pillar of steam rose, engulfing her, and she breathed the scalding moisture deep into her lungs. She had never, in all her life, known such a sense of well-being, of quietude, of peace. It was her proof that she was protected. The rain began to fall.

She stood for hours, a creature of the night, unbound by men's rules. She, Lunica, had done with her spirit what the old fools in their white robes could do only by tyranny and force. She had willed an offering to its death, and it had done her bidding. She was apart from all men now. She was no longer of the tribe, no longer of human flesh.

The enraged waters finally settled as the rain stopped an hour before sunrise. Lun stirred languidly, feeling as sultry and depleted as she might feel after love, and turned back towards the settlement. There, standing in the centre of the village, was Asulicca.

She knew at once that the old woman had seen all. More than that: Asulicca had come out and watched for her. For a fleeting moment Lun felt fear and awe but she quickly swallowed them. Asulicca could not touch her, not now.

The old woman regarded her silently. Black eyes locked to amber, both faces impassive. Finally she spoke.

'So you have found your god, Lunica. Or is it goddess?'

'Goddess.' Lun, in the draining away of the night, felt limp and sated, disinclined for pretence. She smiled lazily at Asulicca. 'You were watching me, then.'

'That is true.' The old woman might have been making casual conversation. Her eyes alone betrayed her; they were hard as flint, watchful and wary. 'It was impressive, young woman. The power grows apace. But do you grow with it?'

The black pupils, impossibly wide in their pools of gold, contracted. 'What does that mean, old one?'

'It means what I asked, no more, no less. It is forbidden for you to hold or use this power, you know this as well as I do. Should the

72

elders learn of it you would die, and die horribly. But perhaps you do not mind that, now that you have found your goddess?'

Lun's pupils were now vertical slits. She did not look completely human. 'Oh, yes, I would mind. But how would the elders find me out? Were you thinking of telling them?'

Asulicca made an odd sound which Lun, incredulously, identified as amusement. '*I* tell them? You speak like a fool. No, I shall tell them nothing. Nor shall Cryth, poor man, though you will destroy him in the end.'

Lun stiffened. 'I shall never harm Cryth.'

'You will. You cannot help yourself, not now. Perhaps Lun would never harm her husband, much as she holds him and his priest's robes in contempt. But you will not be Lun much longer without some wisdom, for the power you crave and now have to hand will eat you alive.'

Lun's smile curved into line of contempt. 'And so?'

Asulicca said harshly, 'Cryth saw you tonight, you know. He watched you, there at the stream.'

Fear struck at Lun like a dagger. 'You lie, old one. I gave him a powder, to make him sleep. He could not wake from that and I not know. I have the Eyes!'

Asulicca's voice was scathing with contempt. 'You have the Eyes. And so? You have not the wisdom, or the weight of years, to show you how to use them. You are like Cel with his bone; it is important to him, he loves it, it is his comfort and his toy. That is what you are like with the Eyes. You are weak, and ignorant.' Again came that sharp snort which was not quite amusement. 'Of what use to the god is a woman both ignorant and weak?'

'You lie,' the girl said obstinately. 'You are a liar. How could Cryth wake?'

'You understand nothing.' The old woman leaned forward until their eyes were inches apart. 'And think, Lun. If Cryth can wake from the sleep of the drugged, what is to keep others, Bel perhaps, from seeing what you do?' She shook her head. 'You understand nothing, I say.'

'Then teach me.' Lun's voice was silky with menace. 'Teach

me, old woman. You have great power. Even I cannot see so far as I think you can. But you can show me how to use that with which I have been gifted. You will show me.'

Asulicca looked into the intent and beautiful face for long minutes. Then she spat directly into Lun's face.

'Learn for yourself, proud young fool,' she said, and smiled. The harsh stretching of the lips made of the lined face a nightmarish death's head. 'You are swollen and drunk with your power. You are no different from those dancing men you watched on the night of virgin moon, the men I saw you spy on, the men you despise. You have a gift and it will kill you in the end. Yes, Lun, go and learn for yourself. I will teach you nothing.'

Chapter 9

As Marian stopped the Range Rover at the foot of Beacon Tor the car stalled for the fourth time since leaving the main road. Once again, she forced back an overwhelming desire to turn it around and return to Four Shields.

The storm was like none she had seen before. It seemed a living thing, with breath and claws of its own, present for some purpose she could not see yet knew to be dangerous. But that way, she thought grimly, lay definite madness; marooned in the middle of a lethal bog in a virtual hurricane was neither time nor the place to give way to panic. So she bit back her terror once again and focussed her mind on the tasks at hand: starting the car and finding Roger Dawkins, wherever he was.

She knew he was out on the moor. The knowledge was complete, as unarguable as the colour of her own eyes, and she wasted no time wondering how she could be so positive. He was out here, and the story she had told him had brought him here. It was up to her to find him, if she could.

The wind was now blowing with such velocity that it drowned out even the noise of the Range Rover's powerful engine. It blew so strongly that she could see the rain, in the Rover's headlamps, coming down at an impossible angle; the drops were enormous and elongated, oddly beautiful. Marian thought they looked like millions of tiny daggers thrown directly at her.

After its fourth stall, the engine took much longer to start up again. The Range Rover, like the Jaguar and the Volvo, was equipped with an expensive defogger; running at full power, however, it was insufficient now to clear the windows of their layer of noxious mist. Marian rummaged in her pockets and, finding a handful of crumpled tissues, wiped the windscreen. Outside the wind roared its dementia through the black night. She could make out the looming shape of Beacon Tor above her, and beyond that nothing at all.

She was, very simply, afraid to get out of the car. The weather was so ugly, seemed so deliberately malevolent, that she was unwilling to expose herself to it. Remembering how she had been slammed against the door in Okehampton, she reached down and gingerly tested the sore spot on her thigh. She nearly jumped at the pain; even the bones beneath the bruised skin seemed to hurt.

Her unwillingness to open the car door left her with only one reasonable alternative. Dropping the clutch into first gear, she eased the car along the rough road towards the settlement, leaning on the horn all the way.

Even travelling at five miles per hour she came upon the rise of the settlement hill so suddenly she nearly sent the car off the road. Making sure that the emergency brake was securely in place, she blew a solid blast on the horn.

Nothing. 'Well', she thought, 'you've just ran out of options, my love. Nothing for it, now, but to take the torch from the glove box and go out into the storm.'

She sat for a moment, irresolute. To leave the headlamps on and flood the hillside with blessed light, and risk draining the battery? It was true that there was a spare battery, in its own steel case, in the back of the Rover. But if the worst happened and the light drained the battery of power, how would she be able to change it in this howling deluge? Yet to go out into that angry dark, with only the torch for light . . .

In the end this unusual fear of the noise-laden dark forced her into a compromise. She turned the car around and, leaving the engine running, switched on the emergency blinkers. Then, with her body stretched to a painful angle in an effort to maintain her footing against the drag of the wind, she slowly climbed the rise. She could barely make out the powerful hum of the engine behind her. As she pulled herself up over the rise and stood blinking into the night, the flash and pulse of the blinkers seemed to pace her very heartbeats.

She stood there, her eyes slowly adjusting. The rain seemed less heavy up here, the wind lighter. It was almost as though this tiny spot in the vast moor was the eye of the storm. She cast her glance around in a slow, methodical sweep, refusing to admit to herself how much the black doorways resembled mouths. On the third attempt her vision suddenly accustomed itself to the murk and she saw, as she had not before, something small and dark lying motionless in the rain.

Marian forced her numbed legs forward, aware of a deep unwillingness to see what it was. Kneeling, she touched it, running chilled fingers over it. It was a knapsack of sturdy nylon and velcro. She picked it up, finding it sodden and very heavy. Awkwardly manipulating the heavy torch, she opened it.

A half-eaten packet of Smarties, twisted shut. A pair of leather gloves. Some tissues, crumpled but clean. And, lastly, a small book, black, bound, old, bearing the stamp of the Oke-hampton Lending Library. She played the torch across the worn cover, ignoring the rain that spattered the binding, and peered at the title: 'Gods of the Elements: A Field Guide to the Ancient Religions of Europe and Asia'.

A sudden gust of wind tore the rucksack's heavy overflap from her slack grasp and lifted it vertically into the air. In the centre was a name scratched in black marker: 'R. Dawkins'.

The bag slipped to the ground from her nerveless fingers. Smarties, tissues and gloves flew out and scattered. The coloured sweets rolled and rested, melted in the rain, running into each other in spots of emotions: red for anger, green for jealousy. She stood still looking down at the pathetic objects, wondering what to do.

He must be near. Roger would not willingly have abandoned his knapsack. The dull flashes of the Range Rover's lights shot the night with amber, illuminating the silent stone huts in a series of freeze-frames. What if he had gone into one of them? What if he had had an accident, was lying hurt, in one of those haunted monuments?

She could not bring herself to do it. Marian turned, slow and unwilling, to regard the circle of buildings. They looked back at her, waiting, inimical. 'No,' she thought, 'I can't. I won't. No matter what, I simply cannot walk into one of those doorways, standing there like alien mouths. No.'

She raised her voice to its highest pitch, shouting his name. Head cocked and hands clenched, she waited. There was nothing but the wind and the rain falling steadily, and in the distance the Range Rover humming expectantly. She took a step towards the huts, and waved the torch slowly. Shadows flickered and froze once more in the dancing beam.

It hit her with the force of a blow. Out of the dark, an arrow of knowledge, came the realisation that she was being watched. There was something here with her, something that watched her, avid, greedy, wanting her. Her eyes hunted from hut to hut and found nothing, no light, no presence, no sign of life. Yet the knowledge was absolute and undeniable. She was not alone.

She began to edge away, never turning her back on the settlement. She could not go yet. There was proof that Roger Dawkins had been this way, and she had not found him. She could not run screaming down the rise, into the safe warm car and home to Four Shields. Yet to stand here was torture, unbearable torture, and she could not bring herself even to approach the huts. That left only the stream.

She came to it slowly, walking in a crab-like scuttle, keeping one eye on the treacherous ground and the other on the village behind her. She had just reached the great flat rock that jutted out over the stream when she stopped in her tracks, bile rising in her throat on a sickening tide. She did not hear her own shriek split the night.

Before her was the rock, and then a two foot drop into the stream, rushing out of control, engorged with rain. And wrapped around the rock's outer edge were fingers, clenched and bony knuckled. In the light of her torch they were livid blue, another indication, if she had needed it, of the presence of death.

Her fear of her surroundings was forgotten, swallowed by the larger panic, and she ran forward, dropping to her knees on the rock. The torch pointed straight down at the living, writhing water below her.

An arm, clad in the sleeve of a leather hiking jacket. A watch, pathetic and futile, strapped to the wrist. She pulled at the arm, scarcely knowing what she did. The sodden leather was incredibly heavy and the fingers, clenched in rigor, refused to let go their ghastly hold.

She was trembling so badly that the torch moved like a living thing. It shone down into the bloated face, the floating tendrils of hair, and fixed in a ray of horror on the ghastly eyes, open and beseeching. Dead, Roger stared back at her above blue lips drawn into a ghastly rictus.

The splash of the torch as it fell was drowned by the deafening crack of thunder above. It was not conscious intelligence that prompted her leap backward. But as she fell, rolling away from the rock and the fingers and the glazed eyes, the sky burst open in a flash of lightening and the world was full of intolerable light.

She had no memory of getting to her feet, of following the blinking car lights back to safety, of driving to Four Shields. It was not until she stood in her own living room, reaching out a hand that shook uncontrollably for the telephone, that the thick crust of panic that had blanketed her mind cracked along the edges, letting in reality and memory . . .

Julian's voice on the other end of the line came sharp and angry. 'Marian! I've been calling you every five minutes for the last two hours! Where the hell have you been? I was worried sick!'

Memory returned like a light breaking through the dark and the fog. Fingers, eyes, a contorted face . . . She began to weep, and the weeping became sobbing hysteria as she cradled the phone as she had not been able to cradle that ruined corpse in the water. 'Julian,' she said. 'Come home. Please come home.' And with that, over forty years of containment and self-sufficiency crumbled into dust and was gone.

'Please,' she said. 'I need you'.

'You're sure he was dead?'

The remark was incongruous when spoken in its present setting. On arriving home some four hours after his call, Julian had found her huddled on the sofa, her soaked clothes stuck to her skin, teeth chattering, eyes vacant. It had taken not only his promise that he would stay with her but a certain amount of bullying to convince her to run herself a hot bath. Now the scalding water worked its magic upon her shocked body and she had calmed down enough to answer his question.

'Yes, I'm sure.' An entire bottle of scented bath oil had been poured under the taps. Marian had given Julian the story in its entirety, omitting only one thing: the dreadful, never to be forgotten smell of roasting flesh. The odour had been hauntingly familiar, fouling the night as the lightning struck the water. The air seemed full of it, and not all the perfume she could lay hands on would cleanse that memory away.

Julian, perched on Marian's delicate dressing stool, watched her, frowning. He had not liked the look of drugged disbelief on her face when he arrived. Without realising it, he began nervously to rub his hands together, caressing the angry pink skin that had grown over the burn.

He said quietly, 'You said you tried to move him, to pull him out. His hand — was it rigor mortis, Marian?'

She leaned her head back against the porcelain, and answered him tiredly. 'I don't know. I — it was all so unreal, like something in a cheap horror film. Blue fingers, holding the edge of the rock. I tried to pull them loose, and they were stiff, tight. And his face . . .'

'All right, darling. All right.' He had heard the surge of hysteria, the sharp rise of pitch, and spoke soothingly. 'Now, will you be all right by yourself for a few minutes? I need to make a telephone call.'

'To whom?'

'The police,' he said gently. 'I know you were too shocked and upset to think clearly. But this is what is known as a suspicious death, Marian. The police must be told of it. In any case —' his voice was suddenly savage — 'I can't stand the thought of his body bouncing around in that stream. The police have the tools to get him out.'

Her eyes felt leaden with exhaustion. 'Yes, I see. All right, go and ring them. They'll likely want to see me, won't they? Tell them to come tonight. I can talk with them whenever they need. The time doesn't matter.'

He was gone for only a few moments. 'They're on their way, said to expect them within the hour. You were quite right. They do want to talk with you.'

'Only to be expected.' Reluctantly she pulled the plug out and lay immobile as the bathwater gurgled slowly down the drain. It was odd, she thought, that water should be at once so comforting and yet so terrible. Refreshed and sane once more, she wrapped herself in her dressing gown and sat down with Julian to await the arrival of the local constabulary.

He seemed restless. Watching him, Marian saw the faint blue shadows under his eyes and the thin grooves, where none had been only a short week ago, running in a tight line from cheek to chin. He prowled the room for a few minutes while she said nothing, merely watched him. Then, with an air of relief that was obvious, he settled to building a fire. Within minutes the room was brightly lit, and full of dancing shadows.

The police arrived a prompt forty minutes later. The storm, oddly, seemed to have died down; the wind was dropping slowly but steadily. When the buzzer from the front gates sounded, filling the room with disembodied voices, Julian was nursing his third brandy and soda and Marian her second. He got to his feet, gave directions and leaned against the wall as if only it had the power to hold him upright.

Mercifully, the man in charge of the delegation from the Okehampton constabulary was a casual acquaintance of theirs,

Sergeant Peter Wilking. The men came in, apologising in their soft west country voices for dripping on the floors. Julian took their coats and their umbrellas and told them not to worry. Drinks were suggested and politely declined; an offer of coffee proved more acceptable.

The five of them settled by the fire, hands wrapped around the large steaming mugs. Glancing around the room, Wilking's stolid face bore an unusually appreciative expression.

'This is nice,' he said. 'It's a bad night out.'

'I couldn't' Marian said drily, 'agree more.'

Wilking twisted his sturdy body to look her full in the face. In the hands of one of his companions, a notebook and pen made their silent appearance.

'That's right,' he said softly. 'Mr Dunne told me when he called that you'd had a bad experience. He said you'd found a body out on the moor?'

Marian shot her husband a surprised look, one that was not missed by anyone in the room. 'Is that all you told them, Julian? Why on earth...?'

He took her hand, giving it a gentle squeeze. 'I didn't want to load them down with information that I might not have got straight, darling. After all, I wasn't there. Better for you to tell them, don't you think?'

'Yes. Yes, all right.' She swallowed a mouthful of coffee and turned to face Wilking once again. Her voice was strained but perfectly steady.

'About a mile and three-quarters to the southeast of Beacon Tor is an Iron Age village. It's built on a rise, a concentric circle of huts around a central clearing. There's a small stream with a pebbled bed running to the north of it. You know the place, I expect.'

'Aye, I do.' His eyes were bright and inquisitive. 'And about this village?'

'In the stream is the body of Roger Dawkins, the Okehampton librarian. I think he's been drowned, but I couldn't be sure. Roger is — the body was bobbing about in the stream, clutching an outcrop of rock with one hand.' She swallowed hard, and the coffee mug began to tremble. 'I tried to pull him out, but I couldn't. His hand — I couldn't unbend the fingers. They were tight . . . ' Her voice died.

'I see, Mrs Dunne.' His genial blue eyes had turned to flint. 'I'm sorry to hear this. It must have been a bad thing for you. When did this happen, please?'

'Some hours ago — I never thought to look at my watch, and I had been driving so slowly because of the storm. Sixish, perhaps, or a bit later. I don't think the exact time is going to matter when you get his body out.'

'Well, Mrs Dunne, we'll have to hold a post-mortem examination, you know. That tells the pathologist things.'

'I don't think it's going to help you,' she repeated. 'A bolt of lightning struck the water.' Her hand began to shake once more, so badly this time that coffee splashed her robe, and left a small puddle on the table as she set the cup unsteadily down. 'I could smell — I really don't think that examining the body will help you much.'

'All right, Mrs Dunne. All right. Try not to distress yourself.' Wilking seemed to have lost any desire for coffee; he was looking rather sick. 'I know this must be painful for you, but if you could just give me some details? It would be a very great help to us.'

Her eyes were fixed on the fire. 'I really haven't much more to tell you, Sergeant.'

'You can begin,' he said quietly, 'by telling me why you went out on the moor in this weather.'

'Oh, I see.' She turned around and faced him. 'I went because I was worried about Roger. I thought he might be there. I knew he wasn't at home.' She drew a deep breath. 'I've been doing some reading up on the history of the Iron Age settlements. Yesterday I went to the lending library to find some books on the subject, and I got into a discussion about it with Roger. He found me some books. I could tell he was interested.'

'Yes?' Wilking's voice was completely neutral.

'Well, I wanted to talk to him about what I'd read. I called him this afternoon, at home, just after the storm started. He wasn't there and I got worried. I don't know why, but I did. I remembered that he likes — he liked — to walk on the moor, and the storm had come up very quickly. I drove into Okehampton to look for him but he wasn't there.'

'So you went to look for him on the moor?' Wilking's voice was still impassive, but Marian felt herself flush.

'Yes. I know it sounds strange, Sergeant, but while I was outside his house one of his storm shutters blew off.'

'So you knew he hadn't been home. Very sensible.' The quiet voice should have been reassuring, yet somehow was not. 'It was very brave of you to drive out on Dartmoor in this weather, Mrs Dunne. Very brave indeed. I don't think it would have occurred to me to do it.'

'I wasn't thinking.' She met his even gaze, and regarded him steadily. 'Roger Dawkins was my daughter's boyfriend for many years, Sergeant, and our two families are very close friends. I didn't intend to go out there, I was coming back here, but I — I changed my mind.'

He said gently, 'Just a feeling, like? A stroke of female intuition, maybe?'

She bit her lip. 'Maybe. I couldn't really describe it to you; I couldn't even describe it to myself. I just had a very strong feeling that he had gone out there, and I went after him. I thought he might have been hurt, might need help. Is there anything wrong with that?'

'Nothing wrong with it. It's a bit unusual, that's all. Now, I'd like you to tell me something, Mrs Dunne. There are hundreds of those old stone villages out on the moor. How did you know he'd be at that one?'

'Because that was where . . .' She stopped abruptly.

For a few moments no one said anything. Wilking watched her impassively, as though some inner suspicion had been confirmed. Then Julian reached for her hand.

'Tell them why, Marian. They won't believe us but it's the truth, and they have a right to know. Roger is dead, and it may be our fault. If we can do anything, anything at all, to help . . . tell them why. Please.'

Marian took her coffee cup and emptied it. Then, her eyes never leaving Wilking's face, she told them.

Chapter 10

'Asulicca.'

The old woman dozing in the warm sunlight heard her name through a thin veil of sleep. The voice was known to her, but not welcome; to acknowledge it was to court trouble and grief, and she wished for neither. She was asleep and wished to stay asleep.

'Wake, old one. I want speech with you.'

Go away, she thought. Go away and leave me alone. I know what you want, and I will not give it to you. You are wasting your time. Get back from me, and let me sleep ...

'No, I shall not leave you be. I say you shall wake and talk with me.' A small foot nudged her, not ungently. Through her own closed lids Asulicca could see the charming smile pricking up the corners of the girl's mouth. 'I shall not harm you, either, so waken.'

With an inward sigh, the old woman abandoned the silent argument and opened her eyes.

Lun, eyes slitted against the afternoon glare, stood in a posture of unconscious insolence. A small brown hand lay flat against one jutting hip; the girl's head, Asulicca noted, was high and straight. There was something flaunting and teasing in Lun's stance. It might have been the pose of a girl who knew, beyond doubt, that she could capture a lover with the wave of a negligent hand. It bespoke a certain kind of power, implicit in every line.

Asulicca, as easily as a bird might fly, could read the thoughts that moved behind Lun's eyes. She felt a great sense of relief. Though the power was growing, the girl had not yet learned to mask her own thoughts and desires. Asulicca spoke dryly.

'Well, Lun? Have you come to trouble me for things I will not give you, or merely to confide?'

Oddly, the girl showed no upset at this shrewd question. 'To confide, old one. You alone can understand what is happening to me. You say you know what is to become of me. I must speak of it or go mad. I can trust you, I think.'

Asulicca spoke wearily. 'Oh, yes, you can trust me. But to what end? I know what it is you should do but no matter what I say you will not do it, because you cannot. You have been given a taste of something that is too strong for your blood, and you will never renounce it now. It owns you, for good or for evil. So why bother me?'

'Come with me.' Lun stooped and lifted her gently to her feet. Her grip was strong. 'Walk with me on the moor, and we will talk together. I wish to be away from these chattering geese, and I must talk with you for safety. You know the pools of scum, how their pressure is given to the air as bubbles? Keep the pressure in, and the bubbles burst. That is what I need, to free some bubbles. You would not deny me something so harmless.'

They reached the edge of the hill and began, slowly, to make their way down. 'No, Lun, I cannot deny you that. What you look to become, dangerous and diseased, is not yet. At present you are still Lun, a young girl I care for, and I will help you in this way.' She stopped and met Lun's eye. 'But only in this way, young one. Take no notions that you can get the knowledge you desire from me by force or by trickery, for you cannot do it. My caution is stronger than your body, and my defences are good.'

'I know. You have told me this before, and I see no reason to disbelieve you. But I want to ask you something, and you can have no reason to refuse to answer.'

Asulicca settled her garments beneath her and sat down. 'I

will be the judge of that, Lun. You take too much for granted. But ask, and we shall see.'

'Very well.' Lun sat facing her. The yellow eyes held nothing now but worry and concentration. 'You saw what happened that night. You saw what I did, how I offered to the goddess and brought the rain and the lightning. You know that Clota of the waterways has given a gift to me.'

'Yes, I know that.'

'And you told me that I would hurt Cryth with this gift. Would such a use not be to desecrate the goddess and what she has given to me?'

'Desecrate?' Asulicca shook her head. 'I am no goddess, Lun, and I cannot answer you. How am I to know what would please or anger her?'

The low voice became urgent. 'Because you are a wise woman, a woman of great holiness. All the tribe knows it. I told you, I know that your gifts are even greater than mine. You can see into tomorrow, and beyond. You need not deny it, old one. I know it for the truth.'

She jumped to her feet, her arms flung wide. 'Can you not see how I suffer, knowing that you have seen my life and death yet will tell me nothing?'

Asulicca said very quietly, 'So what would you have me do, Lun? What would you have me tell you? That I have seen your death in colours that the devils of the earth have never dreamed of? What good will that do you?'

Tears began to course down the girl's face leaving dark tracks on her dusty skin. 'You advised me to leave this gift, to refuse it. Asulicca, you said that as a woman I was forbidden this knowledge, that it would bring me and Cryth too to harm and death. But if I were careful? If I grew to understand it? It haunts me, old one, it will not let me rest, knowing that I have powers that could bring the druids and their rush baskets to dust, and yet I may not show it, or take pride in it. If you would only tell me . . .'

The old woman said harshly, 'Tell you what? How to use your power, or how to hide it?'

'How to hide it, Asulicca. If I may learn to hide this thing, I may yet come to understand it.'

She said pityingly, 'This is the hardest lesson to learn: we cannot change what is to come to us. You cannot hide it now, girl. As it grows it covers you like a bright cloud over the sky at sunrise. If you stay as you are, and where you are, you will die. The elders will see it, even as I have seen it. And let them once discover that you have taken a power to yourself that is greater than theirs, and your life is nothing.'

She added, very calmly, 'And once you have died, in agony and disgrace, what do you think remains for Cryth? He is condemned with you, cast out of the priesthood, a traitor to the elders. At the worst they will kill him. If he is very lucky he will escape with his life and be shunned by our people. This is what lies ahead if your power grows.'

The despairing cry burst from Lun. 'But I did not seek this power, Asulicca, it was given to me. Given! What am I to do? Am I to bring down the anger of Clota upon myself by turning my back on what is almost never given? Can I offer the goddess such an insult?' She bit back a dry sob. 'It is not fair, Asulicca. Can it be fair?'

'Did you not seek it, young one?' The old voice was edged with authority. 'Were you not seeking it those many nights when you went to the stream and waited in the moonlight for the god, any god, to come to you? Did you not seek it when you hid behind the standing stone and watched the rites? Were you not trying to understand where that power came from, and how it was used?'

Lun stared at her, her throat working, her yellow eyes wide and hurt. She made no answer.

'This is why you can do nothing to save yourself, young one. This is why nothing I say to you can be of any help to you. You do not know yourself. If you have not the strength to know yourself, where can you find the strength to know the gods and the world around you? Understanding must begin in you, begin with you. If you do not know yourself, you can know nothing.'

She rose and shakily began to ascend the hill.

'I could run away,' Lun said from behind her. Asulicca stopped, supporting her weight against the hillside.

'That is true. You could go and live alone in the marshes. But in the end it would make no difference. You would die, of starvation perhaps or mauled by wild beasts, or perhaps caught by the men of another village. If they found you living an outcast in the marshes they would say you had run away for a crime, and their elders would kill you.' She moved further up the path. 'I cannot help you, child. I am sorry for you, yes, and sorrier still for Cryth who is blameless, but I can do nothing for you. Do not approach me on this matter again.'

Lun, a forlorn figure in the shadow of the tor above her, watched Asulicca's back disappear over the horizon. Her hands were balled into fists of frustration, her mind a racing freshet of rage and worry.

It was unjust. She had not gone to the gods. She had not said to them, in prayer or otherwise, that she desired to be able to see into the minds of men, to be able to call the rain and the sky fires. They had come to her in dream, they had put an offering in her path and Clota the Mother had waited in full view to see if she would offer it, as was fitting. But Asulicca had spoken to her as though she had willed all these things, and more besides.

Why should a woman not have a right to holy power? Why should it be the prerogative of men to worship and give honour to the gods who gave them all life, men and women alike? She felt her nails digging into her own calloused palms and, with a kind of spite, pressed harder. The pain seemed to embody the helpless frustration she felt.

No, it was not fair. And Asulicca had treated her as a silly child, with a child's inability to control the face she presented to the world.

Well, Asulicca would see that she had been mistaken. The gods had blessed Lun, and she would not throw that blessing back in their faces. It would not be seemly and it would likely be dangerous to do anything so foolhardy. Her offering of flesh and fire had been accepted; was that not proof of approval?

Angrily, she climbed her way back to the village. As she reached the summit a man's hand reached out to her and pulled her up over the edge.

The sunlight seemed shot with flame, dazzling and bright. The hand was not Cryth's but that of an older man, with veins and knotted muscles, the grip painful and cruel. She craned her neck to look into his face and felt her heart freeze.

'A pleasing day to you, young yellow-eyes,' said Bel, Father of the rites of Nemet. 'And what have you been doing with yourself in the marshes this morning?'

The archdruid stood looking down at her. He was a full head taller than Lun, broad and thickset. His face was like a mask wrought of oak, burned almost black by the sun and the religious fires, forbidding and dangerous. He was the most powerful man in the tribe and to Lun, who was well aware of the perils of incurring his displeasure, he was a living symbol of death and peril.

I will not panic, she thought. I must not, for here is danger in all its many skins, and to panic is to die. She blinked up at the chiselled face above her, and managed a slight bob of the knees, accompanied by the most charming smile she could muster.

'A fruitful day to you, Father,' she said, and her voice held nothing but respect and good cheer. 'I have been walking, no more; the heat of the cooking pots makes my head ache, and the wind helps me think.'

Behind him, a shadowy figure moved into her line of vision. It halted, tensed, and began to move towards them.

'And what do you think about, young one?' Bel's voice was deep, improbably calm. The iron grip on her wrist never eased. Please, she thought silently, let go of me...

'What do I think of? Oh, many things, Father. The crops and Cel, mostly. His teeth are coming and he is sometimes fretful.' The distant figure was moving rapidly now. It was Cryth, his face white and set. She lowered her head so that Bel would be unable to see her face, and directed the tiniest shake of the head at her husband. He stopped as if struck and then, more slowly, resumed his progress. She gathered the rags of her courage around her and, tilting her head gave Bel her best smile. His grip loosed slightly.

'I must finish my cooking, Father, else Cryth will be hungry and beat me. I am making a barley mash. Will you honour us and take your meal at our fire?'

Bel did not answer immediately. Cryth was almost upon them now, close enough to hear his reply.

'I thank you, young one, but I have eaten already. I have noticed the way you seek out Asulicca. Tell me . . .'

'Lunica!' Cryth, directly behind them, spoke so sharply and angrily that he might have read her thoughts and heard her silent plea for his cooperation. 'The sun is high and I have had no food yet. You forget your husband, with your dislike of the cookpots. Come back here, and finish the meal at once. It seems I am not strict enough with you. By Camulos, girl, I should cuff you for this!'

Blessed husband, she thought, I thank you and thank you again. Meekly, she bowed her head and scurried off to her pots. Her relief was so great that she was able to ignore the amused and pitying looks of the village women, witnesses to the entire episode. Never had Lun been chastised in full view of the tribe; there were many among them who felt that she would have been better for it. Snatching a heavy iron spoon, she began to pound the mash and feed the fire.

Cryth, his breathing audible, stalked back to the fire and bent over her.

'When we have eaten and it is time for the midday rest, we will talk. You will not refuse me, Lun.'

In all the years they had known each other, he had never spoken to her that way. She opened her mouth to retort and saw, outlined against the light, the heavy figure of the archdruid. He had not moved from where Cryth had left him and was staring in their direction.

From the corner of his eye Cryth saw him too. He lifted one

hand and brought it down in a sharp blow across Lun's cheek. Then he turned on his heel and stalked away, disappearing into their hut.

Lun did not look up. Her face burned, with the blow itself and with the shame of it. Though she knew that Cryth had hit her only to protect her — it was against all custom for anyone, even an elder, to interfere in a man's treatment of his women, and Cryth had known that a blow would deter Bel's intention to approach her again — a paralysing rage began to burn in the pit of her stomach. This is Bel's doing, she thought. By Clota, am I to sit here and suffer this treatment in silence, as though I am nothing but chattel or the village cow, to be chastised at their pleasure?

She remembered Bel standing smug and self-satisfied at the rites of the virgin moon, drawing his power from the death of a goat. He believes all knowledge is his and all power too, she thought, yet he did not even know I was watching. Racked by a sudden spasm of hatred and resentment, she lifted her head and willed revenge.

Across the brilliant sky thunder cracked. She tried to focus her eyes on Bel, somehow to let him know what she could do. Caution and sanity alike were submerged in her triumphant rage, in the excited chattering of the women.

But she did not see him. Between her and the archdruid stood another figure. Asulicca had moved from her seat in the shade against the stone wall and now stood between them. Her black eyes held warning and perfect understanding.

The look brought Lun back to sanity. She bent once more to her cookpots and forced herself to sing as the good smells began to rise from the baking food.

Bel took a step towards her, his face at that distance a black mask. Then he shrugged and turned away. Lun scooped the hot food into small bowls with a trembling hand, and brought it in to Cryth.

The bowls were empty and Cel, rosy and replete, slept in the corner. Lun had eaten hugely, for the tension of the morning's scenes had left her ravenously hungry. Cryth, pale and taut, had eaten his portion in silence. She never once looked up at him, never once met his eye, yet she knew that during the long meal his gaze had never left her face. A confrontation was unavoidable, and long overdue.

Cryth set his bowl down and wiped a lingering bit of the cooled mash from his face. Then he spoke quietly.

'We will talk, Lun. It is time and past time. Had I not been there this morning ...' A long shudder ran through him. 'I cannot even think of that. I am sorry I struck you. I had no wish to do it, but I did so to keep the Father at a safe distance. Later you should go to the stream and wash the bruise. It will swell if you leave it.'

Lun lifted her face to him. All the fight had gone out of her from the moment Asulicca had stepped between her and the archdruid. She spoke tiredly.

'Yes, it is time. I have not spoken with you before this, Cryth, because truly I have had nothing to say. Things of power were moving, coming together, but until now the time had not come. And I was angry at the blow, but I have forgotten it now. It is as you say: I believe you hit me to keep me safe. I bear no malice for that.'

He nodded. She saw with a slight pang of regret the lines that had etched themselves in his brow, the tautness of his body. They were the signs of a man who could not rest. She knew an impulse towards kindness and reached for his hand, closing her own thin fingers over his. He began to shake as if with a rigour. She spoke rapidly, not thinking about what she said, only trying to convey the truth.

'Cryth, I am sorry. I would not harm you or bring you grief. But on the night of the virgin moon...'

'You watched the mysteries. Yes.'

She wrenched her head up to meet his eyes, startled and shaken. 'You knew! But how?'

'It was in the morning ... I knew, when I saw you, that

something had happened to you in the night and I went out alone to think. My steps took me to the place of offering, and I found your prints there behind the standing stone. So I knew.' He shrugged helplessly. 'I wiped the prints away.'

Lun was frightened, and fear made her persistent. 'But how did you know it was me? It might have been anyone. You could not know the prints for mine.'

He smiled, an unexpected lightening of his face. 'They were not a man's prints. And what woman of the Dumnonii would have the courage to do such a thing if not my Lun?'

Tears filled her eyes and, unnoticed, began a slow dance down her face. 'I have been mad, Cryth, mad and sick with the fever of the gods, and I do not know what I should do, what I can do. I have had speech with Asulicca. She is wise, and has powers beyond any I know. But she will not help me, Cryth, and without her help I am like a child in the night, helpless and ignorant, fearful of the dark.'

He began to stroke her hair, long soft touches that were somehow both remote and mesmerising. 'Yes, Lun, the old one has great power but even greater wisdom. She has kept her skills to herself, and herself safe thereby.' He looked down at her sombrely. 'You drugged me two nights past, and Cel too. Why, Lun? Can you tell me?'

His face was indistinct through the blur of her tears. 'I had to, Cryth. I had no choice. The goddess was calling, the way she called to me at virgin moon. I had to do what she wanted; I had to go. And I did not think you would let me if you knew of it, so I gave you something to make you sleep. I never thought you would waken.'

He stiffened, muscles and tendons stretching to snapping point. 'The goddess? What goddess was this?'

'The Mother,' she whispered. 'Clota of the waterways. She came to me in sleep, with her consort. There was a temple, a cup of sacrifice. She came clear as the morning star, and she gave me something...' The whisper died away.

His hands slid down from her hair to her shoulders,

clamping hard around them, fingers digging deep into her brown skin. She stared into his face, not even noticing the pain.

'Clota,' he said. 'What did Clota give you, Lun?'

'I can hear you,' she said. 'I can hear you think, I can hear you feel. When I sit in the settlement, all the tribe moves about me and they think, Cryth, little petty things all bunched together, misty and unclear. But I can hear them. And the sky is mine, with its light and its water. I can call the rain and the sky fires. She gave that to me and I'm frightened, Cryth, I'm so frightened.'

He let go of her. On her shoulders were the livid marks of his grip. He said harshly, 'Frightened? Why should you be frightened? Did you not tell me, here in this hut, that you were waiting to find your power and your god? Was this not what you wanted, what you looked for?'

'Asulicca said — she said the same as you do.' Lun was having difficulty with her voice. 'She said that it had found me. She said that the power, and the goddess too, would eat me alive. She told me that, in the end, I would no longer be Lun. She frightened me, Cryth.' She paused painfully. 'She said that I would harm you.'

They faced each other, saying nothing. Lun's pupils had contracted to tiny dots. Oblivious, Cel shifted and resettled his beloved bone in his mouth.

'So you shall harm me?' His voice was thin. 'And did she tell you in what form the harm would come to me?'

'Cryth, don't look like that. I beg you, don't look at me that way. She is a mad old woman, that's all. I would never willingly do you harm — surely you cannot think I might do anything of my own free will to bring trouble on you?' She was pleading with him now. Her hands shot out and took his garments in a tight clutch. He saw how her fingers trembled, and spoke sadly and slowly.

'No, I do not believe you would. But Asulicca may have meant something very different.'

'Tell me,' she whispered. 'Tell me what you think she meant.'

'Did she not say that you would no longer be Lun? I think perhaps that she was saying this: the goddess has called you, and taken you to herself, but in taking you she will change you past all recognising and this new woman you will become will harm me.' He gently detached her fingers. 'Perhaps the power will eat you, and bring me harm that way. How can I know? Asulicca is not an old madwoman who mumbles with her years, my darling. When you gave me the drug she knew it, and woke me with a dream. I believe she has more magic to her hand than all the elders together, and the fire priests too. A god has her in his hand. I don't know which god it may be but she knows much, and if she says you will harm me then I believe she has seen it.'

'I don't believe you.' Lun's voice shook. 'I will not let it happen. I will refuse the power, give it back to the goddess, turn my back on her. I will be myself. I will!'

A sharp pain went through him, a pain that began in his legs and travelled up his spine with uncanny speed. His temples began to drum with it. Speech seemed difficult, yet he must speak. She was in torment, awaiting his answer.

'And if you do, Lun, what then? You have tasted the forbidden, you have called the elements and bent them to your will. And you killed for the goddess, Lun, Asulicca told me you did. I know more of sacrifice than you do and I tell you that once you have offered life to the gods you belong to them, body and soul. If you abnegate your gift, will you ever know contentment?' He shook his head, wincing at the pain of it. 'My head aches, and I must rest. No, my darling. You cannot give it back now, for you have signed to Clota that you are hers. We can only wait, and watch.'

The pain behind his eyes was blinding. He stumbled to his bed and fell across it. 'Lun, my head aches so. I don't think I can bear the pain. Will you not give me a potion to take the ache away and let me rest?'

'I will see to it.' She went swiftly to the door. With one hand on the hide she turned and looked at him, her eyes dark with hopelessness and misery. 'Is there no road to freedom for me, no way out of this snare? Is there nothing I can do to free myself, Cryth?'

'Nothing,' he said, and bit back a cry of agony as the pain washed through him. 'Nothing at all.'

Chapter 11

The inquest on what remained of the body of Roger Dawkins was held on Saturday afternoon in Dowbridge.

Marian was there, of course. She was the only witness who might even profitably guess what had driven the young librarian out into the storm on the previous Wednesday night. She had told Julian on Thursday morning that she felt up to going, that he needn't be there, that he had business in London to attend to. He had told her not to be bloody foolish and, for the first time since opening his own offices, had called Mrs Potter to say he would not be in London again until Monday.

So just after lunch on Saturday afternoon, they climbed into the Jaguar and drove sedately into Dowbridge, parking directly in front of the coroner's court. They arrived very early, which was fortunate. Roger Dawkins' death had provided the quiet community with a nine days wonder and at two o'clock, when the coroner called for order, the small room was packed with people. It looked as though every adult in the area had turned up to see the show.

Marian was uneasily conscious of a certain amount of pointing and whispering. She settled down next to Julian and muttered under her breath, 'I feel like a circus act. Why do all of their faces look so — look so . . .'

'Hungry? I don't know. They do, though.' Julian, too, was experiencing the sensation of being the focus of public attention for the first time, and not liking it at all. He muttered back,

'Funny thing. I never noticed it before, but Caroline Belling — do you believe that dreadful hat? — looks exactly like a lammergeier.'

'Like a what?' Marian was so surprised that she spoke in normal tones, and nearly everyone in their vicinity lowered their voices to eavesdrop. She felt herself blushing.

'A lammergeier.' Julian was suddenly angry at the crowd, at the situation, at the very fact of Roger's death. He raised his voice. 'A lammergeier is an extremely large vulture. It picks,' he explained as though addressing a boardroom meeting, 'on the bones of death.'

Several large matrons turned their heads hastily away, concealing red faces. The insult had gone home.

'Julian, for heaven's sake,' she whispered. But his studied rudeness had broken the tension. As the coroner called his first witness, the pathologist who had worked on Roger Dawkins' ruined body, she was able to watch and listen with something approaching her usual serenity.

The feeling was short-lived. After droning on about the circumstances of death, prevailing weather conditions, probable time and duration of rigor mortis and other grim facts that surely, Marian thought, only another pathologist could possibly follow, she heard the coroner ask what, in the doctor's opinion, had been the cause of death?'

The answer took everybody in the room aback. 'The cause of death,' the doctor said clearly, 'was coronary arrest. In layman's terms, heart failure.'

Quiet settled on the crowded room like a layer of dust. People who had known Roger since childhood were trying to catch each other's eyes. The coroner drew a breath.

'Can you tell me, doctor, if Roger Dawkins suffered from any condition, congenital or otherwise, that might have accounted for sudden heart failure?'

The pathologist graciously informed the coroner that as he had retired from general practice some fifteen years earlier, and had not been the Dawkins family doctor in any case, he was unable to give an enlightened opinion.

The pathologist was followed by Roger's mother, Mrs Jane Dawkins. Marian, watching her ascend to the box, felt a chill of horror run through her at the nightmare change that had come over the once plump and cheerful matron.

Jane Dawkins, only a week ago, had been the life and soul of the Dowbridge church picnic. Round-faced and tireless, she had radiated good humour. Now, placing her hand on the Bible, she made her responses in a dead monotone. Her hair, despite its usual neat bun, looked somehow faded; her clothes hung loose upon her. In some undefinable way she seemed to have grown small, fragile and old, in the space of less than four full days. Marian heard Julian suck in his breath.

The coroner handled her gently, putting no difficult questions, prompting her when she faltered. No, she had no idea what had taken Roger out on the moor. No, Roger had no heart problems. Aside from measles and winter colds, he had never suffered a day's illness in his life. The Dawkins family doctor, now retired, took the stand and corroborated her statement. The coroner turned to the crowd and called Sergeant Peter Wilking.

Marian, who had not communicated with the Okehampton constabularly since Wilking and his men had left Four Shields on Wednesday night, gave a long sigh of relief. She had been worried that she might be called as a witness before him; now she could frame her answers around whatever information he chose to give.

Julian and Marian had had one of their rare arguments on the subject, Marian heatedly maintaining that to get up on a witness stand with a tale of the supernatural was insane, Julian stubbornly holding that the only thing that mattered was the truth, that to find what had killed Roger was the only fact of any importance. As was usual in their arguments they had finally reached a compromise position. They had decided that Marian would say nothing about it unless Wilking did. In effect, the ball was in the court of the police.

The coroner took Wilking through the essential times, the

efforts to recover the body without further damage, the actions the police had taken so far. Then: 'It is the understanding of this court, Sergeant Wilking, that you acted on information received in a telephone call.'

'That's true,' Wilking said placidly. 'Sometime after eleven on Wednesday night I received a phone call from Mr Julian Dunne of Four Shields, Dowbridge. He informed me that his wife had discovered a body, which she later informed me was that of Roger Dawkins, in one of the old settlements out on the moor. We told him we would need to speak to Mrs Dunne.'

'And did you subsequently do so?'

'I did, yes.' Wilking's voice was still the easy, genial drawl of the west country man. 'I took two men and went directly to Four Shields, the Dunne residence, which is near Dowbridge. Mrs Dunne told me that she had been wanting to do some research on the people that lived in those stone villages, and that she had discussed her interest with the deceased. Mrs Dunne also told us that the deceased had subsequently shown himself interested in the matter, and had given her some books written about it.'

'That is all very clear, I think. Please continue.'

'Well, there's not much more to tell. Mrs Dunne said she tried to call the deceased at his home on Wednesday evening after the storm started, and was worried when she got no answer. She tried his house first, she told me, and then got to worrying that he might have gone out on the moor and got caught in the storm there. So she drove out to the moor, very courageously in my opinion, to look for him.'

'And found him there. Yes.' The coroner cleared his throat. 'And she said nothing else about it?'

Marian found that she was holding her breath; Julian, holding her hand, tightened his grip to the point of pain.

Wilking turned in the hard wooden seat and looked across the crowded court, directly into Marian's eyes. Every person in the room seemed to be waiting, fixed on the invisible line of communication between Wilking and Marian Dunne.

'Nothing,' he said clearly, 'of relevance.'

'I want a drink. I want a drink badly, and I want it now.' Marian, lolling against the leather headrest, kept her eyes closed as she made this statement.

Julian, driving too fast for safety on the narrow country lanes, glanced at her. 'You're not alone, my love. Down to the local in Dowbridge for a half pint?'

'God, no.' Behind closed lids Marian was seeing the greedy eyes of the crowd popping in expectation of some new unsavoury revelation as she stood in the witness box and, as calmly as she could, corroborated the evidence of those who had come before her. She felt soiled and somehow shamed by the experience. 'I can't bear the thought of sitting in a crowded pub with everyone from twenty miles around staring at me.' A small shudder ran through her. 'Let's go home, Julian, please.'

'Home it is,' he replied, and turned the car towards Four Shields.

They were both quiet. Julian, his eyes fixed firmly in front of him, tried to shut out the racing, chaotic thoughts that troubled him. He had noticed in the last forty-eight hours certain new mannerisms in his wife that had never been evident before. He was worried, and with every new and inexplicable challenge to their well-ordered lives, he became more so.

She had always been so serene. Not slow, not someone who was afraid to use her mind, yet serene nonethless, a woman with a deep-rooted belief in herself, her ideas and the ultimate rightness of things. She had had a stillness about her, of body and spirit alike. Now that stillness seemed to be disintegrating before his eyes.

That tiny tic in the corner of her left eye, for example. It was a classic sign of stretched nerves and Marian, in all the many years they had been together, had never hinted even that she possessed nerves. There were other things as well; the habit she had seemingly developed overnight of rubbing her hands together, a very slight stammer in her speech, a sudden tendency to speak too quickly and run out of breath. None of these things had anything to do with the Marian he had married twenty-three years before . . .

And there was something else, something that was worrying him more than all the rest. Since Wednesday night, her voice had changed. It was a subtle change, almost too subtle to put a finger on. But it was there in the tone, the pitch, the very inflection of her speech which had begun to slur, words running together at the edges like a water colour left out in the rain. Julian could not have said why this should so disturb him; he only knew that, as it became more noticeable, his feeling of unease grew.

The first thing she did after unlocking the side door to Four Shields and letting them into the quiet house was to draw every curtain at ground level. She did this without speaking, and with trembling hands. Julian, mixing drinks with more generosity than discretion, felt his mouth tighten involuntarily. Here, too, Marian was doing the exact opposite of what he expected of her. Usually, no matter what the weather, every curtain in the house was flung wide to let the light in.

Now he saw the tic start up in her eye as she fumbled with the wooden shutters of the dining room, the quick glance over one shoulder, the unconscious action of someone who fears the intrusion of prying eyes. He handed her the tall glass and said very quietly, 'No one can see in, darling. The house has twelve acres of land and a high wall around it. Aren't you being a bit paranoid?'

Her answer was so strange that he wondered if his ears were playing tricks on him. 'Walls won't keep the shadows out,' she said, and drained the glass.

His stomach contracted. 'Marian...'

'No,' she said. She went quickly to the bar and measured out a straight three fingers of gin. Julian watched her with a slowly mounting anger, the same feeling that had swept over him at the inquest and led him to insult the crowd.

Oddly enough Marian, who was usually oblivious to the undercurrents of the moods of others, seemed to sense his rage and frustration. She looked up at him.

'I'm sorry, Julian. Am I driving you mad? It's only that my nerves are in a wretched state.'

104

'No,' he said slowly. Now that he considered it, he knew what was making him so angry. 'You're not driving me mad. But to tell you the plain truth, Marian, I don't care for this Watergate rubbish one bit.'

'Watergate?' For a moment she was genuinely startled. Then she grinned, the first honest grin she had managed to produce since Wednesday. 'Ah, I see. Sergeant Wilking and the grand cover-up. Well, we shall never agree on that, Julian. I'm sorry, but I can't be anything but relieved.'

'Can't you?' His voice was savage. 'For myself, I'm seeing the whole miserable business becoming a dusty little open file in the police annals. I'm seeing the police, who were given the inform-ation they needed — at no small cost to us, I might add — politely deciding that Mr and Mrs Dunne both have a screw or two rattling loose because the story is too wild to pay any attention to. I don't like being called a liar, Marian, and by this little conspiracy of silence on the part of the constabulary we are essentially being called just that. And I'm wondering what happens next.'

She had gone very pale. 'Why should you think anything does happen next? I think that's a horrible idea!'

He had never lost his patience with her in all their years together. But now he snapped.

'For Christ's sake, Marian! Will you stop talking like a simpering little fool?' He mimicked her voice savagely. '"A horrible idea." Of course it's a horrible idea. But can you give me one good reason to suppose we've seen the last of this? Because I can't think of one. We seem to be under some sort of psychic attack, a siege almost, and you're being so naive. It's not good, Marian. You won't escape trouble by pretending it doesn't exist.'

He stopped abruptly. He was breathing hard, mouth pinched and nostrils flaring. She sat and stared at him, waiting for him to regain some control of himself, saying nothing. At last she spoke.

'You asked me for a reason,' she said softly. 'I do have one.

You may not like it, but it's logical in a strange way.' She stared down at her hands. 'Roger gave me some books about ancient religions in England. It seems there were once lots of different tribes, scattered all over the British Isles. There were the same few gods being worshipped under many different names and the druids were very much the head boys of the different religions.'

Her eyes seemed wider than usual, the pupils tinged with red. He saw her hands begin their unconscious washing gesture, knuckles twisting over each other in a nervous dance, and swallowed.

'Go on,' he said harshly. 'Go on.'

'Well,' she said, and her voice seemed to him to be unnaturally calm, 'they all had one thing in common; one end, so to speak. Sacrifice.'

'What?' Julian whispered. His throat was dry. 'What are you talking about? I don't understand.'

'Sacrifice,' she said coldly, and a look washed over her features, blurring them, so that for a single heartstopping moment he was no longer looking at the woman he knew. 'They all demanded a blood sacrifice. Roger was a blood sacrifice.'

He wanted to ask her how she knew, why she believed what she was saying, what was happening to the gentle and prosaic woman he had loved for so many years. But he caught sight of her averted face and the words died in his throat. On her face was the hint of a smile, an expression of pure pleasure.

The Red Hart, London, was an eighteenth-century pub nestled in one of the many winding streets between Holborn Underground Station and the vast complex of the British Museum. From the first day its doors had opened the local residents, including the literary pantheon that had made Bloomsbury famous, had loved the pub, cherishing its spacious comfort. It had a charming public bar where one could sit for hours, nursing a half pint and reading.

It also had a saloon bar, nowadays used as often as the public. The tight class distinctions of the eighteenth century had mel-

106

lowed with time, or perhaps those who still adhered to those distinctions in this day and age simply took their half pint elsewhere. It was an unselfconscious pub in an egalitarian age. The booths and chairs were of worn but comfortable leather, and the tables were kept polished to a dull sheen by some private mixture of the owner's wife.

It had, in addition to its other amenities, an upstairs room. This, used for naughtiness in the eighteenth century and for sober political harangues in the nineteenth, was used in the second half of the twentieth century in the way common to other pubs: at least once weekly folk music nights were held in it, and the bars below resounded to the clapping and stamping of people keeping time to a Scottish reel, or singing the chorus of an Irish anthem of war or rebellion. On the second Friday of each month, the room was used for the meeting of the Society of Awareness of the Psyche, affectionately referred to by its members as Soap.

Gemma Dunne, on the second Friday of August, shot through the cutglass doors of the Red Hart. She had been unexpectedly sent by her paper to cover a protest against blood sports in Lancashire, and through a series of mishaps, made doubly exasperating by the intense August heat in the North of England, had only just managed to get back to London in time for Soap's monthly gathering. She had never missed one before, and this time had a legitimate question to ask. She dashed up the stairs, calling a distracted greeting to the owner and his wife, and signed her name on the attendance sheet with a bare two minutes to spare.

The man who presided over the sign-ins also presided over Soap. He was a classmate of Gemma's from university days, a bespectacled and rubicund young man with a sense of humour about everything but Soap itself. This he treated with a solemnity that was slightly ridiculous. Named Peter Fenly-Dill, he was known, appropriately, as Pickles.

'Gemma, my love,' he beamed, 'you do seem to be out of breath. Were you by chance almost late?'

'I've been in the north on a fox hunting protest,' she told him.

107

'Would you believe it, I collected two summonses for doing ninety on the way down, and then the damned car threw a rod or something near Luton? In this heat? There I was, stuck out in the middle of absolutely nowhere . . .'

'You poor baby,' he said unctuously.

'And poor little red mini, so reliable usually. Never mind, let me finish up here and I'll get you a pint. Where's the car now, by the way? In a layby in Hertfordshire?'

'In a horrid little garage in Luton. Totally staffed by Saudi Arabians, or Lebanese, or something utterly macho, they patted my hand a lot and leered. Listen, Pickles, is there anything really specific on tonight?'

He looked surprised. 'No more than usual. Rory McKenna is giving a short talk on the recent UFO activity at Glastonbury. Do you want the floor?'

'I do. Oh, yes, I do.' She suddenly remembered her mother stretched unconscious on the grass. Pickles, watching her curiously, noticed her hands clench into small fists, saw the sudden blankness of her expressive features. 'I need the floor and everyone's cooperation as well. And, Pickles — I ought to tell you, you'll need to be able to believe six impossible things before breakfast. Rather like the White Queen, you know? It's quite a story. Mark me down for it, will you?'

'Consider it done. Now, what will you drink?'

An hour later, after twelve people had politely listened to a learned and very boring talk about Glastonbury Tor and the statistical data compiled thereon, Pickles informed the group that Member Dunne wished to address the floor. Gemma, conscious of a constriction in her throat, stood and regarded the group of school friends and peers who waited, courteously and with interest, for her to speak.

'I wanted,' she said, 'to tell Pickles, and all the members of Soap, that I've had — actually, my parents have had — a very strange experience. I know that we've been meeting for three years now, and discussed every aspect of the supernatural. But nobody here has actually had a recent experience, and so we've

108

never had anything to get our teeth into. I don't know how hard this is going to be for everyone to swallow but I hope some of you, any of you, can come up with ideas for me because I'm worried sick.'

She straightened her shoulders. 'Here goes, then. Stop me if I'm not being lucid, or if you have questions.'

Since Gemma had not spoken with either of her parents since her lunch with Julian on Wednesday, the story did not take long to tell. She finished, aware that her voice was not quite steady, and sat down again.

The long silence was broken by the sound of Pickles clearing his throat. 'Well,' he said vaguely. 'Well.'

Gemma looked at him. 'Well what?'

'Well, this is extremely interesting. And unusual.' He took off his glasses and began cleaning them. Gemma watched him with a strange feeling of impatience. As if he felt her eyes on him, he looked up and met her gaze. Without the thick glasses his eyes looked young, and oddly innocent.

'Gemma,' he said, 'you must have given the situation a good deal of thought. It might help us all if you could tell us what, if any, conclusions you've drawn.'

'Oh, for heaven's sake, Pickles, must you be so bloody pedantic? Of course I've thought about it. I've been thinking about very little else since this began.' She began ticking points off on her fingers. 'One, it isn't poltergeist activity. Two, it isn't ghosts. And, three, I suggested grave spirits to my father. He pointed out that all the graves on Dartmoor that held anything were emptied out long ago. Besides, that might explain what happened to him, but it doesn't even touch what happened to my mother.' She reached for her glass. 'And what happened to her worries me most of all.'

'Why?' The blunt question came from Rory McKenna, who had been leaning forward and listening intently.

'Because it was an invasion of the house,' she said flatly. 'What happened to my father happened out on the middle of the moor; it might easily have happened, whatever it was, to anyone

109

who fell asleep in that particular spot. But what happened to my mother happened inside Four Shields, to her in particular. Damn it, why can't I find the words I want?' She struggled to explain. 'It was personal, Rory. It was as if whatever it was came looking for her purposely, as if something was trying to get at her. The house was no protection.'

'I think I follow you,' Pickles said thoughtfully, 'Your father might have just had the misfortune to be in the wrong place at the wrong time. But what happened to your mother was something directed specifically at her. Is that what you mean, Gemma?'

She nodded. A plump young woman in a bedraggled blue sweater said thoughtfully. 'The most interesting thing about this, to me, is that Gemma couldn't smell the smoke. You said you got up to see what was happening. Do you remember exactly what woke you?'

In her mind's eye she moved backward. She was in bed, sleeping soundly, and then she was suddenly awake. She had sat up in bed, reached for her robe . . .

'Of course! Angela, you're a marvel. I heard a call, a cry from outside the house. I thought it was an animal or something. Then I began to wake up a bit more — you know how disoriented you get at night? — and I realised it was my mother calling from downstairs. At least . . .'

She stopped abruptly, her eyes widening. Pickles said urgently, 'What is it? Have you remembered something?'

'Yes.' She seemed to be having trouble with her voice. 'Yes, I have. It was when I was just getting out of bed. I heard my mother, and I realised that the noise I'd heard wasn't from outside, it was *in* the house.' Her face had gone white. 'Inside the house.'

'Well, wasn't it your mother after all?'

Gemma brought her gaze up to face Angela. Her eyes were wide and blind. 'I heard my mother but I could still hear the other cry. The first one.'

Angela's face was intent. 'Two people calling?'

'Two people calling,' she confirmed. Around her the room

110

seemed to shift then settle, become a changed place. 'Two people calling at the same time. And my father was ten fathoms deep. He never stirred or woke throughout the whole thing. And the only other person in the house was me.'

With the hot sunlight beating down on her shoulders, Marian stood in the moving stream and sang.

She knew she was dreaming, knew that she had for the moment left behind her the symbols and restraints of the waking world. In dreams touch becomes fantasy, sound and vision no more than subjective children of memory. Yet she felt the water move past her like the brush of birds' wings, suggestive, cool, a bit sly. She felt the midday sun and was grateful for its warmth in blood that, after the way of dreams, seemed to be running cold and distant in her veins. She felt a very light breeze flick across her naked arms. Beneath the olive skin of her hands, seeming to float like limp creatures on the bubbling surface of the stream, she saw the delicate tracery of her own veins, pumping her lifeblood to every corner of her body.

So she stood in water that reached her hips and sang, a strange chant about dancing clouds and the giver of the water. She wore a garment that, in waking, she would not be able to properly remember: it was rough against her skin, and its skirt was heavy with water. The stream bed was littered with pebbles, sharp against the soles of her feet. As she looked down into the clear torrent she saw a tiny ribbon of scarlet slide past. One of the pebbles had cut her foot.

She was alone in the water, but not in the dream. Close by, on the rise above her, a group of naked babies played in the incomprehensible rough and tumble of late infancy. They were strange children, small-boned and brown-skinned, with cheeks that were fat and scarlet as poppies. Something that looked very much like an uncured strip of leather had been laid on the ground; on this unlikely blanket, the babies — there were four or five of them — rolled and tumbled.

I am dreaming, she thought lazily, so there is no need to be

111

frightened, no need for anything to seem strange to me. She arched her head to get a better view of the babies playing. They were oddly pleasing, with their brown skins and fat red cheeks. On the edge of the hide a white bone lay gleaming in the sunlight. At the sight of it something, a memory of disturbance that she could not clearly recall, trembled through her. She shook it irritably away and moved her eyes past the children to the village beyond.

Now she saw the others, the adults. She saw an old woman with the blank face of an idiot carefully pouring water from a bronze ewer into a huge iron pot. She saw another old woman, sitting and watching from the shade of a hut. As she watched, the woman with the ewer came and offered the watcher refreshment. The watcher looked up and shook her head, smiling; even at this distance Marian could see the tenderness in her expression.

Another figure moved into her line of view. A man this time; young and very thin, with the same deep-set eyes and thin black hair that characterized even the babies of this place. He emerged abruptly from one of the huts, nearly stumbling over the two old women. The blank-faced woman looked frightened and backed quickly away. Marian saw the young man hesitate and then offer the watcher what was obviously an apology. She waved him off.

And then a young woman, walking very quickly, slipped from behind the young man. She stopped by the children, ruffling hair and pinching cheeks; she called something over her shoulder to the two who watched her. Then, turning her back on them, she walked from the village and came straight towards Marian.

The woman stopped within a yard of the water, with her back to the sun and her eyes fixed on the stream. Marian saw the shock run like a current of electricity through every line of the thin brown body. The eyes lifted from the water and fixed themselves directly on Marian's face.

Several things went through her mind at once, running and blending in a seething mass of emotional conflict. Recognition, awareness, fear and above all sheer surprise. She knew the yellow eyes, knew she had seen them, but did not know where. The girl,

112

too, was familiar to her. Marian felt the jolt of the mind that comes with the sight of a face that is known but cannot be placed. But mostly she felt surprise at one simple and obvious fact. The girl could see her; the girl knew she was there. But that is impossible, Marian thought, I am not here. I refuse to accept that I am here. This is a dream, and I am dreaming of this girl. But she can see me . . .

Marian suddenly heard her own voice, and realised that she was still singing. In this astonishing situation, she thought, I can do far worse than to listen to myself sing. The girl's head moved, tilting, as though she too were paying grave attention to Marian's song, as though this were somehow vital.

Marian sang. She did not know where the words or the tune came from. Her voice sounded hollow and immense, alien, an echo of the wind and the thunder moving through an empty field.

'Rain and light,' she sang. 'Rain falls in me, light moves through me, touch on stone and living bone, you empty vessels all . . .'

With incredible speed, the girl moved. She came off the shore, the flat slab of stone that hung opposite Marian's eyes, and hit the water like a heron diving for food. Marian felt the touch of the honey-brown flesh, hot and evil and as repellent as the touch of an adder. The world cracked and then broke around her as she was knocked off balance, as she sank beneath the water's surface, as she saw the desperate yellow eyes searching her out in the maelstrom. As awareness splintered and scattered like leaves in the wind, Marian became aware of her own voice, screaming.

'Marian. Oh God, God . . . Marian!'

She lay in a grey limbo. Something held her; there was a hand, a strong hand on her shoulder. It was shaking her, moving her, bringing her back to herself from that world of cold and bitter light to everyday things. Her skin crept, then cooled and steadied and suddenly, blissfully, the grip tightened on her almost to pain and she was Marian again.

Her eyes flickered open. Julian stood over her, his fingers sunk deep into the flesh of her shoulder. On the floor around his feet was a spreading puddle of alchohol, and uncountable slivers of broken glass. The room was full of sunshine. In the lines of light that fell on them, the broken glass glittered like myriad fragments of precious jewels.

He let go of her shoulder. Marian, trying to focus her dancing vision, saw that he was grey-faced and shaking, his eyes black and troubled. She blinked and shook her head.

Julian's voice was steady. 'What happened, Marian?'

Annoyingly, her eyesight seemed unwilling to settle. Julian was outlined in a black blur, the furniture behind him a collection of formless shapes that contained no reference to reality. She spoke vaguely, still trying to concentrate on seeing.

'What — I don't know what happened. What time is it?'

'It is approximately eight minutes later than it was when we last spoke to each other.' Julian was holding his temper and his voice alike on a tight rein. 'We were talking things over. You said something . . . something about sacrifice, about Roger being a sacrifice. And then you smiled, and your face went blank, and your breathing suddenly slowed way the hell down. For the past eight minutes I have been standing here shouting at you, shaking you, calling you. I even slapped you. You did not, during those eight minutes, move so much as an eyelash. I thought you were having a stroke.' His voice cracked. 'I have never been so frightened in my entire life, and I want to know what the hell just happened.'

'I don't know.' She heard the note of helplessness in her words, and got unsteadily to her feet. 'I must — I suppose I must have fallen asleep, or something.'

'The hell you did!' Julian reached for her and held her hard. 'Marian, you looked like you had gone into a trance or something. I've never seen anything like it.' He shook her, as if by this contact, this motion, he could snap her into complete wakefulness. 'When I said you never moved an eyelash, I meant just that. In eight minutes, you never blinked, not once.' As she

114

simply stared at him groggily, an angry despair infused him, 'Can't you bloody remember!'

'There was a girl . . .' Her voice trailed off. Why could she not wake up, or remember, or even see him clearly? She felt her muscles tighten, flinch with pain and then relax. Julian felt her slacken in his grasp and, very deliberately, drew back one hand and slapped her hard across the cheek.

Her head snapped back with the unexpectedness and force of the blow. For a moment she stared into his face, her eyes stretched to impossible limits of disbelief. Then she crumpled to her knees and began to weep.

'Oh, Christ,' he muttered. He suddenly realised that, in all the years they had been together, he had never seen her cry before. 'I'm sorry, darling, I'm so sorry, I didn't mean . . .' As he stood staring down at her helplessly, a trickle of blood slid down her leg and he saw that she had gone down on her knees in a welter of broken glass. He stooped and lifted her, depositing her shaking body on the sofa. 'Please stop crying, Marian. Please.'

'You didn't hurt me.' She was coming back; she could feel the difference in herself, in the air itself, in the quality of the light in the room. She became aware that her knees hurt and began to massage them. It was better now; it was almost all right again. The dazzle that had lain like a nightmarish corona across the room and everything in it began to fade. She reached out for the carved Spanish wooden box that Gemma had given her for Christmas the year before and took out a cigarette. With the first familiar sting of smoke, the room righted itself completely and he became Julian, whole and familiar once more.

'You didn't hurt me,' she repeated, and blew a smoke ring. 'It's all right, darling. I'm all right. I simply couldn't seem to wake up properly, and my eyes were doing odd things.' She saw that his shoulders were shaking under the smooth silk of his shirt and added firmly, 'I'm all right.'

'Good.' He slumped down heavily on the sofa beside her. 'Christ, I don't understand. I don't understand any of this. Can you remember anything from when you were — out?'

'I can try.' She closed her eyes, suddenly spent. A jumble of confused images twisted in her memory, refusing to resolve themselves. She began to talk trying to sort out her memories, her eyes still closed.

'I remember a stream. It was familiar, a pretty little stream, just a dancing little burble of water, deep, with a pebbled bottom . . .' She opened her eyes. 'Oh, of course! I was standing in it. It was hot . . .'

'You said something before, something about a girl.'

'A girl.' She was frowning, brows furrowed in the effort to recall. Clarity, on the edge of her grasp, eluded her still. 'Yes, a girl. There was something odd about her, something dreadful. Like stepping barefoot on a spider or finding something nasty in your dinner.' Her voice died away. Julian, watching closely, began gently to prompt her.

'Was the girl in the stream, too?'

'No. No, not at first. At first it was only me. I was watching. There was something — babies, that was it. There was a blanket or something, it might have been the pelt from some animal, and there were some babies playing on it.'

Her voice had taken on a quality of dreaminess, an almost hypnotic intensity that sent a cold thrill down Julian's spine. Yet he sensed that this was the way to get the information that he knew, somehow, was vital.

'Babies, yes.' It took all his concentration to keep his voice even and uninflected. 'A stream, and a woman, and babies. Was there anyone else? Any men or other women?'

Unexpectedly, shockingly, she turned to face him, her eyes wide with a sudden lucid horror, and he knew that the mists had fallen away. She had remembered.

'Julian,' she said wildly, and a sound burbled from her throat, a horrible noise that was part sob, part laughter. 'Julian, it was the settlement. That's where I was, in the settlement. The one where Roger died. I saw the rock that leans out over the water, and the stone huts, and the people. I remember it now.'

Her voice lifted on a note of fierce exultation that frightened him. One thin hand shot out and clutched his sleeve. 'I remember. I was in the stream, I was dreaming. The sun was hot on me. I remember. And there were two old women, one of them was an idiot. And a young man, and then the girl came. Oh Jesus, Jesus, I remember.'

A long shudder ran through her, racking her, twisting her body. Her grasp on his sleeve was like iron. 'The girl. She came down to the stream, she stood on the rock and she saw me. Julian, I wasn't there! I was dreaming, it was only a dream. I began to sing, I don't know what I was singing, it was something to do with light and rain. But she saw me. She *knew* I was there. She came into the water with me, and she wanted me, she touched me . . . oh God, oh God, oh, dear God in heaven . . .'

'What is it?' he took her face between his hands and stared into the wide, panic-stricken eyes. 'Marian, what?'

'She had yellow eyes.' Hysteria took Marian's voice and sent it splintering. 'She had yellow eyes, like a wolf, not like a person at all. And she knew I was there. She could see me. She wanted me.' She let go of him abruptly, exhausted. He was staring at her like a man in a bad dream from which he knows there can be no waking.

'I remember everything now,' she said, and fainted.

Chapter 12

Against all odds, against all Asulicca's predictions that she could neither keep her power a secret nor turn her back on it, Lun had managed to achieve at least a semblance of success at doing both.

In plain fact, she had been badly frightened, receiving three severe shocks in succession. That Bel had noticed her, had paid her any attention at all, was in itself disturbing; the archdruid was not accustomed to passing the time of day with the women of the tribe. He would never have done so had he not noticed, or been informed of, some deviation from the normal in Lun's recent behaviour. And he was dangerous . . .

The second shock had been Asulicca's subtle and very unexpected intervention between Lun and Bel. Lun knew, she had sensed with a feeling of cold peril, that in spite of Cryth's blow and harangue Bel had been only moments away from approaching her, questioning her. He had stopped, had been distracted and turned away somehow, by Asulicca's stepping between them. Lun was not surprised that Asulicca had seen the danger; she was not even surprised that the old woman had intervened on her behalf. That she had enough power to turn Bel's steps away, however, was an entirely different matter.

She had been wondering about her newfound power, wavering this way and that, as early as the night on which she had offered the water sacrifice. She was haunted by the black prediction Asulicca had made for her: that she would destroy herself and Cryth with her in the end. In spite of herself, in spite of the power, she loved Cryth as much as she was able to love anyone, and the knowledge that she was fated to bring him harm stiffened her in her resolve to thwart the fates in all their greed and malevolence.

So when Cryth had suddenly collapsed in pain, falling into agony as they spoke of the power, she had known that the gods were watching them, listening to them, playing with them as the cat plays with the small creatures it feeds upon. She had tended to him, drugged him into a deep and healing sleep, and sat in the quiet of the hut for hours, thinking. And from her thoughts came a gritty pride, a determination that, no matter what the druids might say about man's helplessness against the forces of the heavens and the earth, she would not be the plaything of the fates. She, Lunica, daughter of high birth among the Dumnonii and wife to a priest of Leucetius, would stand against them. She would stand against Clota, against Camulos, against those tenuous rulers from other places who would bend her and use her to her own cost. If Clota was punishing Cryth for it, if she herself was to pay, then so be it. If Asulicca spoke the truth, she and Cryth were to pay in any case. She would not give in.

So for the next two sunsets the tribe saw a great change in Cryth's strange woman. She was first out on those next two mornings, the first to be found bent over the rows of barley, the most sociable in the daily gatherings of the women. Arinicca, who regarded Lun with a species of shy admiration tinged with awe, suddenly found her approachable; Cryth, as the tribe watched curiously, visibly relaxed. Bel, who was rarely to be found in the fabric of daily life, watched without appearing to and began to wonder if, when he had cast portents about the new strangeness he had sensed in Lun, he had for the first time in his life misread the entrails. Only old Asulicca showed no change in her attitude to Lun. Her manner remained aloof, tinged with sadness.

For two days the yellow eyes were permitted to roam anywhere they wished, except in the direction of the stream. Under the hard grip of pride Lun ignored the longing, constant as the pain

119

of a rotting tooth, for the cool comfort of the water. Her chores should have taken her of necessity to the water's edge but by offering to stir the mash, or tend the babies, or even bring food to the elders, she manoeuvred the other women into fetching her water, washing her pots.

It was not easy for her, this time of abnegation. Her power had not abated. She could still hear the thoughts that rang and chattered in those who surrounded her, still sense the colour and texture of their thoughts. But her entire consciousness was directed towards shutting out the endless flow of sensory information that threatened to swamp her.

On the morning of the second day, she woke with a dreadful pain in her skull. Anyone else of the tribe might have been frightened, wondering which power of the red earth or the airy spaces above they had offended. Lun, however, knew instinctively that her body was reacting to her own stubborn self-denial, protesting in the only way it could against the ordeal she was putting herself through. Cryth might have wanted herbs to relieve the pain. Lun, knowing that to drug herself would be to weaken the walls of her self-control, gritted her teeth and bore the ache that hammered ceaselessly between her eyes as best she could.

On the second night Cryth, who since the night of virgin moon had showed no interest in making love to his wife, suddenly became actively passionate. Lunica, feeling the power rising in her like sap, had come to find physical contact with anyone at all repugnant; the power in itself was so sensual a feeling that it was more than any man could hope to offer. She did not rebuff Cryth, however. It was a simple enough thing to close one's eyes and ignore the physical unpleasantness, and the concentration she needed to think of something that would take her mind from Cryth's importunate lovemaking helped her to think away from the power, away from the grinding pain in her head.

Eventually he collapsed against her, exhausted and drained, falling into a sleep like death. When she was certain he would not wake, she managed to push him from her and to roll away from him. Her nerves jangled like wires, and hot tortured thoughts moved too close together, circling in her mind, demanding definition.

After an endless time of staring hot-eyed into the darkness of the hut, her thoughts began slowly to clarify and she understood her new-found disgust with lovemaking. Love and its rituals were far too similar to the druid rites she had seen. It was true that both offered power of a sort. But both were founded on nothing more solid than a brief moment's pleasure, and both were founded in a borrowed mastery over something or someone else.

Yes, she thought, why did I never see this before? Love and death are empty promises both, offering nothing but the illusion of strength; they are substitutes, offerings to the false gods of self. The sense of power to be had from them is a sham and a mockery.

Outside a wind rose, a light summer breeze that ran sighing around the roofs of the huts, lifting the protective hides and resettling them with soft thumps of leather on stone. Lun, surrounded by darkness and Cryth's gentle snores, shifted uneasily on her bed and smelled the fresh tang of rain on the night air. She buried her face in the covers, trying to ignore the voice within her, willing the night to pass, to free her, to leave her in peace. An all-consuming agony beat upon her conscious mind and, as the shore cannot evade the sea, undermined her will and her sanity. The force of her struggle against herself emptied her, filled her, then sucked her dry once more. She slept no more that night.

Alone in her dark home, Asulicca woke suddenly. She was old and confused; for a moment she did not know what had woken her. Then she felt the pull, the agony of mind, the wasted and futile desire of a soul in torment. She came fully to herself and knew that what she felt was Lun, sweating and shivering in a fever of yearning, sending out wave upon wave of misery like a rising storm into the receptive summer night.

Poor child, Asulicca thought, she is trying so hard to be good, and has nothing but pain to show for it. She pulled the covers close to her chin, trying to shut out the shivers that had begun to crawl along her spine. Despite the warmth of the night, her fingers trembled with cold; she had noticed that the older she grew, the less she felt the favour of warmth. Beneath the heavy hides her body was wracked with chills. Yet this was not the normal cold of her age and of the hour; she felt Lun's misery like a snowfall, covering her, distorting vision and hiding all other feeling until the dark room seemed full of Lun and her own head began to pound with the tension of the other. She almost cried out with the pain of it.

Asulicca, too, remained wakeful until the dawn came to ease her. As the first slanting rays of sunlight fell across her bed she got unsteadily to her feet, jaded and exhausted. She dressed slowly and unwillingly. She did not wish to go out among the tribe, or to sit listening to the chattering and giggling of the women; she did not want to see what the onslaught of the night had carved in Lun's face.

But when she emerged into the village, there was no sign of the girl. Asulicca was traditionally the earliest riser of the tribe yet Lun's body, bent over the cookpots or tending her baby, had been the first thing to meet her eyes for two days past. She was not surprised on this hot day to find that Lun had not yet emerged; most likely the girl would sleep sinfully late into the morning and Asulicca, knowing what she knew, could not find it in herself to blame her for it.

She went slowly to the village centre where a few of the women joined her to move sleepily among the pots. The smell of barley cooking wafted temptingly, mingling with the smells of the great mire that surrounded them. Taking a small bowl of the food, she went to her accustomed place and ate.

It was some quality of difference in the light that fell across her face that alerted her. She placed the bowl at her feet and looked around, her muscles taut, eyes narrowed against the dazzle of the sun. The soft pink of early morning was fading rapidly; everything seemed somehow more solid, outlined in black shadow, doubled in density. Her eyes swept the village and found nothing. Yet the pounding of her blood, the hint of cold under the heat of the day, remained with her. Her eyes left the village, moved across the brown earth and came to the stream. The goddess was there. Asulicca, who all her life had spoken with the gods that none other could even see and never known a moment's fear in doing so, felt panic rising like bile, a dark and bitter taste at the back of her throat. She swallowed it down, her eyes fixed on the alien shape in the water. The aching of the night just came back to her, not so much a memory as an icon.

The impossible figure in the stream was banked in mist that glittered and swayed. Asulicca saw the outline shift as the goddess moved, and heard the cold echo of a distant singing. Her flesh moved along her bones. Around her the village women talked, piling pots and mending. Their voices were whispers from a thousand miles off, their bodies moving shadows in the light of the unearthly. She was alone with the goddess, alone in the world.

This, then, was the result of Lun's night. This was what had come from Lun's pain, her suffering, her desire for the goddess to leave her in peace and let her be. She had denied the goddess, and the goddess had come anyway.

A figure, stooped and curiously tentative in its movements, came between her and the water so suddenly that she almost cried out. Bent over almost double, her gnarled and rheumatic hands clenched around the ewer of water, old Cryl smiled nervously down at her.

'Mother,' she said, 'I bring you water. The day is hot, and the barley makes for thirst. I would not presume ...'

'There is no fault in kindness,' Asulicca said. Cryl stood smiling, blocking her line of vision to the stream. As soon as the water was gone from her view her panic eased. She smiled kindly at Cryl, and took the water.

The hide behind them opened. Cryth emerged so abruptly that he tripped over Asulicca, sending him cannoning into Cryl and making him reach for the support of the stone walls. The bronze

123

ewer rocked in Asulicca's grasp. Water splashed over its sides and fell, cool and pleasant, across her feet.

Cryl, whose weak wits led her to fear the power of every man, hastily backed away. Cryth hesitated, then apologised; Asulicca thought that, whatever Lun had suffered in the night, the man who shared her bed had been untouched by it. He looked happy, far more relaxed than she had seen him since the day he first donned the mantle of Leucetius. Once again her eyes flooded with that strange light, so that she could see nothing properly. She waved a hand at him, and heard the hide behind them flap open.

It was Lun. And Asulicca, squinting up into her face, felt a cold hand close around her heart. It had all been for nothing, then. The girl's face was a death mask, graven with passions and a hunger too great for any living soul to hold. The amber eyes were enormous and gleaming in the pinched face; the body was as taut as a bowstring.

Lun saw Asulicca sitting, and Cryth smiling at her. Yet they seemed at a great distance from her for she felt almost as one might feel who had died. It might have been her spirit, detached from its earthly husk, that stood and looked down, empty-eyed and uncaring. She had fought a battle and had lost it and nothing seemed to matter now. In the agony of the night she had come to think that a clean quick death might be best. The idea of suffering what she had just endured, night after night, was intolerable.

Like an automaton, she exchanged greetings with the others. Cryth, glowing with strength and clearly refreshed in spirit, saw nothing unusual about her. Asulicca wanted to weep for them, yet kept silence. Lun moved to the blanket where the babies played and greeted them with that same deadness of the soul. Then, her eyes fixed on the ground at her feet, past all caring, she went directly to the water that beckoned her like a siren's song.

Dark, beautiful, standing like a stone in the eddying water, the goddess of the rivers stood and waited for her.

The shock of it, coupled with purest disbelief, seemed to drain all the blood from Lun's body. For a terrible moment she thought she must faint, yielding her spirit to the time and the day, and go tumbling to the rock never again to awaken. The goddess was pale and tall and impossibly beautiful, edged in bitter misted light, an aureole of the skies that hung around her like a cloak of gold. And then Lun met the eyes of the goddess which were said to hold life and death within their black centres, and got a shock that sent her head spinning.

The goddess was terrified. Terrified of her, of Lun. There could be no mistake.

In a terrible roar, the floodgates of power she had kept damned up for two days burst open. Voices that were the thoughts of the Dumnonii roared into her skull like a spring freshet. Feelings of every dimension, that came from every person behind her, swelled and burst over her. She knew Cryth's relaxation, felt the apprehension of old Cryl as she hobbled to refill the water ewer, tasted the pity and fear that swelled in Asulicca, all for her.

She tried to say something, somehow to prove to herself that she was still truly part of the whole sensual flesh of the world that had invaded her. She swayed, her chest constricting as she fought the voices and the sense of shock inside her. Instinctively she reached out for one voice, one gurgle of basic thought that was Cel. He alone could hold her here. But the avalanche in her mind was too much, and too sudden.

Then, cutting like a fine blade through the roaring confusion that beat against her brain, the singing came. The eyes of the goddess, terrified and confused, still held her. But she was singing a song of rain and light, a hymn of triumph, seductive as a lover's touch.

Lun had no defences against it. She could only follow the dictates of instinct which pushed her forward over the edge of the rock, sent the flush of physical gratification that suffused her skin as the water took her.

She could not have said why she had leaped for the water; she knew only that she must touch the goddess, because of all the sounds, the thoughts and sensations that pulsed against the walls of her mind, the goddess alone was sending her nothing. She had no key to the source of her own power except the goddess's fright.

And then the universe split, water and air merging into a nameless, shapeless torrent as her naked arm brushed against the figure that had somehow faded beneath her. She saw the pale skin, so different from her own, shimmer and dissolve as she touched it, and felt the cold shock, like a finger of lightning, as their skins met.

Then she was going down, spiralling limp and helpless, her lungs drawing in the weight of the water as the goddess, smiling, faded back into whatever limbo had hatched her.

'She is waking.'

The voice was deep and without emotion. Lun came slowly, almost unwillingly, back to conscious life. She was aware of a dull throbbing in her chest, and of a thick pain in her throat; she felt seared and parched, the taste of vomit lying like a pall across her tongue. She kept her eyes closed, quickly becoming alert, not wanting them to know she could hear them. It had been Bel's voice she had heard, the voice of the enemy.

A confusion of voices, some frightened, some calm. There were hands on her, Cryth's hands; she knew his touch well. And a smaller hand, cool and gentle, stroking her brow. Arinicca? Asulicca? She kept her eyes closed, all her wits concentrated on what she would say.

She had acted like a madwoman. No use, to deny it to herself; the sight of Clota, still as a statue in the water, had sent her into the dark halls of insanity. She had gone into the water, thrashing and crying out no doubt, in full view of the village women, in full view of Asulicca and Cryth. And, judging from the cold voice that had accompanied her waking, the archdruid had been watching her, too. If she could not think of something to satisfy them, who knew what her end would be . . .

Lun sighed deeply, and let her eyelids flutter. Cryth tightened

126

his grip marginally, then relaxed as Lun, the picture of frightened bewilderment, opened her eyes and faced the crowd that surrounded her.

'Cryth?' Her voice, she noted, was perfect; a blend of confusion and fear. They were not to know that though the confusion was a sham, the fear was real. It was not fear of what had happened, however; she lay in a sweat of terror at the thought of Bel, towering over her, staring down at her with his cold judgmental eyes. Yet in spite of Bel her mind was clear and moving rapidly. She felt somehow equal to Bel, to Asulicca, to the whole tribe.

'You are safe now.' Cryth's voice was trembling, his grasp hard and protective around her. 'My poor Lunica, you are safe now. All is well. No, you have no need to rise. Lie still and rest awhile.'

'My head hurts me.' She made the statement in a small and wondering voice. It was the truth; whether because she had actually hit herself during her frenzy or as a result of the spiritual turbulence she had suffered, her head was aching unbearably. She shifted, seeking comfort, and winced with the pain of it. Cryth slid one arm beneath her and helped her to sit up. Her garments were sodden.

'What happened, young yellow-eyes?' Bel stood and watched her, his face unreadable. He stood with legs akimbo and his shadow fell between her and the sun. She forced back a superstitious shudder, and tilted her face up to his.

'I — I am not certain, Father. I slept late today, and when I woke I was in a sweat. Perhaps a fever came upon me during the night. I felt hot and soiled. I thought I would wash myself, there at the stream'.

She pulled herself to her feet and winced. Suddenly the tribe was too close to her, encircling her like mountain wolves, ringing her, holding her in. Claustrophobia swept over her, stifling air and light. She was glad of Cryth's comforting arm.

Bel reached out and took hold of her shoulder. 'You slipped? No more than that?'

With the touch of the archdruid's hand, every sense Lun possessed suddenly sharpened. There was danger here, peril she could not name yet might guess at. The powerful Bel had been watching her, had seen her. He suspected something, she could tell. What had she done to rouse his suspicions so?

'I was afraid I might drown. And I — I felt a pain.' This seemed safest. Even as she spoke an idea, breathtaking in its simplicity, came to her. She cast her eyes modestly down and spoke faintly. 'A bad pain, sharp and stabbing, in my belly.' She moved her hands until they rested against her stomach. 'It was the same pains I had before. When I was carrying Cel.'

In the sudden quiet, Asulicca's indrawn breath sounded unnaturally loud. Bel, never taking his eyes from Lun's face, spoke quietly.

'So. The pains of childbearing. You are carrying?'

'I do not know.' Her qualification was swift. If she told the tribe that yes, she was definitely carrying a child, then a child she must produce. And no amount of power would sow fruit in an empty womb. It was better to hedge. 'It was the same kind of pain, only sharper. I slipped . . . '

'I saw you.' The archdruid's voice was cold. 'It did not seem to me that you were suffering from hurt. To my eyes, you were trying to catch something there in the water.'

Close behind Bel's shoulder Asulicca stood like a rock. Lun saw her face darken with warning. Asulicca knew how close the peril had come; the part, then, must be played out.

'Catch something, Father?' She shook her head. 'What would there be to catch in our stream? I saw nothing.' Memory caught at her, memory of frightened eyes and a dazzle of light, and she heard her own voice sharpen. 'Do you mean that there was something there, something I could not see?'

Bel met her eyes. The seconds inched by as yellow met black, as Lun managed to keep her face steady. She was very frightened for, clear as rain falling, she could hear his every thought. She sorted them out, black thoughts, and listened only to them. He does not believe me, she thought. He will never, now, believe me.

128

He has marked me as heretic. And then, as a random thought stood out, he wants me dead . . .

Yet the idea was a sound one, based not only on the hunger for safety from him but on the memory of sober fact. Lun remembered all too well the terrible fainting fits that had plagued her all the time she had carried Cel. She could to this day feel the stabbing pains in her legs, the clammy and frustrating exhaustion, the racking nausea, if she were fool enough to call them up in her mind. She had sworn to herself never to bear another child. All the tribe would remember, full well, how hard a time she had had of it. But Bel . . .

'No.' He turned from her, as though he knew she was inside his mind, had come to that hinterland of thought and feeling behind his eyes. 'There was nothing in the water.'

He went quickly from the circle. And Lun, her body shaking, got to her feet and stumbled to her bed.

Chapter 13

On Saturday afternoon, sweltering on the London tube and cursing the loss of her car, Gemma took up her briefcase and headed for the British Museum.

She had been planning to go home for the weekend. Had she taken the time to telephone Four Shields, she would have learned about Roger Dawkins' death but, as it was, she decided to get some solid research done on the shadowy people that had inhabited Iron Age Britain. Then, if time allowed, she would take the train down and spend Sunday in the country.

The Museum, on a summer Saturday, was packed with eager tourists. She showed her library membership card, skirted a crowd of German tourists who were ogling at an enormous Chinese vase and headed for the quiet of the Reading Room.

She was used to research. Methodically, she consulted the list of subjects she had compiled in the small hours of the morning and began to gather the volumes she wanted. When she finally sat down and began to read, she had amassed a large pile of books, some on supernatural phenomena and others on life in ancient Britain.

The day drew on. People came and went, talking in hushed whispers. Once an elderly man stumbled against her chair and murmured an apology. She did not notice. She read steadily, stopped, jotted down notes. A pattern was slowly emerging, a disturbing impression of blood and fire. She frowned over one passage, checked a cross reference, added to her list of notes.

Yes, she thought, this could be it. It makes sense, it all adds up. If it's really possible . . .

She looked up at the light tap on her shoulder. It was the librarian, very apologetic, informing her that the Museum was closing, he was very sorry, and she needn't worry about the books because he would see them back to their proper places.

She glanced down at her watch. Half-past five. Good grief, had she really been here since before noon? She gathered her notes, apologising to the librarian and left the building slowly. Heading for the tube, she suddenly changed her mind and instead found a local coffee bar. She had discovered that she was ravenously hungry.

Making short work of a plate of pasta and two cups of coffee, Gemma began to sort out the mass of information she had sifted through. Lines of script lingered in her memory, fresh and clear. 'Rites of the ancient druids revolved around a central concept, the importance to religion of living sacrifice. . .' '. . .smoke from the sacred fires. . .' '. . .burnt their sacrifices alive in baskets made from rushes and straw . . .' And, in a nineteenth-century treatise on the place of the supernatural in history, 'Logic and precedent show us that the places used for worship throughout history are never randomly chosen for their beauty or convenience of locale. Modern churches are very often built on the same spot where, in earlier time, an earlier arm of the species had sensed a special quality that would be called holiness . . .'

Her coffee had cooled. She ordered another, and a glass of wine with it, and searched through her notes until she found what she wanted. She had copied the paragraph verbatim; it came from the same book on supernatural history, and was underlined and starred in red ink. She read slowly and carefully, trying to understand not only the written words but the sense that lay behind them.

'There are numerous records throughout modern history,' she read, 'of spiritual invasions or visitations that can best be categorised as religious in origin. It may well be concluded from these occurrences that what has invaded the modern man was not a conventional ghost, but rather a lingering essence, as though memory was not, after all, a one-way function but worked for both past and future. If a religious belief was powerful enough in its time and sphere of influence, the strength of that belief, as opposed to merely the spirit of those who believed it, may linger. Indeed, when many have believed strongly enough, the lingering power in combined form may well be said to punch a hole in the fabric of time itself. In the realm of the everyday, racial memory may be used as an example of this power. It is interesting to note that the great majority of these so-called "religious invasions" occur in or around those very areas that once hosted the ancient rites.'

Gemma gathered up her briefcase, now crammed with loose bits of paper, and went back to her one-room flat in Chelsea. She was unsure, now, about her decision to head for the country; besides, she wanted to digest what she had read, somehow to clarify her own growing suspicions before she put them before her parents. They were dear people yet they had great difficulty in believing in anything they could not see or touch.

She spent most of the evening thinking. When her head was aching with the effort of clarifying her thoughts, she went to the cinema. The next morning she called home. There was no answer.

Marian was wandering, in another place, another time.

She knew that there was something seriously wrong with her; she did not seem to be able to feel anything properly, and the sounds of the night came muddied and indistinct. There seemed to be some kind of muffling layer between her body and her surroundings. Yet her vision seemed uncannily sharp. Everything seemed larger than usual and crisper in outline. The grass beneath her bare feet was wet and cool.

Very gradually she became aware of a remote feeling of confusion. She was outdoors and it was dark; the long curving shape on the edge of her vision was the garden wall of Four

Shields. She was in the garden then. But Julian had carried her up to her bed, her own warm lovely familiar bed, after she had had some kind of attack and fainted. The sun had been shining then. Yes, that was right. It was coming back to her now. It had been daylight, golden sunny day, and she had drowsed under the warmth of her down quilts. How had she come to be here, out in the garden at night? And what had happened to the hours between sun and shadow?

She stopped in her aimless wandering and looked back at the house. The windows were black, lightless. Julian must be sleeping, uneasily dreaming perhaps, of bodies and eyes and gleeful expectant voices. Even as thought came to her the walls of the house seemed to dissolve momentarily and she saw him, curled under the covers, his dark head moving restlessly on the soft pillows. Then the vision faded and she was alone in the garden once again, Four Shields a dark looming shape before her.

A soft call sounded above. Jerking back her head, she saw the winged shape, vast against the moon, of some bird of prey. A hawk, perhaps, or an owl?

The call sounded again, loud and terrifying in her ears, and she knew that this second cry had come from her own throat. The bird swooped down, in a silent rush of folding wings, and came to rest on the dark grass not a yard from her feet.

It was a sparrow hawk, a large male. The grey-blue feathers of its back glinted with a metallic sheen in the moonlight and she caught a glimpse of its buff-coloured underbelly. The hawk regarded her steadily.

The knowledge went through her like a spear, searing her with its implausibility. I called it, she thought incredulously. I echoed its cry right back at it, and it came to me . . .

The hawk lifted its wings and shot upward. She saw the primaries, razor-edged as they spread to catch the breeze, and then the hawk dropped once more. She threw up her hands and then, led by an instinct she could not identify, dropped them. The hawk, light as air, landed on her shoulder.

133

She looked into the creature's mad eye, flat and yellow and only an inch from her own. One hand crept slowly up to touch its head. The hawk sat motionless, the crazed yellow stare never wavering from hers, as she began to stroke the soft feathers, crooning to it, odd little bird sounds falling into the dark air. Through the heavy cotton of her bathrobe she could feel the strength of the curved talons, cruel daggers as strong as iron, resting lightly against her shoulder.

In the thick grass behind her, something rustled. In a flash of power, silent and dark, the bird was away. It lofted upward, moving in a straight line. She saw the wings tuck in against themselves for the dive; far above her she saw the glare of its eyes and knew that she had seen them somewhere before. Then the bird dropped like a stone, a graceful arrow of economic movement. It struck the grass behind her, hopped, and settled. A frenzied squeaking was suddenly cut off. Then it lifted itself, the titmouse dangling limp and bloody from its great beak, and settled its solid weight on her shoulder once more.

The night was alive, it was a singing, breathing demon that swelled inside her until she felt the blood must burst out at her eyes, staining the grass with the force of a dam breaking. The bird sat, not eating, dangling the mouse from its beak.

Everything seemed to be happening very slowly. She reached up one hand and, taking the warm tail of the mouse between her fingers, gently pulled. The bird released it, never stirring from her shoulder. Its eyes were absolutely flat with an oblong pupil; the vicious beak was partly open, the claws relaxed. Eyes, she thought, yellow eyes. These eyes have watched me before. If I could only remember where and when . . .

The universe was a weight on her, compelling her, telling her what she must do. The actions were spelled out for her, known to her in the way she knew her name or how to breathe. She raised her trophy, both hands lifted to the heavens, and a cry burst from her throat — inhuman, savage, triumphant. The bird shot straight upward into the sky on a current of air. The blood of the sacrifice ran down her wrist.

Then her fingers had closed completely around the small body and she was ripping at it, tearing it with hands and teeth, chanting something in a language she did not know, yet had heard before. The taste of blood was warm and coppery. The hawk hovered directly above her head.

Why am I doing this? she thought dimly. What in the name of heaven can be happening to me? And why is my head full of noise and voices and names?

'I accept the sacrifice,' she said, and her voice was the voice of a stranger; blurred, different with a dangerous edge to it. The voice of a young girl. 'I accept the sacrifice. Clota! Camulos! I accept . . .'

The bird wheeled, screaming. It shot across the night sky like a flash of lightning and was gone, beating its way to the south across the great moor. Marian sank to her knees in the wet grass, screaming, trying to shut out the moving cascade of vision and sound that inundated her. In the bedroom window above her head, the lights began to burn.

Julian, sunk in the profound slumber of exhaustion, did not hear Marian rise from her bed in the small hours. He slept dreamlessly as she moved across the room, going soundlessly across the lush carpets, down the stairway, through the darkened house. The well-oiled brass hinges of the front door made no sound to alert him; her bare feet, slapping against the grass wet with dew did not penetrate the walls of the house or the depths of his sleep. He lay like a stone beneath heavy quilts as something pulled his wife through the mists of time into another reality.

He edged sluggishly up towards the waking world at the first scream of the bird. But animal cries are common at night; in sleep he noted the cry, and dismissed it again. A bird or a fox perhaps, was going about its rightful business in search of food. No need to wake for that.

Yet the quality of his sleep lightened, and he swam closer to the surface. The chanting, high and eerie, brought him up a step further. But it was the screaming, shocking and unexpected and raw with a species of terror that could find no expression in words, that finally chased the last vestiges of sleep from his body and mind and brought him fully awake and on the alert for danger.

He stumbled across the room, calling, and found the light switch. The sudden light flooded the bedroom, blinding him. It fell on Marian's empty bed. Julian, standing for an endless moment frozen into immobility, thought that no bed had ever seemed emptier.

The screaming grew louder, filling the room. He ran to the windows, fumbling with the heavy curtains, wrenching them half off their rails, and shouted into the night. There was no answer. The screaming continued, sickening and intolerable.

Barefoot and clad only in his pyjama bottoms, Julian ran through the house. Custom and familiarity stood him in good stead; he took the stairs and reached the front door without even barking his shins, pausing only to snatch up the heavy flashlight that was kept in the cloakroom. The front door was closed, and the latch resisted his efforts.

The screaming was laced with sobbing now, a deep and despairing sound bubbling downward and then soaring into fresh hideous shrieks. With a savage curse Julian wrenched the door open and flew across the dark garden, the rose bushes and ornamental hedges scratching him as he went.

He found her halfway between the house and the front gates. She was huddled in a knot, arms wrapped tight around herself in a small foetal curl. The screaming had stopped only to be replaced by a desolate wailing that lifted the hairs at the base of his neck. The sound grated against him unbearably. Listening to it he was somehow reminded of lepers cursing their fate, pleading for pity . . .

'Marian,' he said, and knelt to put his arms around her. 'Marian! It's me, Julian. Can you hear me?'

She lifted her head slowly, as though the weight of it was a burden too great to bear. He looked into her dazed face and wondered at whatever trick of the moonlight turned her brown eyes to wicked amber. She began to shake, long wrenching tremors that wracked the full length of her body.

Her voice was weak. 'Julian?'

'Yes, love, it's me. Come on, now. We've got to get you out of this wet before you catch your death.'

She allowed herself to be helped to her feet. There was something about her stance, however, that disturbed him. She stood with her toes pointed outward, in the manner of a ballet dancer, and her head was cocked to one side in a movement she did not usualy adopt. Some compulsion that he could never afterwards explain made him turn the flashlight on her so that it shone directly into her face. She gave a stifled cry, throwing her hands up to protect her eyes, and Julian saw that they and her mouth were smeared with some dark noisesome substance that, incredibly, looked and smelled like blood.

'Come along.' He held her firmly by one arm and let the light play along the grass at their feet. He saw the shreds of fur and skin, the remains of some small animal, and a few dark feathers. Perhaps a bird had ripped the mouse, or whatever it was, and she had stumbled upon it? Then he remembered the foul-smelling stains on her face and hands and his gorge rose. 'Come along,' he repeated firmly and, leading her back to the comfort and safety of Four Shields, closed the heavy doors upon the night.

Once indoors, Marian's recovery was dramatic; the familiarity of her own elegant furnishings, of the small things she had chosen to decorate her home with, seemed to act like a tonic. Julian, brewing coffee and lacing it liberally with cognac, had the satisfaction of seeing the confusion fade from her face, and that indefinably alien look that lay like a film of grease across her features ebb and disappear. As he handed her the coffee and sank wearily down on the sofa beside her, she gave a deep sigh.

'Better,' she said, and took a heartening sip. 'This is good,' she added, and streched her legs out before her. In the soft light of the living room Julian took a closer look at the marks on her skin. There was no doubt about it; it was dried blood and, from the look of Marian herself, the blood had not come from her.

137

Remembering the shredded mouse on the law, an explanation came to him. He rejected it immediately; it simply wasn't possible, it couldn't be. Not Marian. Not his gentle Marian.

Still, he must know. Perhaps this time, in spite of her lapse of memory earlier in the day, she would remember what had happened. He kept his voice calm and reasonable. 'Can you tell me what happened out there, Marian?'

Her answer took him off guard. 'Some of it, yes. Not all of it. I don't remember getting out of bed, or going out into the garden. But I remember the rest of it.' Her face grew tight. 'I wish I didn't, but I do.'

'Tell me about it.' He forced his gaze away from her slender fingers with their hideous rusty blotches and met her eyes. Funny, they seemed a lighter brown than usual.

'All right.' She swallowed a mouthful of cooling coffee and grinned. Julian saw that grin and felt his heart freeze. It was a cold expression, utterly unlike her usual smile. 'If I begin to get hysterical, feel free to knock me about. As I say, I don't remember waking up or getting out of bed. I'm not sure I actually *did* wake up — it was more like walking in my sleep. But when I came to my senses I was out in the garden, barefoot.' The smile grew dark and deep then vanished. 'I heard a bird call very close by.'

'I heard it too.' He gulped, hearing his own voice emerge thin and strangled. 'Go on, darling. About the bird?'

'Yes, the bird.' He stared at her in horrified fascination. Her eyes now looked almost completely yellow and her mouth had thinned to a dark gash, a travesty of a smile. 'It called, the bird, and I heard it call again. But it wasn't the bird, not the second time. It was me. I had answered it, and it came to me.'

'It came to you?' Julian whispered. 'What do you mean, it came to you? It came into the garden?'

She was still smiling, that terrible slanting smile that was not her own. The yellow eyes gleamed. 'It did. A sparrow hawk, lovely, a big male, I think. It came into the garden and landed on my shoulder.'

There was something very frightening about her. As he

138

watched one slender hand reached up and stroked the shoulder of her cotton dressing gown in a gesture both reminiscent and oddly tender. 'It caught a mouse.'

He was flesh and blood and could bear no more. He reached out and took the hand, still moving in the sensual stroking movement against her own shoulder. He held it brutally tight. Her eyes darkened, the wide black pupils contracting to nearly normal size. Julian said harshly, 'The mouse. What did he do with the mouse, Marian, this hawk of yours?'

'He gave it to me,' she whispered. She was staring into his eyes, seemingly unable to break his gaze. 'He sat on my shoulder and gave me the mouse.' As he tightened his grip her eyes cleared a little more. 'He held it out to me. I saw the tail dangling form his beak ...'

There were livid marks on her wrist now where the soft skin was crushed in his grasp. He held her gaze. 'Let me see if I've got this properly. A full-grown wild hawk answered your call, caught its supper, sat on your shoulder without leaving a mark and gave you its meal?'

The words were deliberately sarcastic but Julian was more afraid than he had ever been before. Behind Marian's words, her every look, waited the abyss of the unthinkable. And both of them stood at the edge of that chasm, not knowing what might topple them inside.

'It offered—it ...' Something terrible seemed to be happening to her face. It was crumpling, falling apart and reassembling itself, the features dissolving like print on a wet newspaper. Her voice, too, seemed oddly distorted. 'I—I took it ...'

'There is blood on your hands.' His voice was flat and cold as he watched her, noting the eyes that had been first brown and then yellow and were now brown again. 'Blood on your mouth.' His voice, no longer controlled, soared to a crescendo of raw violence. 'What in hell did you do!'

She cried out, wincing away from the rage and agony that poured from him in suffocating waves. 'Julian, you're hurting me, you're frightening me! I'm trying to remember, I really am, but I'm frightened . . .'

'Christ', he muttered, and let go of her. All the fight, all the strength that his terror had lent him, had gone out of him in a single debilitating rush. Suddenly he was a man approaching middle age, who had had a gruelling day and less than his allotted eight hours of sleep. He rubbed his eyes. 'I'm sorry. I'm sorry.' He turned his head, resting like a dead weight now on the sofa cushions, and said very quietly, 'You killed the mouse, didn't you? You ate it.'

'No,' Marian said strongly. 'I did not. It was a sacrifice. I remember now.' She held her hands out, looking wonderingly at the dried blood. 'I can't believe this. I simply cannot believe any of this is really happening. Julian, I swear to you, it happened the way I said. It gave me the mouse, not alive, it killed it before it came back to me. But it was for me. The hawk did what I told it to do.'

Julian was vaguely pleased to see that his hands lay quiet and steady on his lap. They wanted to hold something, to grip something, anything that was real and normal and had nothing to do with whatever was happening to them. 'You could understand the hawk? And it understood you?'

'Yes.' Tears welled in her eyes, her normal brown eyes, and began to pour down her cheeks. 'I don't know how. It just came to me, like the names . . .' She knuckled her eyes like a child.

'Names?' The room, quiet and gracious, settled around them. 'I heard something, thought I heard something, just before your screaming woke me. It sounded like chanting.'

'You did hear it, and it was chanting.' She began to cry, naturally and with a great sense of relief. 'I offered my sacrifice to the gods. No, don't interrupt me, don't ask me what gods. Maybe I dreamed it all. Maybe I'm going mad, Julian. But they were the names of the gods that I read in those books that Roger gave me before he died. Camulos, I remember that one. And Clotis, or Clota, something like that. I said something about accepting something, I don't remember what.' She got to her feet, her

140

bathrobe pulled tight around her, shoulders sagging. She looked into his bleak face.

'Julian,' she said, 'am I going mad?'

The question, the tone of voice that eloquently told him that she was afraid he might say yes, nearly broke him. He got to his feet and gathered her in his arms. She fell against him, her tears streaking his bare chest. She seemed to weigh no more than a child as he picked her up and carried her upstairs.

He laid her on her own bed, and tucked the blankets up around her chin. Her eyes implored him for an answer.

'No,' he said. 'I don't think you're mad. I think you're possessed, or perhaps we're both possessed, or the house is. And until I can find out exactly what the hell is happening here, you are going to come to London.' He moved around the room, closing curtains, dimming lights.

'London?' She looked doubtful. 'Why there?'

'Because,' he said grimly, 'I don't think Four Shields, or anywhere near Dartmoor or those filthy settlements is safe for either of us right now. And until I know just what is happening to you, I prefer not to let you out of my sight.'

Chapter 14

It was not surprising that Bel had become archdruid.

His had been a strong and dominant personality from childhood. His strength and presence were outstanding, even judged by the harsh standards of the men of the Dumnonii. He was not a deliberately cruel man, but he had a cold clear-sightedness that enabled him to examine a circumstance from every possible angle, sweeping aside any consideration of human weakness or frailty as irrelevant and obstructive. He was, in short, a good judge of character, and possessed that most invaluable of qualities, the ability to smell out a lie a mile away.

He was austere, emotionally twisted and something of a misanthrope. All in all, he was the perfect man to lead the druid elders in their law giving, in the meting out of their cold justice. And did he not bear the name of the great god himself? It was obvious to the tribe from the hour of his birth — he was marked for power.

Given the manner of man Bel was, it was perhaps not surprising that he had begun to hate Lun. She was opaque, different from the others, and he had not been able to intimidate or even to understand her. He had known, as she lay dripping by the stream and hinted to the curious tribe that she might be carrying a child, that she was lying. To know was easy; to make her admit that she had somehow taken a power that was forbidden to her by law was another matter, and harder by far to do.

Complicating this problem was Cryth. It was true that the boy was a highly favoured and very promising priest of Leucetius, cold and obedient in all matters of ritual. But he was also a husband who doted on his skinny, evil-eyed woman to a degree that Bel considered preposterous. The only sensuality Bel knew was the religious onanism of his worship, and how Cryth could feel so about a woman was something he could not comprehend. That the bitter stirrings of his own blood whenever he brought the image of Lun into his mind might come from a similar wellspring as Cryth's emotion was beyond his capacity or willingness to understand.

He had mishandled the young yellow-eyes, he knew that now. He could have had her taken up for the questioning of the druids, under which each lie is burned into the transgressor in blood and fire. But she had lain there in her husband's arms with her hands around her belly, outfacing him with her yellow gaze, hinting unerringly at the one thing that would keep any woman from the wicker coffin, and his gaze had fallen first. She had bested him.

So he strode from the settlement to the holy place, the locus, battling with his rising temper and trying to clarify his thoughts. She had been careful, he thought bitterly, very careful indeed. See how she had not come out and said boldly, 'I am carrying and therefore sacrosanct.' A clever little witch, young Lunica. Had she made that statement and been unable to produce a child, her fate would have been sealed. She would have burned, Cryth or no Cryth. And the power that he smelled in her like musk, the power that no woman had a right to, would have burned with her.

He came to the locus, ignoring the soft breeze, the blessing of the summer air, incapable even of appreciating it. He stood in the cold ashes of the holy fire and the standing stone, silent and black in the hot sun, watched him like a sentinel. The nine oak trees that ringed the locus stood still and calm. Eyes closed, spirit open, Bel waited for the intuition that would tell him what to do. His concentration was distracted by his anger, however, and after a long, frustrating wait he gave it up as hopeless. He sat back against the stone and thought about Lun. He did not believe for one moment that the girl was pregnant. A few nights past he had woken from an odd and disturbing dream in which a white wolf stood at the waterside and called lightning down to strike down all the people of the Dumnonii. Dreaming, he approached the wolf on his knees, barely conscious of a desire, a sensuality, that he had no way of recognising, and the wolf had looked down at him with bright, contemptuous golden eyes. Eyes that he knew only too well ...

He had come awake, staring into the night that was fading now to sunrise with a feeling of impending disaster. Naked, he had gone from his hut to the stream and stood on the washing rock. When the morning sun, pink against his flesh, had brought the first of the women sleepily from their homes, he had still been staring at the great charred streak where the lightning had struck. Dressing with haste, he had gone to the pens. There, as was his right, he had taken a young kid and, after cutting its throat, had dragged the bloodied corpse to the locus. He had spread its entrails in the ashes, reading, interpreting, shifting.

What he interpreted from the mess of entrails he kept, as was his wont, to himself. But the portents were too obvious to miss, peculiar though they were: a woman gnawed by hunger and thirst, a fathomless distress of body and spirit, and a power that if taken and understood would dwarf even the power of the elders. The interpretation, taken with the dream, could mean only one thing.

He had watched Lun, secretively at first and then more openly. Bel thought that he knew all there was to know about power, knew intimately the taste of it and even more the potent smell of it on the skin. He saw that Lun held it on a short string, wrestling with it, trying to know it. He was almost amused by her obsession, amused in a cold fashion because any power she might possess could lead only to death.

So he had confronted her, secure in the knowledge that he was archdruid and an object of fear to such as she. And Lun had reacted in a way he could never have expected, a way that had

144

shaken him badly; she had smiled, showing no fear of him at all, and lied with easy skill. And who was to say, if she was allowed to hide the power and nurture it, that she might not some day be able to summon the druids' own power, the goddess, She of the Sacred Grove, Nemetona herself? It was not to be borne. He, High Elder of the Groves of Nemet, would stop her.

Yet she had beaten him once again. He had wondered these two days if he had completely misread the portents. She had seemed so different suddenly, had played the part of a normal young wife of the tribe so well that even he had been almost convinced. Then she had emerged this morning, and had gone to the stream . . .

He shook himself like a dog, sitting in the shadow of the standing stone, the Guardian of the rites. The force of his realisation that there was something of great holiness in the water, and that she could see it clearly while he, Elder by right, saw nothing at all, would stay with him until his dying day. He pictured her, long-legged and slender, and the muscles of his groin tautened almost to pain.

Could she really have expected him, as she lay there prating about her aching belly, to believe that she had merely lost her footing and fallen? It was ridiculous, an insult. Did she think him blind? She had stood on that rock and stared, her body a flaming and tempting line of shock and recognition. She had dived, taking the water like a heron, reaching out for something, someone. He had seen it.

Small thick clouds moved above him and hurried on once more, shadowing the flight of the marsh birds to the south. Even as his eyes followed them, reflecting nothing, his mind dismissed Lun for the time being and moved on to the other woman, the older woman, the stranger.

Bel knew, as did everyone of the Dumnonii, that in other tribes there were women of power and position. The people of the Dubonii, he knew, paid great tribute to the goddess Brigantia, and her priests and acolytes were women. Among the Catuvellauni the priests were one step below the healers, and

145

these, too, were women. It was from the Catuvellauni that old Asulicca had come as a young bride, from a barbaric people, from a society where women were powers, warriors and leaders, within the tribe . . .

And Asulicca had power. Bel knew it, had always known it, yet somehow it had never before bothered him as it was coming to bother him now. He closed his eyes, remembering things that had puzzled him about the Catuvellauni wise woman, things both remembered and experienced.

He knew, for one thing, that old Cryl the idiot would not now be alive had it not been for Asulicca's intervention on her behalf. It was the custom among his people to give those whose wits were afflicted to the Goddess. Bel's own father, Styth, had been archdruid when Cryl was examined. The sacrifice had been set and accepted by the tribe, over the tears and hysteria of Cryl's mother.

And Asulicca, a stranger to the hearth of the Dumnonii and with no standing at all, had calmly gone to the Elders and told them at their own fire that the Goddess would not be pleased if Crylicca died, that to sacrifice a flawed and simple young girl was to insult the gods and in retribution great rains would follow and devastate the crops and the harvest.

They had believed her. Such things, the memory of incidents that formed the lore of the Elders, were passed from father to son, and this had been passed to Bel by his father before him. He had never been given what he knew must be the full tale; Styth had merely told him, on passing him the myrtle and the white robes of power, that the Circle had considered her words, had consulted the portents, had found that she spoke the truth. To Bel, the single oddest thing in the legend of Asulicca was that no one had asked her how she had known. They had taken her at her word because, he realised now, although she was but a girl at the time and had likely spoken meekly and without emphasis, they had sensed the power that lay behind her words.

Bel suddenly gave his tensed muscles up to the bittersweet luxury of warm summer air and a soft sky. Yes, Asulicca had lived to be an old woman, had lived and thrived, and none had felt her power used against them. She was a clever old crone. She spoke softly and kept her gifts hidden from men's sight. They sensed the gifts in her yet she was subtle in their use, as subtle as this hot day with its air of false calm and drugging lassitude.

Yet it was false, Bel told himself. It was false because behind the clear sky is always a threat of storms to come, because power is elemental and the elements are nature and nature cannot be controlled, on earth or in the spirit of woman. Power is strength, and when the strength is hidden it can bring nothing but danger . . .

On the still air came a distant peal of laughter, high and charming, the enchanting chuckle of a baby. It acted on Bel as a kick, a spur, a touch of guilt that he was dreaming the day away. He climbed quickly to his feet and stood surveying the stone, the ashes, the scattered bones. Then, because he was a man who greatly respected secrets and worshipped method, he took the entrails from where they lay stinking in the sun, and buried them beneath the ashes.

In the cool shadow of the huts another figure sat silent. Asulicca, however, was not thinking. She had followed Bel in her own spirit, had hovered over him like a wisp of smoke as he slit the goat's jugular vein, had stood at his shoulder as he arranged the entrails and read their meaning. Now, protected in her trance from the solicitude and interference of the village women, she lost track of her own breath and bone and slipped like a blade into Bel's mind.

It would never had occurred to the old woman to call the archdruid a misogynist, for such an idea had no part in the philosophy of the times. Men were as they were, and women were as they were, and though other tribes might differ in their opinions of the respective sex's strength and weaknesses, each tribe lived by its own rules. Bel was an extremist in his dislike of women; certainly it would never enter his mind that at heart he feared them, despising them for their darkness and their difference. He would never realise that he was forever tainted with

147

the need to crush what he could not understand. But moving among the shadowy pillars of thought that were holding Bel in his seat against the standing stone a half mile from her, she saw the fear and knew it for what it was.

A fool, she thought remotely, but a dangerous fool, a blind asp among the mistletoe. He is frightened of me, and blackly resentful with it; how he would love to bring me to ruin! But I have moved in darkness and silence always, never misusing what I have been given, never revealing my power, forever acting by instinct and by touch. But poor confused Lunica, she has no such weapons, no protection against him and his malice and his all-consuming fear.

And, like a cold hand upon her heart, she felt a new thing rise up in Bel, basic and irrevocable. Like a dark strand running through an even darker background she smelled his lust, a picture of sexual mastery over Lun, a way to defeat her that was purely male, and in her cool place and moving trance Asulicca suddenly cried out, low and tormented. The women stopped their chattering and turned to her, their eyes curious, fixing her with their beady concerted gazes like birds avid for food.

The spell was broken. Asulicca, her body suddenly waking and wracked with the stiffness that this travelling on the wind always brought, opened her eyes into a greedy silence. She rose slowly to her feet and, producing a smile, called across to the group of women.

'Did I disturb you? I am sorry for that. It was only a cramp. I had been dozing in the heat, and the cramp woke me.' She shook herself, first one leg and then the other, feeling the blood restart its painful needling through her veins. She moved towards the stream, her bare feet slapping and recoiling from the hot ground, and in a corner of her mind noted that Lun was nowhere to be seen. Doubtless the girl was still resting, trying to recover her body and wits from the soaking and from the heavy hand of the goddess.

The water was deliciously cool. Alone by the stream, Asulicca felt the first throb of a headache coming and edged herself a few

148

inches further into the current. She cupped her hands and gathered two palms full of the precious stuff, her eyes on the glittering stream bed below her.

There was something in the water. Sight and flesh ran together and merged, the small ache in her head suddenly turning to vicious and merciless pounding. She breathed heavily, trying to dispel the vision, not believing that she saw again what she had seen briefly and from a great distance on the night that Lun had stood here, arms open to the sky, calling down its fires.

There was a body in the water. He wore the garments of another time, another world; things that were recognisable even to Asulicca as thick boots of animal hide were sodden with water, holding him down and keeping him from rising to the surface. His face was a rictus of incomprehension and terror, his eyes open, his tongue a swollen and blackened serpent protruding pitifully into the clear flow. The flesh had already begun to rot from the bones; one hand was gone, dissolved away. The white bones gleamed dully. Through the solid flesh she saw the stream bed, the bits of effluvia, moving beneath him. He was a ghost, a demon, a tragedy.

I will not call out, she thought, and held the thought fast. Her heart was pounding, the noise and pain in her head was the echo of her heart swelling, preparing to burst from her in a wash of agonised fear. I will not call out, for if I do they will run to see and Lun will burn. To cry out is to give Bel the weapon he wants . . .

'Old one,' said the smooth voice from above her head, 'you might easily hurt yourself. Let me help you out.'

A cold hand, brutal in its strength, reached out and took her by the shoulder. She pulled her fascinated gaze away from the cycling, rhythmic motion of the corpse in the water and looked up at Bel. He stood, his face set in its usual mask, watching her. She saw his eyes move to where hers had been only moments before, and then come back to her face. He had seen nothing and would see nothing; he was blind to what she saw.

She reached out a hand, gnarled and fragile and wet, and he pulled her back up to the dry ground.

'Thank you, Father,' she said. 'That is kind. I think I am wet enough for one day.'

In the darkness, the soft touch on her neck and the tiny whisper came together.

'Wake, young one. Wake and follow. Power is on us.'

Lun swam to the surface of consciousness. The long nights of struggle and acceptance had given her the art of waking with no noise. She opened her eyes and spoke quietly.

'Asulicca.' It was a statement, not a question.

'Yes, it is I.' The old woman was a black shape on a blacker background. 'Cryth must not wake. Come softly.'

Lun got to her feet. The night had grown very cool and she was naked, her flesh prickling. Yet her eyes, catlike in the dimness, glowed hot and aware. She went silently out of the hut, following Asulicca.

Lun had no idea where Asulicca was leading her. The old woman seemed to know precisely where she was going on this strange night expedition; she walked briskly and with unusual speed, her thin robes fluttering in the wind. And Lun, her teeth chattering, suddenly knew that she had never seen these robes before, on Asulicca or anywhere else. They were black, woven from fine cloth, the seams showing green with age. She wore a girdle of heavy bronze, ornamented with symbols that spoke of things Lun could name only in her blood.

Asulicca stopped and turned to her, her face seemingly carved of stone. And, in a flash of intuition, Lun knew that these things, the robe and girdle, were objects of a power that the Elders knew only by hearsay and innuendo, a power that she herself had longed for. These were the symbols of the knowledge of the gods, of the future, of oneself. With the insight of vision Lun saw the young Asulicca, child of Brigantia, daughter of the High Priestess of the Goddess Protector of the Catuvellauni. She saw the young woman, beautiful and disturbing and self-contained within her chrysalis of power, taken from the shrine of the goddess and given to the son of a high-born man of the Dumnonii in wedlock, as a beautiful bribe to bring peace between the tribes. She saw the young still face, the long fingers hesitating over this robe, this girdle of office. She saw them folded and taken, kept separate from the dower she brought. She saw them hidden from the prying eyes of the Dumnonii women beneath the straw of the marriage bed.

In a curiously humble gesture, Lun reached out and tentatively touched the fabric of Asulicca's gown. The old woman stood like a stone, motionless, her eyes holding Lun's. The younger woman saw the encouragement there and let her hand move to the girdle.

The power, a tangible streak of pure energy, hit her like a swordthrust. She leaped backwards, fingers pulsing, eyes wide with disbelief. She saw Asulicca's smile, cold and triumphant, a frame of strength around the blackened teeth.

'You wished to learn of power from me. I denied you, for I saw your death, and Cryth's, and the trouble you must bring on us all. A bad time is coming, full of pain, and it is for you and through you. But I can deny you no longer, young one. I will give you what you wish. I must.'

'Why?' Lun whispered. A tiny current of wind lifted the free-flowing white hair that hung down Asulicca's back. 'Why now? If what is to come cannot be changed, why hasten its coming? What have you to gain, Asulicca?'

'Gain?' The smile was chilling now, barely human. Lun could hardly stand to look at it. 'I gain nothing. And what I will show you will change nothing. But all things must come in their place, and at their appointed time. You are in danger, and I too, because Bel has the greed of man and cannot wait for the stars to move. He must needs push them. And that is dishonour to the gods, something I cannot permit.'

Asulicca turned her back on Lun and continued to walk, covering the open distance with a long, loping stride. She climbed down the rise and walked away from the village, not even lifting her skirts, and suddenly Lun knew where they were going. Her arms wrapped around herself as a shield against the cool breeze, she followed as quickly as she could.

In the faintness of the sinking moon, the standing stone was a giant out of legend. It loomed over the field, over the dead ashes, over the sacred locus. Asulicca went directly to the site of the cold pyre and stood, hands held at an angle across her belly, fingers spread to their fullest, palms resting lightly on the intricate buckle of her girdle.

'Come here, young one. Come and share my eyes with me.'

Asulicca's voice was hollow, enormous, deeper than any man's voice could have been. The sky shuddered in Lun's eyes, the clouds wheeled above them in the winds of the upper air. Asulicca lifted her face momentarily to the heavens and called, low and deep, a strange animalistic sound. Above their heads a great shape, its wing feathers arched, circled in silence, watching, waiting. 'Come and taste of the goddess of the grove. Come and taste of her glory.'

There was no gainsaying that voice. No disobedience was possible; the enormity and unexpectedness of what was happening to her filled Lun. She moved toward Asulicca and wondered why, in her mind's eye, she suddenly saw the young demon that she herself had given back to Clota in a ritual so disturbingly like this one.

She was close to Asulicca now, her face inches from the older woman's. Asuliccas's eyes were black pits in her frozen face; her voice rolled like an ocean surf against Lun's ears.

'Lay your hands on me,' she said. 'Lay your hands on my hands, lay them flat, lay them easy.' The voice, never changing in volume, began to alter, intoning high and low, a voice from the depths of time itself. 'Rain and light, rain falls in me, light moves through me, touch on stone, living move through living bone.' The gnarled hands shot out and took Lun's in a hard clasp, drawing them close, drawing them in, and taking them at last to rest against the bronze of her girdle. Her voice was flat, mesmerising. 'Move through bone,' she chanted. 'Living move through living bone . . .'

152

I know this, Lun thought, I have heard this before, and then her hands were pressed against the carved buckle and the night went blind with pain and glory, split into a million bright fragments, and she was sinking, drowning, and somewhere close by and far away a bird was screaming . . .

'Make no sound,' said a calm voice that came from the sky, from the earth, from inside her own skull. Asulicca, Lun thought, what have you done to me? And the old woman who was somehow within her answered her thoughts, grim and unsmiling, speaking not with her voice but with her senses.

'They cannot see us, but ears can go where eyes cannot. So make no sound. The pain is nothing, and will soon pass.'

Lun, her eyes dark with pain and fright, looked down at the locus below her and saw the High Ones, the Circle of Five. Their white robes glimmering in the rosy firelight, the Elders stood within the sacred ring of mistletoe. In the heart of the leaping fire were bones, withered branches, small amorphous objects that Lun, through the mist of vision and the smoke of the fire itself, could not identify.

She could feel the breeze run like a finger through the hair on her neck; her nostrils caught a sharp, acrid whiff of the smoke and she smelled the foulness of blood, the hot pungency of ashes that were once wicker. Something had died, screaming, for the Circle's sake tonight.

'Leave go of yourself.' She was safe now, hidden and protected in the cloak of Asulicca's power. She was irrationally soothed by the small passionless voice that was the old woman's hand on her rein. Lun had ceased even to notice the pain; Asulicca was her shield and her mentor and all was well. 'Leave go of yourself, Lunica, forget yourself. There is no other way for you to follow me. Leave go, young one.' The inner voice sharpened. 'Quickly.'

Perhaps Lun was more adept even than she guessed. It may have been that her attempt to abnegate her gift had in some way strengthened her hold on it. For in the end it was easy, a simple thing indeed, to slip from herself and follow the dark clear-cut

153

shadow that she recognised as Asulicca into the black and tortured corners of Bel's mind.

And then she was Bel, and Asulicca was Bel, they had become one with Bel and she heard her own voice speaking, Asulicca's voice, Bel's voice, gathering the attention of the Elders. She felt his scorn for them, his rage and contempt and, with incredulity, his madness and the lust for her he would not admit even to himself.

'My brothers,' he said, and Lun felt the heat of his body in the firelight, 'there is trouble coming to us. We have a traitor, a creature of blasphemy, among us.'

Lun felt him savouring the words, the deep pleasure he took in them. She sat inside him, body and soul, and with a wonder tinged with nausea felt his testicles tighten. His voice took on a greater resonance.

'It is known to us that among the tribes of the north and east, women are given power. It is known to us that among them, are women raised to revere and nurture that same power. But we are not the savages of the Dubonii, we are not the blasphemous scum of the Catuvellauni even if we have one among us that first saw daylight among them. I have read the portents and they do not lie.'

Terror ran momentarily through Lun. Even as she fought it back from her she heard Asulicca's voiceless warning and felt Bel's head suddenly shake, as though from pain. He raised his voice a tone louder, enjoying the effect.

'After the night of the virgin moon, I dreamed, my brethren. I dreamed that a white wolf stood on the rock of our sacred water. I came to the water's edge to drive it off and it looked at me with yellow eyes, knowing its power, glorying in the death it would bring. Death not only of the body, my brethren. The white wolf brings death to the order, to the balance of the natural world. It must be defeated.'

Lun, a feather on a moving current, felt the weight of his lust like a tangible thing. She felt the pressure between his thighs, the pressure of blood flowing molten through the veins of his skull, distending them until she thought they must burst.

Giddy and disoriented, a fleeting thought passed through her like the voice of the wind. If he dies, she thought, if he dies here and now, do we die with him, Asulicca and I? Do we disappear, body and flesh, winking out as if we had never been?

Bel's fists were clenching and unclenching now, his face salty with sweat, his muscles knotted. The smile on his face was a wide mad stretching of the lips, carving deep grooves into his brown cheeks. The glow of the holy fire, dying now, streaked his face with crimson intersected with the shadows cast by the nine oak trees at the edge of the grove, which stood like ghosts in the moonlight.

'Yellow eyes, my brethren. The eyes of the wolf coveting the power to bring us all to ruin. The wolf who would burn the holy trees and savour the taste of the ashes. And the entrails, the holy entrails of the virgin kid I killed for the goddess – they said the same.'

His voice soared, manic and triumphant. 'It is Lunica who has broken our laws. Lunica, wife of Cryth, she who gazes upon the holy ritual with the eyes of the wolf. I tell you it is so, brethren. I, Bel, High Elder of the Circle of Five, tell you it is so!'

Four pairs of eyes, slitted and peering like the eyes of the hawk that hovered high above the circle, fixed on Bel. With no perceptible effort, Asulicca led Lun out of Bel and into the moving air above, into the body of the hawk who danced now, in silence, its great wings arched like a lover's arms to catch the currents of mobile wind.

'Listen now,' said Asulicca. Lun, her spirit folded small and motionless within the vicious and ancient skull of the great predator, saw the bodies beneath her through the creature's black-slitted pupils and heard the thoughts of the men blow, each different, each wary.

'He is strange tonight,' thought the smallest of the Five, 'strange and chancy. I hear something in his voice that smells of desire to me. Can it be that he wants her, and she has denied him? Jealousy is a potent enemy . . .'

'So young Lunica has overstepped herself at last,' thought the

155

one who was the most just and therefore the most wholly dangerous of the Elders. 'I have always thought she might; power pours from her like rain in summer. Yet Bel has offered us no proof. He tells us of his dreams, and arranges the portents to fit what he wishes them to say. I have often remarked it. I think perhaps he is slowly losing his wits. Should that happen we will need a new High Elder, and who better fitted than me?'

'What nonsense is this?' This came from the youngest of the Five. 'A threat, perhaps, but from a mere girl? And a girl who is high-born, and wife to a priest of Leucetius! Bel has run mad. Even he cannot read the portents so well as I, and I have seen nothing, nothing at all.'

'Perhaps,' thought the last of the Five, the oldest, who had seen eyes like Lunica's before and knew in his blood what she was, 'Bel may be right in this matter. He is mad for his power, and plays with sacred things. Yet he is no fool, and nor am I. Lunica, daughter of the moon . . . He wants her, that is certain, and it is equally sure that she does not want him. Yet here is more than spite.'

The bird lifted wings edged with royal darkness to the moon and screamed, filling its throat with the night in a call of rage and derision. It plummeted like a stone, curved over the heads of the men, and was gone into the night sky like a comet. The startled outcry from the Elders faded and became a part of the night, and then Lun was curled on the hard ground of the settlement, retching and disoriented. Asulicca held her and was silent unitl the spasm had passed.

'Here,' she said, and handed the girl a ewer of water. 'You are sick only because this is so new to you. After long years it becomes painless, as easy as walking.' She hesitated. 'Tell me what you heard, and what you felt.'

The girl raised her head as the nausea ebbed. Her voice was low and very weak. 'I was you,' she said, and her voice grew stronger as the memory of her wonderment came back to her. 'I was you,' she repeated. 'You, and then I was Bel.' She suddenly bent her face to the earth once more and was violently ill. 'I was Bel. I could feel what he felt.'

'Ah.' Asulicca's voice held inexplicably a note of deep satisfaction. 'Then you felt it even as I did. Madness, and a lust in chains. You know, young one, whom that lust was for, do you not?'

'For me,' Lun whispered, and tears began to trickle down her face. 'I felt it, old one. It was for me, desire but with hatred in it, such hatred.' She said, with sudden violence, 'It made me sick.'

'Yes,' said the old voice, suddenly weary, 'it would sicken anyone. Now I must speak with you seriously, and you must listen to me. Much will depend on your obedience.'

Lun splashed water across her mouth with fingers that trembled, washing the taste away. She said thinly, 'Speak, then. I will listen, I promise you, and listen well.'

'That is good. I told you, when I roused you tonight, that I would teach you all I could of power. I did not wish to do this, young Lunica. And make no mistake, I still do not wish to do so. But among my people, the people of my heart's blood, we are taught that to sit back and simply accept so great an evil as that which Bel has in mind is to desecrate the gods. And among the priests of the Catuvellauni, such desecration is the greatest of sins.'

She moved towards her hut, beckoning Lun to follow. The girl, reaching for the full meaning behind Asulicca's words, fell into step behind her. 'Yes, I understand this. But Asulicca . . . your girdle. When I touched it . . .'

'The girdle is only a girdle. If it holds magic it is the magic of communication, between ourselves and with the world we cannot see.'

'But when I touched it — I felt something come from it.'

'Yes. What you felt was me, whatever it is that is the best of me, reaching out to you and drawing you in. It is everywhere, this power, and though we cannot reach it with our sight or hearing, it runs through the world. It is in the air we breathe, it shivers in every storm, it runs like gold through the waters. It is there for everyone, child, yet few can touch it because they can believe only their senses, and to harness it the adept must learn to

157

disregard those very senses we need to keep the body alive.'

They entered Asulicca's darkened hut. As the old woman stripped herself of her strange trappings, wrapping them in tanned hides and slipping them beneath the straw that littered the floor, Lun spoke slowly.

'I think I understand what you are saying. The power is everywhere, even in ourselves; yet it is of a kind that we cannot hope to understand in the world of our bodies because our senses distract us. And somehow your robe and your girdle help you to shed your distractions, and thus to free your power.' She looked at Asulicca, a small shape in the blackness. 'Is this what you wished me to understand?'

'Yes. You understand it perfectly. Now heed me, Lun. I followed Bel into his shadow world today, followed him into the cold dark places where madness and murder grow. And his madness is growing; he is no fool, the archdruid Bel, and he has hidden his madness well. I understand this, for how else could I have survived if not by keeping my own power hidden and secret? But Bel is different. He has kept his own counsel too well, for he has kept it from himself. He does not admit to himself that he fears you, he does not admit to himself that his fear is shot through with a desire for you.'

Asulicca's eyes, burning through the darkness, held Lun in helpless thrall. 'He is ravenous for you, young one, as hungry as the wolf in the iron hills for the tender lamb. He is a hard man, cold and in his own eyes austere, and if he ever admitted the truth to himself it might well kill him. He will never understand that the caged beast only stinks in the bonds of captivity. So he will try to destroy you for, in destroying you, he will serve many purposes.' She broke off abruptly, her head slanted to one side. 'The Circle has broken, and the Elders are returning. Quickly, Lun. Get back to your bed. And whatever happens, make no sound. Cryth must not wake.'

Lun did not stay to question her. She turned on her heel and fled across the settlement towards the comparative safety of her own four walls. She stopped only to snatch up the water ewer, which might have betrayed their presence out of doors to the men, and climbed beneath her covers. Stiff with apprehension, she huddled as far from Cryth as she could.

'Lun. Close your eyes, and keep very still.'

Asulicca sounded faint and strangely muddy, as though she spoke through layers of water. Yet her presence was palpable, far more real to Lun than Cryth who lay sleeping a few feet away. She closed her eyes, obedient to the old woman's commands, and sent her thoughts out through the night.

'Asulicca? Wise woman, can you hear me?'

Asulicca's presence, acknowledging the use of the title of honour, drifted into Lun's mind like falling rose petals. 'Yes, young one. You learn quickly. To send your voice on the wind takes much effort and learning, and many years. You have already mastered it, it seems.'

Lun was conscious of a patina of pride in her mind and hastily sought to subdue it. Surely, with mystery and magic so close at hand, pride in oneself was unworthy? 'Asulicca, what can I do?'

Lun was beginning to interpret the shades of mood that inflected Asulicca's thoughts. Now she felt regret, a soft tinge of rue that fell across the senses like a fleeting scent of lavender, and tensed, waiting for an answer.

'I cannot tell you that, young one, not at this time. This madness of Bel's, it has a feel to it that is strange and unsettling. I must learn more of him if I am to hold him off.' The regret deepened. 'You must know, Lunica, that I cannot hold him off forever. In the end, he must win.'

The thought of Bel's triumph, of her own death, had panicked Lun no more than an hour earlier. Now, enveloped in Asulicca's passionless pity, she felt only a remote acceptance of the inevitable. For the first time in her life she was in the grip of power she could understand. It was maturing her, imbuing her with strength of mind and courage of body as nothing else could do.

'If that is what must pass, so be it,' she thought, and felt the satisfaction in Asulicca, felt the old woman's relief at her understanding, her compliance, her acceptance.

'If you understand this, truly understand this, you have more wisdom than I suspected. There is no point in worrying any further tonight. If we can speak in this way we have gained time, and time, young one, is what we must have.' There was a pause, a kind of mental readjustment, and Asulicca's thoughts took on a brighter tint. 'The men have returned from the locus, and all is well for now. I shall be near should you need me. Sleep now.'

Lun, with a calm she had never known before, closed her eyes against the coming day. Outside the great hawk folded its wings with a gentle rustle and settled its body atop the hut where its new mistress, her yellow eyes veiled by sleep, took what rest she could.

Chapter 15

The telephone was ringing for the third time in less than an hour.

Marian, ensconced on the Habitat sofa with a plate of excellent cheese and a mystery story, looked across the sitting room of Julian's London flat and wondered whether to follow her instincts and let it ring. No doubt it would be him again; fussing, worrying, wanting to know if she was still all right. It was very sweet of him to keep dashing out of conferences to call her but it was also very irritating. She eyed the phone with loathing, wondering why she had never noticed what an ugly sound it made, shrill and unpleasing.

Seven, eight, nine. No, it was no good hoping the bloody thing would simply stop. If that was Julian, he would probably let it ring until doomsday. She sighed, dropped her book on the coffee table and reached for the phone.

In the manner of telephones the world over, the harsh jangle stopped the moment her hand closed over the receiver. She thought for a moment, aware that Julian would probably be frantic; she should, she really should pick up the damned phone and dial his office. But she had been in London for forty-eight hours now and, during that two day stretch, she had become sick of the sound of her husband's voice. She had not spent this much time in his proximity since the early days of their marriage. Now, forced into close quarters with him, she was actively missing her usual privacy and finding him an irritant.

With a sudden decisive nod she took her purse and her keys

and let herself out into the street. The buses roared busily up and down Sloane Street, seeming to rest on two wheels only as they took the roundabout. The bookshop at the corner of Sloane Gardens was packed full of schoolgirls in their hideous uniforms. Overhead the sky was bright and the pigeons loud. She stood in the sunlight, conscious of a sensation of guilty pleasure, and wondered idly which way to go. Down the King's Road, perhaps, for a good long look at the punks who posed for tourists, spots of brilliant and idiosyncratic colour along Chelsea's main thoroughfare? Or up Sloane Street to Knightsbridge, where Harrods waited in one direction and the green spaces of Hyde Park beckoned in the other? No matter. The day was hot, the streets active, and she had time to kill.

In the end she opted for a long walk eastward, along Knightsbridge to Piccadilly and on to the National Gallery. She strolled past Cadogan Square, smiling at the children in the private park, and for the first time since arriving in London allowed herself to think about the chain of events that had brought her to a city she had always despised.

She had not wanted to come here. The morning after the incident in the garden, she and Julian had launched into the first real fight of their lives. She did not want to spend time in London, she told him. It was noisy, and dirty, and full of tourists. The west country was in the full glory of summer, and no place on earth was as beautiful, Julian knew that as well as she. It was no use; to each objection she put forward, Julian grew more truculent, more didactic. It was as though whatever was happening in their lives was slowly stripping away the layers of civilised protective colouring, leaving their true personalities bare to one another.

Can it be, she thought as her eye was caught by an astonishing confection of feathers and brocade in the window of Harvey Nichols, that we are really more like the people who quarrelled than we are the rôles we have acted all these years? I have always been so serene, not wanting to get involved in pettiness. Yet I sat there and dug in my heels, my mouth tight with fury. And Julian, always so calm and self-possessed, so reasonable, is he really as he suddenly seemed two days ago? Stubborn and obstinate, a peevish, opinionated child?

What in the world can be happening to me? she thought, as a group of tourists jostled past her in the crowd. And why, with every reason in the world to be worried half out of my mind, do I feel so free, so happy?

She stopped for a gâteau at a French pâtisserie on Piccadilly, thought briefly about exploring Bond Street, and continued east. The statue of Eros, covered with ugly scaffolding for repairs, nevertheless seemed to smile at her as she scampered through the traffic that spiralled in an endless circle around the Circus and turned down Shaftesbury Avenue. She smiled back at him, nasty chubby little god that he was, and went briskly onward towards Trafalgar Square and the National Gallery.

In the distance between Sloane Gardens and the famous picture gallery, she had somehow become attuned to London, in much the same way as a long walk on the moor would absorb her. Now, standing amid the fountains and the lions of Trafalgar Square, she looked up at their carved paws, at the thousands of pigeons begging for food and attention, at Nelson standing pompous guard on his tall column, and was filled with a sudden upsurge of delight. Had she truly not wanted to come here, to this surging lovely madhouse of life and movement? How could she have been so stupid? Giddy with the pleasure of the moment, she closed her eyes against the strong sun and flung her arms out, opening her mind and spirit to her mood and the warmth of the day.

Something brushed against her face, against her hair. There was a weight on her arms. Time moved over her, around her, shifted and then steadied, a sensation both cold and unpleasantly familiar. She opened her eyes, bringing her mind back to the present, and found herself gazing into the face of a stranger.

He was a sharp-faced little man, barely reaching her shoulder. Quintessentially cockney, his clothes were loud and cheap, his

163

face pinched. But as she focussed her gaze on him, she saw that his eyes were concerned and kind.

'Here, you all right, lady?'

His voice, she noted hazily, matched the rest of him; thin and sharp with a knife-edge of pertness to it. 'I think so.' She turned her head away from his bright enquiring gaze and stared into another set of eyes, an uncanny yellow with vertical pupils. And then another set, and another.

Pigeons. She had put her arms out to the sun in an instinctive gesture of welcome and now her arms were loaded with pigeons. Mechanically she counted them: one, two, no, three on her right arm and three on her left, and the one on her shoulder that stared into her face with its beady look that was as old as the world. There were four more hovering just above her head, watchful, ready for something. Suddenly frightened, she jerked her eyes away and shook her arms in a violent, abortive gesture. The pigeons rustled and shrilled but did not budge.

'Never seen anything quite like that before,' said the stranger. At her first movement he had stepped quickly backwards, eyes narrowing, brows lifting. He spoke in a chatty manner, familiar and confiding, but the narrowed eyes and tensed shoulders spoke of curiosity and caution. He watched the birds that formed a soft blue corona around Marian's head and cocked his head at her, inviting response.

'Haven't you?' She spoke vaguely, wondering why she could not bring herself to care about this little man, about what was happening, about anything except the soothing potent presence of these creatures. They surrounded her like a guard of honour, and she no longer wanted to rid herself of them. 'Well, I'm country bred, and birds do seem to like me. And of course the Trafalgar pigeons are used to people. Perhaps they think I have food for them.'

'Ah.' The monosyllable managed to be indefinite and knowing at the same time. 'Well, as long as you're all right, then ... mind they don't muck you up. Pigeons don't much seem to care where they drop their loads, dirty things.'

164

He jumped back just in time. The pigeons in the air above Marian's head suddenly darted at him in a concerted rush, forward and down. He flung up a hand to protect his face, leaping and swearing. Through the flurry of feathers Marian saw a bright streak of blood where a beak had gone home just under the cuff of his sleeve. Then the birds returned to their post. Marian turned her head and looked thoughtfully at their softly beating wings. The birds looked back at her, silent now. Their gazes held rage, knowledge, obedience. She sucked in her breath softly.

'Bloody hell,' said the little man very quietly and then he was running, shouldering astonished tourists out of his way. At the entrance to the Strand he looked back at her and she saw him rubbing the blood from his arm. Then he was gone, just another shape in the moving tide of humanity.

'Shoo,' she said gently. 'Shoo, scat, go away now.' She waved her hands, twitching her shoulders lightly, and saw the feathers, blue and grey, ruffle and spread as if for flight. Something she could not name made her add, just under her breath, 'If I need you, I'll call you. Go now.'

They obeyed. Clucking and flapping they took the air and were gone, flying in a huddled formation south towards Whitehall. She looked down at her clothing, brushing absent-mindedly at herself; a solitary feather, slate blue and very clean, fluttered off her shoulder and fell to the ground. She looked around her at the press of people. They were taking pictures, laughing, splashing in the fountain. No one looked her way. Smiling the cold dark smile that was not her own, she entered the National Gallery for a good long stare at the Leonardo cartoon and a cup of milky tea.

'I'm sorry to disturb you, Mr. Dunne, but your daughter Gemma is on line one, and she says it's urgent.'

'All right, Mrs. Potter. Thank you.' Julian brushed a lock of limp hair from his face and turned apologetically to his client. 'Sorry, Peter, but I really ought to take this call. My wife hasn't been well, and it could be important. Excuse me a moment, will you?'

He slipped out of the conference room and into his own office. The fan, circulating hot air, was more a hindrance than a help; the windows were closed against the enormous bluebottle flies that buzzed, hungry and frustrated, in the heat of the Indian summer. He sat down and took the phone.

'Gemma? It's Dad. Mrs. Potter said it was urgent?'

She sounded distraught. 'Daddy, I've been calling Four Shields for the last two days! Where the hell is Mum?'

'She's in town with me this week. Gemma, you sound dreadful. What's the matter? Why do you need her?'

'I've been reading.' She sounded breathless. 'I've been reading a lot. We had a meeting about it, about what was going on at Four Shields — you know, with Soap. And they got together and gave me a list of research materials. I've been following it up.' She stopped so suddenly that for a moment Julian thought she had rung off. When she spoke again her voice was tight with tears barely kept at bay. 'I'm scared, Daddy. I'm so scared ...'

'All right.' Sitting in a patch of sunlight, all the trappings of the twentieth century surrounding him, Julian felt a brush of cold fear and wondered at it. He kept his voice level. 'All right, Gemma. Calm down, there's no need to panic. Your mother is fine. She came up to London with me for this week. I tried calling her about an hour ago, and got no answer; I'd lay you odds she's gone off to Harrods or one of the museums. If I wasn't in conference with one of my best clients, I'd be very tempted to go and lie on the grass in Hyde Park myself.'

'Oh, Daddy, I'm sorry. I got you out of a meeting.' She thought for a moment. 'Look, can I come over tonight? I'd really like to talk to both of you.'

'Yes, come over, we'll send out for something. I'll be home about six. If there's no answer, wait for us.'

'I'll do that.' Under the voice, steady now with a kind of determined gaiety, he heard the rasp of nerves scraped raw.

166

'Daddy? Can I ask you something, please?'

The phone slipped in his sweaty palm. 'Of course.'

'Has anything happened since the last time I spoke with you? You know – anything, well, peculiar?'

To tell, he thought, or not to tell? What could he be thinking of? She must find out eventually. Better to hear it from him. 'Yes,' he said levelly. 'Something rather awful has happened, Gem. If things hadn't been so bad and hectic, I would have called you. But you couldn't have done anything anyway, and I didn't want to worry you.'

Her voice went flat. 'You're using that dreadful, gentle voice of yours, the one you use when someone dies. Is that it? Did someone die?'

'Yes,' he said quietly. 'Roger Dawkins was found dead, apparently of heart failure, in the stream at one of the Iron Age settlements. Your mother found him.'

There was silence on the line, a silence pregnant with pain, aching and somehow alive. Finally she spoke.

'Daddy – did it have to do with all this?'

'Yes.' The answer came from him immediately, and so naturally that he surprised himself. How, he thought, can I be so sure? 'Yes, it did. There was an inquest.'

'I'll be there by six,' she said and he heard the phone drop heavily back into its cradle. He got up and, shaking his head to clear it, went back to his meeting.

As he totalled figures and discussed options the same thoughts ran through his mind in a ceaseless dance. Where was Marian? Why had she not answered the phone? Surely the danger was only at Four Shields, only near the settlement? Please God she was not at risk in London itself . . .

On the ledge outside the conference room window, several pigeons gathered. They leaned against the glass, cooing and settling. They watched Julian's every move, eyes following him with uncanny precision as his arm swept back and forth across the chalk board, as he tapped the table for emphasis or scraped back his chair. They never looked away. And it was not until he

167

had ushered out his guest at five-thirty and closed the conference room door behind him, that they lifted their wings and left their perch.

The first thing Julian heard on entering his flat was the reassuring sound of Marian singing in the shower.

He took a purposeful step towards the small bathroom, thinking that he really ought to tell her off. How could she simply pick up and go out, or stay home and refuse to answer the phone, when she knew how worried about her he was? Women could be so inconsiderate at times . . .

His anger evaporated as suddenly as it had risen. He tilted his head to one side, listening to her. Her voice rose, happy and triumphant, over the drumbeat of running water. How amazing, he thought, she sounds like a bird. She sang steadily and clearly, her voice lilting and trilling in loops of pure enjoyment. It had been far too long since he had last heard her sound so relaxed and peaceful.

No, he thought, I won't disturb her. If she's managed to put herself in a good mood in spite of everything, it would be a shame to upset her. But Gemma was coming over, and she had something she wanted to discuss with them both. He went and rapped lightly on the bathroom door.

'Julian? Is that you?' It was astonishing, she sounded absolutely ecstatic yet when he had left the house this morning she had been as close to a fit of the sulks as made no odds. What could have happened to lighten her mood?

'Hullo, darling. Can you dry off? Gemma's coming.'

'Gemma?' Julian, who had moved away from the door, stopped and turned sharply on his heel. Could that really have been confusion he heard in her voice? No. Ridiculous.

'Yes, Gemma,' he called. 'Your daughter. Remember?'

'Don't be silly.' She sounded light-hearted again. 'I'll be out in a minute. I hope you don't expect me to cook tonight. Did she happen to say what she wanted to talk about?'

'No.' He went into the sitting room and poured himself a gin

168

and tonic. 'But I expect she's come up with more theories. Anyway, she'll be here any moment.'

'She can wait.' There was no mistaking it this time; that was definitely amusement he heard in Marian's voice. He swallowed his drink, keeping one eye on the bathroom door.

After a few moments it opened and she came out. She was wrapped in her dressing gown, and her hair was covered by a terrycloth turban. She looked dear and familiar to him; looked, in fact, precisely the way she had every morning for more years than Julian wanted to count. He looked across the room, smiled, and then met her eyes. And, in that meeting, an icy hand took a firm hold of him, robbing him of sanity and speech.

The eyes that looked back at him with cool amusement were not his wife's. They were not the deep brown slits that had watched him across the breakfast table for more than twenty years. They were yellow, a bright, unsettling shade of amber, the pupils elongated and blurred. They were not Marian's; he was not even sure they were human. And they watched him with blatant amusement and challenge.

'Whatever's wrong, Julian?' The voice was the same; the face was the same. Yet the fact that she appeared normal in every other way only made it worse. This was not her, it could never be Marian so long as those impossible yellow eyes stared out of her face. 'You look as though you'd seen a ghost. Are you all right?'

'Your eyes,' he said. 'What happened . . . ?'

'What are you talking about?' She looked at him, one corner of her mouth twitching. And that was all wrong as well. That was not Marian's smile, not the generous expression that etched laughlines into her face. It was the smile he had seen before: after her seizure, in the garden, in his nightmares. 'There's nothing wrong with my eyes.'

He strode across the room and caught her by the shoulder. Then, as she fixed those dreadful eyes on his face, he spun her around to face the enormous mirror that hung directly over the dining table.

'Nothing wrong with your eyes?' he said harshly. 'Funny

169

thing, my dear. In all the years I've known you I would have sworn they were brown. What do you call this?'

She peered into the mirror, then back at him. There was no mistaking the honest bewilderment in her expression.

'Julian,' she said, 'aren't you feeling well? My eyes are just the same as always.' She became aware of his grip, tight and painful on her arm. With a quick, graceful motion she shrugged herself free and went to the whisky decanter. 'You're hallucinating, or something.'

As he opened his mouth to reply, the doorbell rang. Gemma had arrived. Tight-lipped, he opened the door and let his daughter in.

He saw at once the marks of sorrow. She had powdered her face but no amount of makeup, however artfully applied, could hide the tear tracks on her skin. And there was something new about her, a determination that sat well on her, quite different from her usual cheerful obstinacy. She came in with her eyes cast down; under her arm was the shabby leather portfolio, stamped with her initials, that had seen her through her university days.

'Gemma,' Julian said loudly. She looked up, startled.

'I want you,' he said carefully, 'to do something. I want you to look at your mother . . .'

Marian's voice was sharp and angry. 'Oh, for God's sake, Julian. Will you give it a rest?'

'. . .to look at your mother,' he continued, as if she had not spoken. 'Look at her and tell me what you see.'

Gemma looked blankly up into his face. Then, brows lifted, she turned to face her mother.

Her shriek was not loud. Still, in the small room that was already overwarm from the heat of the day, it was as nerve-wracking as anything could be.

The three people stood like a waxwork in an elegant museum display. No one moved; no one spoke. Marian, her eyes on her daughter, stood frozen in the act of mixing a drink; the glass she held did not even quiver, so still was she. Gemma had both hands pressed to her mouth, a gesture of stress that dated back to her

170

childhood. Above the knotted fists her eyes were wide and horrified.

Julian, separate and alone, watched them both. He, too, was perfectly still, his arms wrapped tight around himself as if for protection against the unknown. Sounds of the city below drifted lazily in; horns, footsteps, traffic going about its business in the world outside. The tiny pulse that jumped at the corner of Julian's mouth was the only moving thing in the quiet room.

'Mum?' It was a scratchy whisper, a flute of breath. 'Mum, what happened to your eyes?'

The tableau broke into moving fragments. Julian let out his breath in a noisy gust. Gemma, with her hands till raised to her mouth, sank on to the sofa behind her. And Marian set down her glass with a slap that shook the table. Her voice was cold, tinged with scorn.

'There is nothing wrong with my eyes,' she said. 'You and your father may have something wrong with yours. I don't know what nonsense you're going on about, and what's more I don't want to.' She turned to face them, the yellow eyes gleaming with anger. She had a presence, an air of dominance, that she had never possessed before. 'I hope I make myself clear?'

Gemma opened her mouth and shut it before her father's look. The warning was clear, implicit in the tiny shake of his head. She sat back on the sofa, her hands trembling.

Julian's manner matched his wife's for chilliness. 'You do. I, for one, am more than glad to oblige. Gemma, I suggest that we leave your mother alone for a bit. Would you care for Greek food? Good. Don't forget your papers. Let's go.'

Marian was still standing and watching them, smiling that strange inimical smile, as the front door closed behind them.

'No,' said Julian, as he pushed Gemma into a taxi. 'No, don't say a word yet. Athena Restaurant, driver. North end of Marylebone Road. You and I, Gem, are going to sit down and eat and then you are going to talk all night. You are going to tell me what you saw and what you think and I am going to listen with an open mind. All right?'

171

She said nothing. Julian, glancing at her where she sat huddled against the far door of the taxi, saw her look of shock, of betrayal beyond tolerating. His heart ached for her.

The Athena Café was a fashionable restaurant that managed, in spite of its popularity and high prices, to avoid pretentiousness. It also served some of the best Greek food in London. It was roomy and very dark. Regulars insisted you could pinpoint its location from half a mile away simply by following your nose, and indeed the smells of roasting lamb and fresh pitta bread were noticeable at some distance.

It was also, rather uncharacteristically, fairly empty this evening. Julian took his daughter by the arm and led her to a corner table. Without consulting either Gemma or the menu, he ordered a carafe of wine and souvlaki for two. Then he leaned back and lit a cigarette, watching Gemma under lowered lids. He did not like the limpness of her body.

'Tell me what you saw,' he said suddenly.

She lifted her head and looked at him. In the dim light her eyes were enormous. He saw her hands tighten convulsively and, leaning across the damask tablecloth, covered them with his own. She began to shake, a steady shivering that she seemed unaware of, unable to stop.

'Her eyes,' she whispered. 'Daddy, what happened to her eyes? And why did she lie to us about it?'

'I don't know.' He spoke reflectively. 'All I do know is that she was fine when I left for the office this morning. I called her four times during the day. The first two times, she was home and she answered. The last two, no answer. She either went out or simply decided she didn't want to be bothered. During the day something happened. She won't tell me what, as you heard. She won't even admit that anything did happen.' He regarded his daughter, noting the quivering lips, and said gently, 'And I do know something else. I know how glad, how unspeakably glad I am that you saw what I saw. If you hadn't seen it . . .'

'I saw it.' Gemma refilled her glass. 'It made me sick. Yellow eyes. And that smile as we were leaving . . .'

'It's happened before.' At that she looked up quickly, frowning. 'Twice. I think I should fill you in on what's been happening since the Dowbridge picnic. It's time.'

'Yes,' she said flatly. 'It's certainly time. But before you tell me about Mum, or Four Shields,' her voice broke suddenly, 'I want to hear about Roger.'

'All right,' he said quietly. She rubbed her cheeks angrily, blew her nose and poured more wine. This was her third glass, he thought, and Gemma had never been much of a wine drinker. To still his racing thoughts he began to tell her, as precisely and unemotionally as possible, every detail he could remember of Roger Dawkins' death. She listened in silence, her fingers beating a nervous tattoo on the table. As Julian finished his account of the inquest, the waiter deposited two steaming platters before them and withdrew.

'Well,' he said, 'there you have it. And I should like to know what you make of all that?'

Still she said nothing. Her fingers stopped their drumming and took up a fork. Then the fork was deposited back on the table, and she looked up at him.

'Mother said that Roger was a sacrifice.'

'Yes,' he said. 'She did. I can't remember her exact words. I wish I could. Something about a blood sacrifice. She stated it, Gem, quite unemotionally, sounding very much as though she knew what she was talking about. But I can't be sure of what she said; it was just before she had that odd fit when she dreamed of the girl . . .' He stopped with an exclamation.

'What is it?' Gemma saw his face tighten, and said urgently, 'Daddy! What is it? What's the matter?'

'The girl.' Julian was having trouble controlling his voice. 'I told you, Marian went into some kind of trance or fit. When she came out of it I kept pushing at her to try and remember . . . she did, finally.' He stared at Gemma's blank, desperate face. 'Yellow eyes.'

'I don't understand you. What yellow eyes?'

'The girl, the girl that knew she was there in the stream – your

173

mother said she had yellow eyes. I was digging at her, being deliberately nasty, trying to rouse her. She looked so drugged and lethargic it scared me. I tried . . . '

'Yes? Go on, Daddy, for heaven's sake!'

'All right.' He sat back abruptly, taking control of himself and the situation. 'All right. Let me see if I can remember exactly what happened, what Marian said she saw. She went into that trance, it lasted about eight minutes. When she came out of it, she was − disoriented. Blurry, vague. She couldn't seem to focus properly. I made her talk it out. She said,' − he closed his eyes in concentration, − 'she had been standing in the stream, the one at the settlement.'

'Where Roger was found.' Gemma spoke harshly.

'That one, yes. Marian was standing in the stream, singing. There was an animal pelt or something spread on the ground, in the settlement itself, with babies playing on it?'

Suddenly his eyes widened. 'Got it!' he said triumphantly. 'Babies playing! And two old women, she said. One of them looked like an idiot − you know, brain-damaged. She said a young man came out of one of the huts and tripped over them. And then the girl came down to the stream where Marian was.'

'And the girl could see her?'

'More than that. She said the girl not only knew she was there but actively wanted something from her. She said the girl saw her and dived into the water after her.'

Gemma was thinking rapidly. She moved back in time to a meeting of Soap held at the Red Hart more than a year ago. It had been an unusual meeting because, whereas Soap usually kept itself to itself, this particular night it had featured a guest speaker. An American author, who professed to have had personal experience of supernatural phenomena, had spoken on how normal flesh reacts to the touch of possession. He had spoken extensively and in detail . . .

'Daddy. Did Mum happen to say whether this girl made any attempt to touch her?'

'Yes.' Julian was breathing heavily. 'She said the girl came

174

into the water and reached for her. She said it was like –
damnation, what did she say? She said it was like stepping on a
spider. Hot and repulsive.' He suddenly noticed the waiter
hovering, staring anxiously at his cooling plate of food, and
pulled it towards him. 'Gemma, does this convey anything to
you? Anything at all?'

'Yes, it does.' Gemma, too, reached for her food; the souvlaki
smelled wonderful. She suddenly realized that she was ravenously hungry. Speaking through mouthfuls of rice and lamb, she
talked quickly, without thinking too hard about what she was
saying.

'Listen, Daddy. This bears out, or at least I think it bears out,
the idea I've been turning round at the back of my mind. I spent
a day at the BM, just researching, and all the books I came across
on the subject say basically the same thing – that this kind of
spiritual invasion is like racial memory. It isn't a ghost or a spirit
attacking the living. I suppose you'd have to define it by saying
that it's a tear or tunnel in time. And it happens because an old
power, or an ancient belief in that power, is so strong that it
lingers.' She reached for the bread and butter. 'Want to hear
something interesting? They say it happens most often around
ancient holy places. Temples and things. Now, we don't know
nearly enough about what went on then . . .'

'I think I understand what's on your mind.' Julian pushed his
empty plate away and nodded at the waiter. 'Yes, we'll have
another carafe of wine, please. All right, what you seem to be
saying – correct me if I'm wrong – is that this girl, this woman
with the yellow eyes, has somehow managed to push her way
through time and leech on to your mother. Perhaps the girl was a
priestess – no way to tell that now. But if she had power, or only
wanted it . . . yes, I see. Her desire, or strength, or whatever
emotions or feelings were driving her, gave her the ability to
reach through time. That makes sense of a sort. But why
Marian?'

'Mum's a pure Celt,' Gemma said simply. 'Maybe she's just
sensitive to it. Who knows? We can only guess.'

'True. Do you know, Gem, I'm inclined to agree with your ideas.' He smiled faintly at the astonishment on her face. 'Don't look so surprised, I'm not totally a creature of the material age, you know. Yes, I think your answer is the right one. It smells right somehow. Nothing else makes any sense, or offers any answers at all.' His voice turned cold. 'And, besides, there's the little matter of your mother's eyes. That needs explaining.'

'I think it's the girl.' Gemma spoke flatly. 'I think the girl had something, or wanted something. I think she got hold of Mum somehow, in some weird esoteric way I can't even begin to understand, and have taken her over. I think she's got hold of Mum, body and soul, and is pulling her in.'

'Yes, but pulling her into what?' Julian brought his clenched fist down on the table so hard that the glasses rattled musically against each other. 'So much has been happening, Gem. So much and so fast . . . the inquest on Roger wasn't the end of it. That night I woke up in the small hours because I heard Marian out in the garden.'

'What on earth was she doing out there?'

'Screaming.' Julian drained his glass and refilled it. 'She couldn't remember getting up. When I found her she was huddled in the grass, wailing like a banshee. And Gemma, you won't like this but I think you ought to know — she had blood on her. On her hands, and — and on her mouth.'

'Oh, God. What . . . ?'

'A mouse. She didn't remember what happened but it was plain enough for anyone with eyes to see.' He swallowed. 'She said the same thing, or almost the same thing, that she'd said about Roger: A sacrifice. Except she claimed this one was given to her.'

'Jesus. Sweet Jesus.' Gemma had paled. 'Given to her by who? Did she remember that?'

'Yes, indeed. Would you believe a wild hawk?'

Silence fell. They stared at each other but neither was seeing the other's face. Each was occupied with private thoughts. Julian was remembering Marian's voice. 'A sparrow hawk, I

176

think. A big male. Lovely.' He remembered how, in the brutal gleam of his torch, her eyes had looked bright yellow, and how he had dismissed it as a trick of the moonlight.

Gemma was turning pieces of research over and over in her mind. Druids. Their belief in control over the natural world. The sacred hawk. Sacrifice . . .

'She claimed that the bird had brought her the mouse.' Julian was speaking with painful slowness. 'She said she didn't kill it, that the hawk did. But she claims she heard the bird call, that she called back, and that it came to her.'

'She says that the bird came to her when she called it? Daddy, there was something about that in one or two of the books I looked into. They said the old religions – they lumped them all together and called the ancient worships geomancy – believed that with enough power you could control the natural world. Would that mean animals, do you think?'

'Animals – and weather. Christ! Gemma, the storm, the freak storm the night Roger died. Do you think . . . ?'

'That Mum called it? Created it? I don't know, Daddy, I just don't know.' Gemma once again saw her mother standing in the Sloane Gardens flat, a figure of doom, somehow taller, infused with a dangerous presence that was completely new and different, out of Gemma's experience. She saw again the yellow eyes, her mother's flat sneering denial. A wild hawk, a freak storm, a young man's body submerged in a swollen stream . . . The pictures, implacable and remorseless, melted and ran and then, at last, merged into a clear pattern.

'That burn on your hand.' Gemma was using words the way she had used them as a student, as a means of clarifying her thoughts. 'Mum smelled smoke inside the house. You smelled it out on the moor. You fell asleep and dreamed. And your dream – wasn't that also about babies, and a girl? When we talked about it . . .'

'Yes. Damnation, it's gone fuzzy. I can't remember much of it but there was something . . .' He screwed his eyes up in an effort of memory. ' A baby, a boy it was. And there were two people. I

177

assume they were the parents. A young man and a girl. I think they were arguing about something. They were speaking a language I didn't know.'

Gemma watched him closely. 'How were they dressed?'

'Rough clothes. Homespun stuff, it looked like. Bare feet.' He jumped. 'That's right – I remember now. We discussed it, didn't we? And you laughed, and said something about dreams suitable to my surroundings. Yes, I recall it now. They looked like Iron or Bronze Age people. Villagers.'

Her voice warmed with excitement. 'We're getting closer. Can you bring them to mind, Daddy? What did they look like? What did she look like?'

But Julian shook his head. 'It's no good, darling. You want to know if the girl had yellow eyes, don't you? I honestly don't remember. They weren't that distinct. I do remember that they looked much alike – thin and brown. And the baby was very vivid, with his bone. Beyond that, nothing.'

'Never mind. You had the dream anyway. But that was the last thing that happened to you, wasn't it? Everything that's happened after that happened to Mum.' She began to tick the events off on her fingers. 'The smoke in the kitchen that Saturday night, the storm, Roger's death, the fit when she saw the girl, the bird in the garden. Nothing else happened to you. Except for the time you fell asleep and got your hand burned, this thing – whatever it is – seems directed straight at Mum, and only at Mum.' She repeated it thoughtfully. 'Only at her. Now, I wonder . . .'

'You think this is happening to your mother because, for some reason, she's the most sensitive to it? If that's true, how did I smell the smoke? And what about my hand?'

'It could be the time and place.' She struggled to explain. 'What I mean is, the place where there's this hole or bridge is likely to be out on the moor – probably right in the middle of the village. Perhaps the initial contact was made when Mum smelled the smoke, but maybe the dream and the burn would have happened to anyone who happened to fall asleep in the middle of

178

the village at precisely that moment.' Momentarily, she forgot the gravity of the problem facing them, carried away by her enthusiasm. 'Fascinating, isn't it?'

'I am not,' her father said dryly, 'in the mood to appreciate its complexities. To continue: something, maybe the shadow of some religious rite performed thousands of years ago, sent some kind of sensory impression of smoke into Four Shields. Your mother was receptive to it; it's a point, by the way, that none of the gas people smelled anything. This smoke drifted in through a gap, for lack of a better word, in the fabric of time. Your mother's receptivity helped widen that gap, rendering her even more sensitive and receptive. A kind of vicious circle. Is that the idea?'

'Got it in one,' she replied. 'This girl with the yellow eyes – we ought to find a better name for her than that, I think – established some kind of bond with Mum. And the bond has been growing. Whatever happened today . . .'

'We don't know what happened today,' Julian pointed out quickly. 'And I don't think she intends to tell us. But I'm scared, Gemma. Until she walked into the room tonight and looked at me with someones else's eyes, I firmly believed that the trouble was the house, or the countryside. I never for one moment thought that she could be in any kind of danger from this thing here in London. What happened today proves me wrong. Your mother is no safer a thousand miles away from Dartmoor than she would be at Four Shields.'

The waiter dropped the cheque on the table with the air of a magician performing a conjuring act. Julian pulled some notes out of his pocket and turned to his daughter.

'I don't know about you, Gem, but right now I don't want to go home until there's a damned good chance your mother is sleeping. I can't even imagine going back there right now, knowing what we think we know. I can't imagine trying to make conversation with her, staring into those yellow eyes. Can I treat you to a film, or maybe a good long pub crawl?'

'I'm not in the mood for people. Why don't we go back to my

179

flat?' She saw his hesitation and added bluntly, 'Look, Daddy. I'm not enjoying this any more than you are. I'm just as shaken up. I cared a lot about Roger Dawkins, and I care about Mum. But this thing isn't likely to go away just because we want it to. If we go back to my flat, I can show you the notes I made. Maybe if we read them over together, it will give us both some ideas about how to cope with it. There's another plus, too.'

'There's no plus for anyone in this situation.'

'Oh, yes, there is,' she said grimly. 'By the time we've gone over everything, Mum ought to be fathoms deep.'

'I hope you're right. Grab your purse and let's go.'

Chapter 16

Lun woke to the first strains of a lark singing, and the sound of Asulicca's voice in her mind.

'Wake yourself, young woman. Morning now.'

Lun stretched herself and brushed against Cryth, who was still deeply asleep. She was aware this morning, as she had never been before, of the play of each individual muscle of her body as she stretched her limbs to their limits. She was aware, too, of the tingle of her nerves; they seemed to have taken voice in the night and spoke to her now, declaring themselves. She noted these things with a kind of surprise, which was tempered by Asulicca's gentle amusement. Closing her eyes once more, she queried the old woman amiably.

'You are laughing at me, wise woman? Will you tell me what amuses you, then?'

'Oh, it is nothing very much. Only that people who think they understand the workings of power always seem to believe that to have power of the mind means they must subdue the body. That is untrue, of course.'

Lun opened her eyes, holding fast to her thoughts. Much to her surprise, Asulicca's presence was as strong and potent as before; not even the sight of Cel, lying awake and smiling at her, seemed able to distract her. Her mind felt as open as the wild moor itself.

'Why is it untrue? Is the body not a distraction?'

'It can be one, if you let it. But you must know your body as well as you know your spirit. Body and spirit go hand in hand, and to deny one is to lose control of the other.'

'I understand you, and I believe you are right.'

'I must go now, and deal with the day. Cryth will wake in a moment, young one. Let him learn nothing.'

'Of course not.' Cryth stirred then and yawned cavernously. Lun felt Asulicca fading and thought quickly, 'How did you know he was waking, Asulicca? Can you tell me?'

'I can, yes. But this is not the time. We will speak further, when the waking world does not require us.'

Blue to grey, and grey to nothing. Asulicca was gone. Lun, learning with uncanny speed how best to interpret her new eyes and ears, was beginning to understand that thought was painted, much as a mood on the landscape itself. She smiled and reached her arms out to Cel, who gurgled with pleasure. From behind her Cryth spoke, sleepy but content.

'A new morning you, my Lunica, and a fine day too. Is that young Cel who makes such noise?'

She hoisted the baby up against her hip, vaguely aware of the rose tint in Cryth's mood; it was the colour of fondness edged with passion. How safe I feel, she thought, nestled in power, wrapped in the cloak of a wise woman's care. Her voice was light. 'It is. A new morning to you, Cryth. Here, young boy, stop this kicking at once, or you will have me blue with bruising. I must go tend to our meal. Cel, if you will not stop kicking I shall put you down and make you crawl for your food. Enough, now.'

She turned the baby sideways under one wiry arm and left the hut. The first person she saw was Bel.

He was standing just outside the hut, staring up at the roof. His eyes were narrowed, his mouth taut. How mean he is, she thought, how narrow, how avid, how ugly. I shall not be bested by him. I shall not. She shifted Cel to the crook of her arm where he promptly chuckled and wrapped his arms around her neck. She nuzzled his hair and turned to Bel.

'A new morning, a fine morning, Father. Forgive my young

one's lack of manners, I beg. I must cook the mash this morning, Father. Will you take your meal with us?'

'There is a bird nesting on your roof.'

The words were so unexpected that she simply stood and blinked at him. Then, puzzled, she turned to face her home and craned her neck. Yes, there it was. She could just make out the edge of a feathered back, grey and blue.

'Why, I believe that is so, Father. A hawk, I think it is. Oh, Cryth, come and see — there is a bird, making its nest on our roof! Is that not said to bring good fortune?'

'It is. A good morning to you, Father.' Cryth, taller by far than either Bel or Lunica, lifted his eyes to the roof. The slitted eyes of the bird, mad, dangerous, impassive, glared back at him.

'There is no nest there, not yet. Doubtless he — or she, it may be — will make one soon. Yes, Lun, that is a good omen. It is said to bring fertility.' He moved his hands in the ritual gesture. 'May that be true for all the Dumnonii.'

'May that be true for all the tribes,' Lun corrected, and turned back to Bel. Like the blue of woad his mood was visible to her: bewilderment at her, irritation with Cryth, distaste for the baby. And under it, a scarlet streak among the others, two darker things lay submerged. Superstitious terror of the hawk that watched them, and his constant, controlled desire for her. This was true power, then, to know as much as this and yet not to fear it. Nor to fear him. Amused, catlike, she smiled charmingly and repeated the innocuous question he had left unanswered.

'Will you not honour us and share our meal, Father?'

'I thank you,' he said slowly. His eyes never left the hawk. Perhaps the bird, too, sensed something of how he felt for it stared back at him, eyes inimical, beak open. 'I thank you, young yellow-eyes. But I will not trespass on your hearth. I have things to do this morning.'

It was stronger now, that line of scarlet, and closer to the surface. He could not bear to have her so near ... She put her free arm around her husband, smiling lovingly up at him. A charming picture of domesticity, to be sure. She dropped a slight

bow to him and was brought up short by Asulicca's voice, loud
as a clarion in her mind.

'Take care, young one. You dare too much, too soon.'

With a rush, Lun came back to reality. Asulicca was right.
Was she mad with her power, then, to risk so much? She must be
more careful; Bel, wanting her, was yet dangerous, his desire
tinged with madness and death. It would not do to forget that so
soon. She spoke humbly.

'I am sorry, Father. Some other day, then, if you will honour
us. You are always welcome at our hearth.'

'My thanks,' he said coldly and, turning on his heel, strode
away from them. Cryth stared after him, puzzled.

'The High Elder is angry,' he said, and glanced down at
Lunica. 'Do you know why, Lun? Did you say something?'

'I said nothing,' she replied sharply. Why must he always
assume that, if there was any trouble caused, she had been
responsible for it? 'I found him where you found us, standing
and staring at the bird. If he is upset about the bird, or lays the
blame for its presence on me, then he is unjust. I neither know
nor care why a hawk has chosen this place to nest.' She stopped
as Cel, drumming his heels against her hip, made it very obvious
that he wished her to set him down. She stooped and detached
him from her, adding plaintively, 'I didn't put the hawk on our
roof, you know.'

'Such an accomplished little liar,' said the voice in her mind,
austere but with a certain amusement nonetheless. So clear was
Asulicca's voice that she nearly jumped.

'I am not lying,' she flashed back indignantly. 'I know
nothing. What should I know about a bird?'

'You should know this bird well enough. You rode within him
this night past, and set him yourself upon the elders.'

'Asulicca! That bird? Why has he come to me then?'

The colours deepened. Warning; alarm. 'Cryth watches you,
young one. Have a care. The bird has returned to you because he
is yours now. You took him last night, much in the way you
would have taken a man in love. He is yours. You will use him if

you wish, and he will protect you. And something more: he will be your voice. He is a sacred bird, and as such he can speak with the gods for you. But first you must learn to speak his language, and know how to understand him even as he understands you. Enough of this, now. Tend to your chores and forget this for a time. I will instruct you further when the hour is better.'

Blue, grey, nothing. She was gone once more. Lun lifted her eyes to Cryth's face and smiled at him, blinking in the strong sunlight. Beyond his shoulder, in her usual shaded place, Asulicca sat alone. She was not looking at Lun, or at anyone; she appeared, in fact, to be dozing in the way old people do. Lun wondered at Asulicca's extraordinary capacity for deception, for survival, for self-preservation.

She went to tend the barley, simmering and aromatic in its iron pot. On the roof above their heads the bird settled itself in a tight ball of feathers, its eyes following her every movement, awaiting her pleasure and command.

Bel, turning his back on Lunica with more haste than dignity, had scarcely left the confines of the settlement before the shivering began.

It started as a tremor in his hands, the fingers jerking and opening in spasmodic, uncontrollable twitches. The muscles tightened and loosened, sending the motion up his arms and into his back and legs in a wave of pain that was no more terrifying than the black choking rage he felt. Cold sweat beaded across his brow and dripped down into his eyes.

He bit back a curse. The village was behind him now; if he could force his uncooperative legs to bear him as far as the locus, he would be all right. The tribe must not see him this way. She must not see him, the yellow-eyed demon. He must reach the locus, the standing stones, the sacred oaks. All would be well if only he could get there . . .

He stumbled across the bracken and heather, long years of practice over this dangerous ground instinctively guiding him through the soft and boggy patches. Then he had reached the oaks, and there were the stones, and he had crumpled to his knees, gasping and fighting for breath against the waves of giddiness and nausea that engulfed him.

After an eternity of time the world began to right itself once again. He ran a hand across the back of his mouth, swallowing hard on the bile that had rushed into his throat and spilled on the dewy earth. Moving his body away from the stench of his own vomit, he leaned his aching back against the stone, his favourite place to sit when something he could not rationalise came to haunt him, and closed his eyes. With the passing of the sickness, he found himself deep in the trap of impressions and random unnamed feelings that could not be called thought.

Lun, he thought, Lun the lawbreaker, the enchantress, the seductress. She danced behind his lowered lids, a mocking, taunting succubus; she was all he wanted, all he hated, the sum of all he could never have. He thought of her until his head went around in a drunken spin. The eyes of the witch. Of the wolf. Of the bird who kept watch over her.

The dizziness mercifully eased. Yes, that bird. It had not been there the previous day, he would have seen it. But it was there now, a sparrow hawk, the creature of the Old Woman of the waterways, the goddess of death. Mother Clota's emissary. Bel took a long draught of the summer air and followed the images running in loops and whorls through his memory.

A skinny young witch, her body a spear against the sun, diving into the stream until she fainted and the water gave her up to the land again. Asulicca, staring into the same depths, seeing what was invisible to Bel. And the voice and wings of the Mother, Clota, dark and feathered and mad, guardian of the woman who dwelt in the sunlight below . . .

He had known the bird was there. Not yet awake, his senses and perception at their lowest − he had sensed the hawk's eyes on his back as he had stood in a white heat at the door to Lunica's hut. Even through the haze of the morning he had felt a look like iron. The memory of that shock of fear, of absolute terror, would stay with him until the hour of his death . . .

186

Oh yes, he knew what the bird was, and why it had come to roost on this of all the village roofs. Not for nothing had he been High Elder since the coming of manhood. If Lun thought he would not know what rode on this particular wind, she very much underestimated her enemy. No, he understood nearly all of what he needed to about that guardian spirit. What he wanted to know now was who had summoned it.

He did not believe that the guiding power had been Lun. He knew how excellent was her mask of innocence, he knew the danger that walked hand in hand with her power. She had the power to call it, yes. But there was no gainsaying it: she had been surprised, as surprised as he. He had watched her as if he could see straight through her skin, and he did not believe that the mask was false. Her surprise had been genuine. Who, then? Who had such power?

Cryth, perhaps? The idea that the young priest might not only know of his woman's sacrilegious behaviour but might actually be aiding her was both new and unwelcome. Bel considered the possibility only to dismiss it as unlikely. Experienced priest of fire through Cryth was, he had no true power, no control of his knowledge, nothing of that elusive quality of intuition so essential an attribute for the person Bel was seeking.

No, it could not be Cryth. On the nights of fire he painted himself blue and led the sacrifice, he danced and he chanted, he gorged himself on the blood and flame and holy smoke. But he did not have the power to summon a guardian.

Not Lunica, not Cryth, certainly not himself. And the idea that the bird's presence was coincidence only was too foolish to be seriously considered. Someone had called it. And if Lunica and Cryth were exonerated, Bel thought with grim satisfaction, there was only one possibility remaining.

Was it not rumoured that the old woman had been a priestess among the savages of her own tribe? Had she not bearded the Elders of her day in their own circle, and got them somehow to do her bidding? And was she not obviously watching Lunica, even as he was? Only Asulicca could have summoned the guardian. There was no one else to do it.

He ran one hand over the stone, smiling. The sickness had passed now, replaced by a sense of deep satisfaction. He thought of what must come to pass with a joy that was almost passion. He would find the old witch out this time, find her out and exact the payment of the grove.

What she had done in her youth, among her own people, he could not touch her for. Among the Dumnonii, however, a woman who interfered in the sacred rites was given to the gods. She would not escape him, not this time.

Asulicca, deep in the trance that passed for sleep in the eyes of the tribe, felt the presence of the Old Woman, the guardian of the water, the destroyer, the mother of death, and prepared herself for battle.

She was not afraid of death. She had never been a servant of Clota; her gifts had come from another source and she paid the bulk of her homage there. But she had been, was, a priestess, and none who walked with the gods could fear death for to do so was to insult them. Submerged in the hinterland of consciousness, watching Bel from the shadows of his own soul, she saw the shadowy figure of the crone and knew she could not submit. The time was not yet.

She pulled herself away, gathering mind and spirit in an arrow of concentration both vital and dangerous. That arrow she laid before her so that it lay between herself and the hag who watched her, features formless and indistinct, from the edge of time.

'No,' she thought. 'Not now, Mother, not yet. Go back to the water, and wait there; I have some days yet.'

The shadowed figure did not move. Asulicca, who was accustomed to seeing the gods, found herself vaguely disturbed. Clota it was, it could be none other, but there was something here that was not right, something that hung like perfume on the outskirts of memory. What was it . . . She scoured her knowledge of herself, for that knowledge was the basis of her hold on

188

life, and repeated 'Back to the water, Mother. Go back, I say. I cannot go with you; it is not yet the time. I am not yours, yet.'

The hag moved, lifting her arms up and outward to the sky. Asulicca knew, without hearing, that the goddess had begun to sing, to chant, and suddenly she knew what had disturbed her and what difference she had noted.

She had seen Clota in the stream not many days past. She had seen her, not vividly yet clearly enough to know her shape and form. And this was not the figure she had seen.

The hag suddenly broke off her singing. Throwing her head back she began to howl, a silent horrible gesture that resembled nothing so much as the wolf who courts the moon. Asulicca felt the cold settle on her as the hag's power over her life and death grew, and fought back with all the silent and murderous power she could muster.

Her body, immobile and dislocated, gave a sudden heave and then settled once again. In the shadowed place where her spirit hung, the grey air parted with the howling of the goddess. With a rush and a beating of wings, the world was suddenly filled with birds. Hawks, pigeons, doves, they hovered and watched, watched and hovered, their presence and obedience to the goddess adding to her power.

The life spark was flickering wildly now, the cold sinking through skin and into bone. No, Asulicca thought, no, I cannot go, not now. She exerted herself, beating at the crone with her mind, bracing, screaming soundlessly at the birds. Huddled in the doorway, her empty body chilled.

There was a scream, a flash of light, an upsurge of life and strength that was extrordinary in its potency. And then she was no longer alone, no longer cold, and a male sparrow hawk, blue-grey and white, was cutting through the masses of its fellows. Bright blood dripped from its talons.

The hag's features contorted and she was gone. In the moments before she faded entirely from Asulicca's vision, the old woman caught the barest suggestion of her features, contorted, inhuman. She felt the warmth come back to her as the grey air took on colour and light. Sunlight filled the sky.

'You were almost gone from me,' said the quiet voice in her mind. 'A very near thing. You are safe now, I think?'

'For a moment.' Asulicca, drained and exhausted, had just enough spirit left to feel a vague amazement. 'I thank you, Lun. I am deep in your debt. The Old Woman would have had me but for your help. You sent your guardian?'

'Our guardian.' Lun's voice, clear and high, had a calm to it that she had not possessed a bare three days ago. How quickly she learns, Asulicca thought. 'Our guardian, wise woman. He keeps watch for both of us.'

'Yes. How did you know that the Old Woman was near?'

Lun's voice took on the tint of puzzlement. 'I heard her, and you too. Screaming, arguing. I heard her singing.'

'You heard her?' Asulicca's interest sharpened. 'Do you mean that you heard the words to the death chant?'

'Very clearly.' The meaning of Asulicca's question abruptly came clear. 'Could you not hear what she sang?'

'No, young one, I could not. I saw her, I knew that she sang, I knew what she sang. But of the words, nothing.'

Lunica was silent a moment. 'She sang words I knew; the same words I heard her sing when I found her standing in the stream. I heard her as well as I can hear you.'

'But you did not see her.' Odd how it had suddenly come back to her, so many long years after she had lost her priesthood. 'You heard but saw nothing. Is it so?'

'Yes. How . . . ?' Lun's thoughts went from blue to gold, the gold of understanding. 'And you saw, but heard nothing.'

'You cannot do both. It is forbidden.' Asulicca was young again, a slender and beautiful girl draped in the sacred vestments, eyes and ears straining toward the goddess she had chosen to serve. She heard her own voice, raised and ringing across the years, crying out with frustration that she could not hear, the goddess would not speak or give the portents . . .

Lun was very quiet, very gentle. 'You learned why, in the end,' she thought softly and Asulicca, with a jolt, knew that

190

Lun had travelled back those years with her.

'I did.' How it came back: the holy rock, the water dripping, the smell of the herbs as the answer to her lament was given. 'No one is allowed the gift of both hearing and vision; to no man do the gods give so much. We take what we are given, and in the end we learn not to yearn hopelessly after what is withheld.' Wonderingly, childlike, she added plaintively, 'How could I have forgotten this?'

'It has been many years. Age taking its toll; no more than that.' Asulicca felt the brilliant flash like hot embers coming suddenly to life. 'Asulicca! The song, the one you called the death chant — it was your song!'

'My song?' Momentarily at a loss, the old woman cast her mind back. 'What is my song? When have I sung for you?'

'Last night. Oh, Asulicca, think back — it must mean something! When we joined together, when you drew my hands to the girdle you wore — you sang to me. And it was the same, the same! Three times, now. Once in the stream, once last night, and once when she hungered for you.' The colours were flickering with fright and excitement. 'Three times. Asulicca, what can this mean?'

'I do not know. You are certain, then, that my song of power and the death chant are the same? There can be no mistake?'

'I would stake my life on it, wise woman.'

'That speaks of certainty to me,' Asulicca thought with a flash of grim humour. 'As to what its meaning may be, I am in darkness, even as you are. But I will find out. What is it, Lun? You have turned dark.'

'Bel, coming back from the locus. Blackness pours from him like rain on the moss; I can scarce bear to look at him for fear of choking on his poisons. I must go, Asulicca. He is thinking of evil and I have a mind to learn more of him.'

'Do not.' An idea was forming in Asulicca's mind, a vagrant memory coming to the surface. 'I kept watch on him this day already. He was thinking about me, something dark that I cannot remember, when Clota came. No, leave Bel be for the time, for I require your aid.'

191

'It is yours, wise woman. Say what you need of me.'

Asulicca kept her thoughts slow and as lucid as possible. 'Hear me, young one. You were so certain that the goddess who gave you this power was the Old Woman. I am not so sure, not after what you have told me. I must seek the truth from my own goddess, and I dare not attempt it with Bel's eye on me. I do not fear death but what use can I be if my tomb is of wicker? So you must help me.'

'I have told you, my help is yours. What must I do?'

'You have great skill with the things that grow. Use that skill, and give Bel a dose that will keep him from waking until I have called my goddess. I dare not try else.'

'I can do it. But Asulicca . . . listen a moment.'

The old woman felt the change in the girl as the idea came to her. Blue, dangerous and opaque; a diminishing in the light, in the quality of the air of that dreaming place of the spirit. She shivered, and steadied herself.

'You have a notion. You had best tell me, Lun.'

The girl's thoughts had sunk to a horizon of the spirit. 'I can do as you say — easy to give him enough to set him deep in dreams. But it would be just easy to give him more than enough.'

'More?' Asulicca froze in place. 'Do you mean . . .'

Lun's whisper was like cold air. 'Why not give him enough so that he would not wake at all?'

Chapter 17

Marian, safe and deep in the velvet palm of a dream, felt the cool water lap against her legs and knew that, in some mysterious way, she had come back to Dartmoor.

The first time she had come here there had been a sense of vagueness, of dislocation. This time the transition was smooth and painless. The journey from a comfortable sofa in London to the darkened village of a time long faded into history was as simple and natural as sleep itself.

The village, settling into sleep for the night, was mysterious under a moon approaching fullness. Marian let herself relax under the gentle touch of the water as her eyes grew accustomed to what she saw in the moonlight.

Darkened doorways. A distant unease rose in her and was gone. Surely, once before, she had seen those same doorways and had been frightened by them. But how absurd, how could she have been frightened? She shrugged off the memory and let her eyes transmit their messages to the brain.

The thatched roofs, lush and dry, looked like burnished flame under this vivid sky. On one roof was a huddled shape; a bird, deep in the moult. As she watched it the creature turned its head towards her, perhaps sensing her presence. She saw the gleam of eyes extinguished as it turned away.

And there – she felt no surprise, only a deep sense of satisfaction – there was something in the centre of the clearing. It was nothing physical, nothing she could put a name to.

Rather, it appeared to be a line of colour, moving and floating like mist, nebulous in its deepest parts but more distinct at its ends. And it seemed, to Marian's heightened perceptions, to be linking two of those doorways.

How peculiar colours look under the moonlight, she thought. And how much this eddying dance of shades seemed to change from minute to minute. One moment a deep scarlet, the next moment flickering to rose and then to blue . . .

She knew that she was being watched. Distracted by the colour cloud, it took her a few moments to pinpoint the watcher at its source. She closed her eyes in concentration and, after only a moment, the image burned itself into her mind like a brand. It was the bird, watching with beak at the ready. She had seen it before . . .

The silence of the slumbering village was absolute. Not a whisper, not a step, not even the call of a nightjar on the wing disturbed the quiet which seemed to have a life of its own. Power, magic perhaps, lay across the glimmering thatch and worn earth like a soft, fine blanket. It was tenuous, she thought, but also dangerous.

The hawk watched her, its feathers ruffled, its beak open in a bitter parody of a smile. The line of colour pulsed in the air, now darkening, now flaring. It was all very beautiful, completely out of Marian's experience. Yet it was somehow familiar. It gave her, in some fashion she could not identify, a sense of great power.

She cupped her fingers, allowing water to dance over nail and knuckle. It was then that she noticed the humming.

It had been there, she realised, all along. It was not a sound in itself; it was, rather, a darker counterpoint to the immense quiet that surrounded her, a part of that quiet. She fixed her eyes on the web of colour and, with childlike delight, heard the words that ran beneath that colour.

A plea. Someone was pleading, begging. Her memory moved and she was back in this same stream under a sunny sky, watching an old woman sitting in the shade of a doorway. And from that doorway, she knew, one end of that lovely cloud of changing tints now stretched like a corona into the night.

It was an old woman's voice that she heard now. There were no words, no reference point for the brain to hold and decipher; only the cold humming that, as it shifted in pitch and intensity, seemed to alter the colour cloud along with it. But the tone was obvious to Marian. She was hearing a plea, a question, a prayer for knowledge and information.

And the prayer, the question, was being asked of her.

Recognition of the truth seemed to trigger something in the ancient recesses of nerve and bone. I am being called, Marian thought, summoned and needed. I have something that is wanted; I must answer if I can. But what can I do?

Without further thought, with no conscious effort, she reached her hands out to the flat rock level with her eyes and pulled herself easily out of the water. At the precise moment that her feet touched solid ground, the hawk lifted itself from its post on the moonlit thatch. Floating in silence across the clearing, it came to rest on her shoulder.

Touch, that most obvious of senses, seemed to have gone away. She could feel the soft brush of feathers against her cheek while the bird seemed weightless; she could feel the cold of its talons on her naked shoulder but no sharpness.

The ground beneath her bare feet was warm, a repository of the day's heat. But the sharp pebbles that littered the ground here might just as well have been a blanket of silk; her feet touched them with no sound and no feeling. She might have been floating, weightless and insubstantial. Sensation and intuition had stayed with her, sharpened with time, even as the reality of the tactile world deserted her. The powerful creature on her shoulder was as light as air, its presence and response to her desires something she already took for granted.

Hands dangling loose and relaxed at her sides, she followed the web of light to its nearest end. The bird's heartbeat, that rapid dance of blood, pulsed warm and quick against her ear. She pushed gently at the thick animal hide which formed the doorway and entered the hut.

So, she thought with deep satisfaction, I was right. Standing in the doorway, she could see the old woman. Shot through and surrounded by that haze of light, the kneeling figure looked at first glance like something out of a Rackham drawing, a kobold, inhuman, unearthly, utterly charming to the eye. Then Marian saw what she had missed in the classic oddness of the woman's posture; gnarled, bent, aged beyond the normal span. This was a woman who walked near to death.

The woman raised her head, eyes veiled, and saw Marian.

For a moment, as Marian remembered who she was and where she came from, the entire scene dimmed and blurred. What am I doing here, she thought, what am I thinking of with this bird on my shoulder, this old woman who is staring at me with such recognition? I was asleep on the sofa in Julian's flat. How the hell did I get here? And then she met the old woman's eyes and the bird tightened its claws against her and the twentieth century, with all its determined worship of the physical world, drifted around her like smoke and was gone into the night once more.

The old crone had not moved from her knees. Their eyes were locked into a small circle of acknowledgement, Marian's mysterious, ageless; the old woman's pleading and humble yet wiser by far than her own. Marian broke the exchange of glances first and turned her head to face the bird. Its eyes reflected the uncanny light from her own yellow irises.

She had wondered what to do, what to say, how it could be possible for herself and this dream figure to communicate. But in the end it was easy. The medium was thought.

'What do you want from me, old woman?'

'An answer, great mother. I am confused, and afraid, and I beg for an answer from you.'

The thoughts, with their overlay of great power kept in firm check, were unsettling. Marian thought sharply, 'I'm not a dictionary,' felt the complete confusion in the other woman, and tried to clear her mind. 'Ask me what you want to know,' she thought more calmly. 'I don't know if I can help you, or tell you what you want to know, but I'm willing to try. And I have a question or so for you, too.'

'What could the mother wish to learn from her servant?'

'Well, for one thing, I would like to know your name.'

'I am Asulicca, high one, daughter of the sacred grove.'

'Asulicca. All right. What is the bird doing on my shoulder? I don't remember that I called it.'

The puzzlement in Asulicca — 'What a funny name,' Marian thought, and felt rather dizzy — was growing. But the old woman thought with a clarity and precision that was worthy of a mathematician. 'The bird, holy one, came back to you when it saw you. He has been my servant, and young Lunica's too, but he is ours only so long as you permit it. When you come he returns once again to his ruler and mistress.'

Marian lifted a hand to the creature. It shrilled, and nuzzled against her cheek. 'This is all true,' Marian thought, this is true, it's truly happening. I don't know how, or even what it is, but it's all true. I'm here, wherever here is. This is no dream...'

She became aware of the old woman, still waiting on her knees. You need not kneel, Marian thought. 'A woman as old and wise as you need not kneel to me. Get up now. Yes, that's better. Now, I said I would try and answer whatever questions you wanted to ask me, but first I have a few more questions of my own. I want to know who you are. I want to know who you think I am. And please tell me — where am I?'

Asulicca's stupefaction hit Marian like a gust of wind, nearly knocking her off her feet. 'What is this?' the old woman thought slowly. 'What are these things you ask of me? Do you seek to torment your servant, I who have served you faithfully my whole life long? Do you doubt my faith in you, that you should test me so? I am Asulicca, as I told you, as you already know. You know who you are, high mother, goddess of the night, for all your testing of me. You stand with your messenger upon the soil of the Dumnonii, on my hearth.

'And now I have given you my answers as best I can and I beg that you let me put my questions to you. My life depends upon it.

197

I have risked my life to call you to me tonight; I am woman and forbidden from worship, forever barred from power. The High Five of our people are ruled by Bel, and Bel has darkness and evil in him. He would destroy me, and destroy your chosen daughter Lunica too. He desires her, holy mother, desires her but will never know it, and his desire is the running sore of malice and madness.

'Listen to me, high one. Listen, and know the truth: he would kill her to give himself a moment's pleasure, for his pleasures lie that way. He would kill her because for him desire is death, because he cannot take her any other way.'

Asulicca stepped forward. Frozen into fascination by the old woman's urgency, Marian thought that she had never seen eyes so dark and deep. The words 'chosen daughter' came back to her and she knew with certainty that this Lunica, this chosen daughter, was her link to this dark place where she now stood. Not the old woman, but the girl.

It was the girl who had sent the smoke, and burned Julian's hand. The girl who had called her from her warm bed so short a time ago, into the gardens of Four Shields where a sparrow hawk waited, its offering dangling warm and bloody from its beak. The girl who had somehow linked with her, called to her, touched her in mind and spirit and now in body. The girl in the stream, water moving cold and easy across her yellow eyes . . .

'I must do something,' she thought. The room had begun to move, corners where wall met floor cycling into whorls and loops like fingerprints in time. 'No,' she thought, 'no, I can't go yet. I can't. I understand now, I understand all of it. The girl is me. She called me, she touched me, she needs my help. I don't know how or why I could hear her or come to her, but the girl Lunica is me, I *am* the girl Lunica. She thinks, the old woman thinks, they both think I'm a goddess, that I can help them.

'I can't betray them this way. Please,' she thought, and the thought became a frantic plea as the old woman's eyes, black and desperate, merged with the shivering web of colour and splintered it into screaming fragments. 'Please, not yet . . .'

The bird was gone from her shoulder, the night air had warmed into something dense and black that sat like a dead weight on the heart. She lifted her face, wet with tears, from the soft leather of the Chesterfield sofa and stared around the darkened flat. From the concrete ledge outside came a rustle of wings, a sly, suggestive brush of sound.

She went quickly and unsteadily to the window. Three pigeons lifted their bodies into the sky and wheeled out of sight toward the park. The headlights of the passing cars in Sloane Street reflected like yellow eyes on the windowpane.

No, it couldn't be. It was monstrous, horrible. The same old story, a man with the power of life and death in his hands, a woman with no protection against his spite and his frustration. She had breathed the midnight air of a life now faded out of time, had somehow been transmuted into something outside her own flesh. She had no way of knowing whether or not she could have provided the help that Asulicca had begged her for. She had no way of knowing what, at the last minute, had pulled her back to her world, her own time.

But one thing she was certain of. If she could help them, she would. And she couldn't do it from here . . .

She looked at the mantel clock. Just before midnight. Julian was still out, it seemed, probably moaning to Gemma over a bottle of wine somewhere. Unless, of course, he had come in very quietly and was sleeping in the other room . . .

She tiptoed across to the bedroom and peered in. Good, the bed was empty and she had some time yet. Praying under her breath, Marian opened the coat closet. The jacket Julian had worn to work that morning hung rumpled and limp on its wooden hanger. She found what she was looking for tucked neatly into the inside pocket.

She had grabbed her purse and was reaching for the door when the thought struck her. Julian and Gemma were already suspicious; if he came home and found her gone, he was perfectly capable of figuring out what had happened and following her. Some deception would be necessary. Where did he keep his writing paper, and the pens?

The note took her only a few moments to write. Without stopping to think too much about wording, she wrote rapidly.

'Dear J., Sorry about this evening. I had a scare today but I'm feeling much better. I'll tell you all about it after a good night's sleep. Can you take the sofa tonight? I'd like the bed to myself. Love, May.'

She scanned it and was satisfied. Yes, it would do. If the tone of the letter didn't do it, the use of the pet name she had abandoned years ago surely would. Taping the note to the bedroom door, she picked up her bag and the keys to the Jaguar and let herself quickly and quietly out of the flat.

It was one in the morning before Julian realised that he was very tired, and very drunk.

Gemma's flat, a large bedsit over a shop on the Kings' Road, was furnished with an astonishing array of furniture picked up at auctions and closing down sales, augmented in places with oddments donated from Four Shields. While none of the pieces matched, they all shared a quality of comfort, combining to make the flat extremely easy to relax in.

Julian, unused to the experience of facing up to the world that hovered, ghostlike, just outside his own, had been far more shaken by the evening than he was willing to admit to his daughter. He had lived his life through reason, and he had brought what reason he could to bear on a situation that was totally outside anything he had ever thought to encounter. But just below the surface of his calm language and rational thought was a howling demon, a cold shadow of hell, waiting to pounce on his carefully ordered ideas and beliefs and blow them away on the wind of the impossible.

So, when Gemma had declined a pub crawl, Julian had followed his instinct far enough to insist on stopping at an off licence for a bottle of Gilbey's. To this Gemma had added a half bottle of brandy left over from a party. Now the gin sat in his blood like a dead weight, dulling perception and blunting the edge of reality. Gemma, draining what remained of the brandy,

200

had hoped that it would perform its accustomed magic by granting her the same relief. As a result, they were both reeling, from exhaustion as well as alcohol.

They had talked themselves, through three hours of drinking and repetition, to a standstill. Julian, through the fog that lay across his brain, thought vaguely that they had in the end accomplished nothing at all. They were agreed on what was happening, it was true, but they had come no closer to a solution. Ghosts, imprints, spiritual memories, he thought, all very grand terms. But when I get back to the flat Marian will still be the unknown woman I left there. And the scar on my hand won't fade simply through acknowledgement . . .

He looked blearily down at his watch. 'Good grief, it's after one. Gemma, I must go home. I have a full schedule at the office tomorrow, and if I don't get some sleep I'll be useless. Can you call me a minicab?'

'Yes. Daddy, what are we going to do?'

The tone was plaintive, the voice reminiscent of a little girl asking why she had to get the measles, why didn't someone else get them and leave her alone? Julian felt a lump in his throat, of affection and fear combined. He took her hand and swung it gently, a gesture he rarely used.

'I don't know, love. I really don't. But surely knowing what's happening is better than blundering about in the dark? Whatever happens, we can at least take a little comfort in just understanding it. Can you call that cab?'

She reached for the phone, watching him as she dialled. 'Daddy, will you call me here tomorrow and let me know what happens? I'm taking the day off, just in case . . .' She blinked, gave her address into the receiver, and set the phone down with a thump. 'The cab will be here in five minutes. He says he'll ring the bell.'

'Good. Yes, of course I'll call. I must go to the office tomorrow, unless something drastic happens. Good night, darling.' He pinched her chin gently. 'What's that revolting expression the Americans use? Hang loose?'

She produced a feeble smile, 'That's fairly revolting, all right.

201

Oh, there's the bell, you'd better go down. I shall hang as loose as possible. Talk to you tomorrow.'

Five minutes later Julian climbed out of the cab, looked up at the darkened windows of his flat and felt a surge of relief. Good, Marian was sleeping. He would not have to face her tonight; he could sleep off the gin and the worry and cope tomorrow. He let himself in as quietly as he could.

Rooms in a city home, however thickly curtained, are never completely dark. The note on the bedroom door, a pale flutter in the air, caught his eye at once. Switching on the table lamp, he read the message and his relief deepened.

God, that sounded so much more like the Marian he knew. She must really be feeling better to sign herself with that pet name, abandoned with advancing years. The sight of it, in Marian's taut and economical handwriting, evoked an entire set of memories and emotions he thought long buried.

He took one step towards the bedroom door. Perhaps he ought to just check on her, make sure she was all right? Then he turned towards the sofa. Marian had always been a light sleeper; even to open the door might waken her. It was better by far to kick off his shoes and make do with the bumpy sofa. Better by far simply to let her sleep.

The sun burning through the east facing windows woke him just before six. For a moment he lay on his stomach, uncomfortable and disoriented; one cheekbone tingled where it had rested against a leather covered button. Then memory dawned and he sat up, rubbing his eyes and stiff legs. Marian's note lay where he had dropped it.

She was still asleep, then. Well, he would have to take a chance on disturbing her, since his electric razor, not to mention all his clean clothes, were in the bedroom. He could hardly go to a meeting in dirty socks and yesterday's shirt. Perhaps if he moved very quietly she would not wake.

Smiling, relaxed, he softly opened the bedroom door.

For a moment he stood, bathed in a shaft of sunlight, staring at the empty bed. His eyes told him that the bed had not been slept in, that Marian had not been there while he snored dreamlessly on the sofa. His brain told him that the note had been placed there for no other purpose than to deceive him. But the frivolous little clock on the table beat away precious seconds while he stood motionless, refusing to accept the evidence of his senses.

At last he turned and fumbled through the pockets of his jacket. The keys to the Jaguar were gone. Moving like an old man, he reached slowly for the telephone and punched up the number of his parking garage.

'George? Julian Dunne here. Tell me, have you — what? Oh, she did? I see. Yes, that was fine.' He gulped down nausea, fighting to keep his voice normal. 'Just a small emergency at home. Can you tell me what time she left? Thanks, yes, I'll wait. Just after midnight? I see. No, there's no problem. Thanks again.'

He dropped the phone and sat silent, cradling his head on his arms. The walls were dappled with bright sunlight. Around him, the room continued its sickening spinning.

After a time the habits of long years — tea, shower, clean clothes — began to reassert themselves. With the return to ritual came clarity of mind. He set the kettle on to boil and began, as cold-bloodedly as possible, to think.

Sometime during the night, while he emptied a bottle of gin for courage and relief, something had caused her to sit down and pen that note, to go through his pockets in search of the car keys, to leave London. She had almost certainly gone to Four Shields. No point, now, in wondering what had happened last night; no point in searching for reasons. What he must contend with was the end result. Marian had gone.

The kettle began its cheerful singing. After pouring a cup of tea, he sat down with the telephone and began dialling.

He tried Four Shields first. After twelve rings he set the phone down. No answer but, after all, he had not thought there would be. He thought for a moment, considering whether or not to phone one of their neighbours and ask them to check on Marian, but dismissed the idea as useless. The gate would be locked whether she was at the house or not. If she was there but refusing to answer the phone, she would be very unlikely to answer the buzz from the front gate either.

Gemma, sounding groggy, answered on the second ring.

'Gem? Dad here. Listen, my love, your mother's gone. Four Shields, most likely; she left while I was with you. What? Of course I'm still in London. Because she took the damned car, that's why! No, I don't know what happened. I got home and found a cheery little note taped to the bedroom door, asking me to sleep on the couch so that she could get some rest. When I went to get my clothes this morning, it was obvious the bed hadn't been slept in at all. The porter at the garage says she took the car out around midnight.'

Gemma had woken up speedily. 'Dad, you must go to Four Shields, and I'm coming too. Can you call and rent a car − a good fast one?'

'I could, but why? Why don't we just use your Mini?'

'Because it's in the bloody shop, that's why, with a broken clutch. Dad, please. Get hold of a Mercedes or something, tell them to deliver it and wait there for me. I'll be round in twenty minutes.' The phone went dead.

Julian swallowed his tea in one scalding mouthful and took the fastest shower of his life. He was waking up now, the hangover fast receding, and beginning to feel the sharp edge of the same urgency that had infected Gemma.

The Mercedes sports coupé and his daughter arrived simultaneously. He signed for the car, showed his licence, and waiting only long enough for Gemma to fasten her safety belt set the great car to the road at a speed that, under normal circumstances, he would have condemned as lunacy.

The city gave way to green countryside. Julian, wrestling with an unfamiliar and powerful automobile, had little attention to spare for it. Gemma sat staring straight ahead of her, silent and preoccupied.

At a small town in Somerset, he announced that he was hungry

204

and thirsty and suggested stopping for tea and an early lunch. Gemma, pulling her thoughts back from the dark hinterland of surmise and mythology she had allowed them to wander into, realised with surprise that they had been on the road for over two hours. She, too, was ravenously hungry.

Julian put the car on a tiny side street and led his daughter into the only tea shop in sight. Having spent the first part of her life in the country, Gemma was not surprised to be served an excellent and hearty meal. She made short work of sausages and chips, and toast and marmalade, and emptied an earthenware pot full of strong tea. Wiping her mouth, she looked up and found her father smiling faintly.

'Isn't it astonishing,' he said, 'what odd things a calamity can do to the appetite? So very inconsistent. When Marian was in labour with you, and having a very difficult time, I was wretchedly nervous. I remember that a nurse offered me a cup of tea and I smiled and thanked her, and then promptly went to the loo and was sick just from the mention of tea. I feel every inch as nervous now as I did then, and look at me: I've just eaten an enormous plateful of food, and I could easily eat another.' He shook his head. 'I'll never understand it. Pass me the toast, will you?'

She nibbled on an apple, so red and glossy that it looked like plastic. 'Calamity is the word, too. Daddy, we've come tearing down here after Mum, and we haven't said a single word to each other about anything at all. What are we going to do when we get to Four Shields? Suppose Mum isn't even there? And what shall we do if she *is*?'

Julian drank the rest of his tea as if he needed it. His face was bleak. 'I honestly don't know. I can't answer any of those questions. If she's at the house, and still in this − this bizarre state, I'll do whatever I must to get her free of it. If that means knocking her on the head or tying her down, I'm perfectly willing to do it.' He looked intently at her. 'I had rather hoped that you might have a few ideas of your own, my girl.'

The slight twist of Gemma's lips acknowledged a hit. 'Touché.

I do have an idea, but I hadn't wanted to mention it. You'll likely think it silly beyond belief.'

'This entire situation is beyond belief. I assure you, my dear girl, I'm willing to listen to any suggestion that won't land us behind bars.' He added, with a certain grim humour, 'And if the suggestion is good enough, I'd even risk getting arrested. So you just forget every opinion and attitude you think I've got, because no normal course of action can possibly apply in this situation. Suppose you tell me what you've got in mind?'

'All right, then, I will.' She took a deep breath. 'We've been over this from every possibility, every angle, that concerns Mum. But there's something we haven't even touched on. She's not exactly cooperating, she's hardly even Mum anymore, so I can't suggest this to her. Suppose we try to contact the girl who got us into this?'

Gemma looked, he thought irrelevantly, like a puppy expecting to be kicked. He said slowly, 'It's a thought, certainly. Do you mean a — a seance, or something?'

'Yes.' She was speaking urgently now, in an all-out effort to convince him. 'I said last night that Mum might have been open to all this, whatever it is, because of her bloodline — you know, being unadulterated Celt. You're all sorts of things, aren't you? Some Scot, some Irish?'

'With a smattering of French and German thrown in for good measure. About forty percent Celt, the rest a mess. Yes, I'm the textbook genetic mongrel. So?'

'What I'm saying is that, with all that Celt from you and nothing but Celt from Mum, I'm about seventy percent pure Celt myself. Maybe in the right setting, I could get open the way Mum somehow did. Maybe I could contact the girl that way. I'm certainly willing to give it a try.'

'I'm on for it.' Julian suddenly got the full gist of what she was saying and jerked his head up. 'Wait a moment, Gemma. When you say the right setting . . .'

'I mean the settlement. The one where you had the dream and burned your hand. Where Roger died, was killed, whatever happened to him. That must be where the girl lived when she was alive. That must be where her power still is.' She met his eyes. 'It's probably our best chance, Dad.'

'I don't like it, Gem.' Julian spoke flatly and decisively. He got to his feet. 'Come along. We've got another hour or so of driving to do. We'll discuss this some more in the car.' She gathered up her belongings and followed.

They had been driving for some fifteen minutes, and the Mercedes was cruising at over eighty, when she spoke again.

'You said you didn't like it. Why not?'

'That settlement is a dangerous place for any of us, perhaps for anyone. There is something there that should have faded to dust hundreds — God — maybe thousands of years ago. But it didn't. It's still there, Gem, and it's hungry, God knows for what.'

He stopped abruptly. Gemma looked thoughtfully at his strong profile, at the planes of cheek and brow cast into even stronger relief by the afternoon sun etching its way through the windscreen. His hands trembled on the wheel, the pink burn showing sickly against the leather.

Gemma reached into her purse for a cigarette. Making a complicated business of lighting it, she mumbled around a mouthful of smoke, 'I'm not afraid of its being dangerous. And if I don't mind trying it, why should you?'

His lips were compressed into a tight, uncompromising line. A little frightened at her own temerity, for Julian was not a safe person to nag, she persevered.

'Anyway, Daddy, we may not have any other choice. If Mum's not at home when we get there, what else can we do?'

'For God's sake, Gemma will you give it a bloody rest! We'll cross that bridge when we come to it.' As if suddenly irritated beyond tolerance, he pressed the accelerator. The Mercedes jumped forward with a roar of the engine, bouncing Gemma back in her seat. She shook her head and gave her father a long, reproachful look. For the rest of the time it took to reach the front gates of Four Shields, she sat in deep, contemplative silence.

Chapter 18

The world of light took Lun into itself, as it had not done before, with a single and very painful pull.

She had lain awake long after the tribe had settled itself for the night. Her eyes were wide and staring, the slaves of memory. Over and again she saw herself, the bowl and the stone pestle in hand, grinding to a fine paste the purple flowers of the monkshood, mixing with them the tiny particles of other plants that would bring sleep. Against the darkness of the walls that surrounded her, she saw her own hands, the brown knuckles taut and trembling, grinding and mixing, smoothing out, mixing the lavender paste with the thick barley mash. Bel would sleep. Yes, he would sleep.

And it had been easier by far than she could have hoped. It seemed to her, as if the very gods themselves were ranged behind her in their approval, so easy had it been.

The men of the Dumnonii were not hunters by habit; they preferred to till, to raise their game. But today, when the sun was at its zenith, Mydd had completed the beautiful spear over which he had laboured so long and hard. Nothing would do but for him to test it, and he had taken a heavy sack and the spear itself and gone out into the gorse and the heather.

Just before sunset he had returned, flushed with the triumph of the successful hunter. In his sack were four fat hares; slung across his shoulder a brace of quail. The spear had the touch of the gods in it, so magically did it move, and the tribe would have meat with their barley tonight.

Of all the women of the tribe, Lun was by far the most skilled in the cleansing and preparation of meat. The other women were slow, and some even turned sick at the blood and the entrails. Lun could clean a hare with uncanny speed, and her knowledge of plants provided her with a vast range of flavourings that made a tough bird taste like ambrosia. So, as was the custom, the bounty of Mydd's hunt had been turned over to Lun to cook and prepare as she saw fit.

She had prepared the lavender-coloured paste in the early hours of the day, while the people slept. And, lying wakeful in the darkness now, she remembered her struggle with Asulicca.

Who would have thought that one so old and wise as Asulicca would balk at the only reasonable solution to a problem that might well kill them? It had seemed, and still did seem, utterly clear and sensible: let Bel die, and the threat was gone forever. Yet Asulicca had run nearly mad at the mere suggestion. Lun could not understand why. The old one had said something about fairness and purity. Lun had dismissed it. It was all incomprehensible.

But she had not deliberately disobeyed Asulicca. Though she might disagree, her respect for the old one's knowledge was too strong to allow any possibility of disobedience. She had gone to the meadow to gather the plants before first light, taking enough for what she had wanted to do only, she told herself, in case she mixed it wrong and needed to make up another batch. And she had not deliberately put a lethal amount in Bel's food. She had given him only the barest touch more than was necessary, so she told herself, to make certain that he would sleep and give Asulicca the time she needed.

The paste, kept in a separate bowl from the benign mess of herbal pottage that held only simple seasonings, had been stirred into Bel's barley. She had not looked at him, and she had not served the food herself. Two of the other women had handed the bowls around. She had given Bel a dish she could readily recognise, a krater of bronze. It was the finest of the bowls and only fitting to the elder's rank.

209

She had sat, eyes cast modestly down, throughout the meal. She had not needed to look up for instead she had looked inside Bel, listening with all her soul for the faintest hint that he knew of his own drugging. Had she detected even the smallest of suspicions in him, she would have stopped him eating, fainted perhaps, or fallen into his lap if need be. Spooning up her own barley, her thoughts moving busily behind demurely lowered lids, she had tried to picture what he would feel if she toppled suddenly into his arms. The result was hysterical laughter barely kept in check. But of suspicion there had been nothing; only the varied hummings of the human mind going first here, then there, as all minds do. And, under it all, the cold shock of the latent madness that was devouring him body and soul.

But if Bel's thoughts were aimless and undirected, his body was worse. His eyes seemed to be constantly moving, edging sideways as if he was peering at the tribe around a corner invisible to them, fixing abruptly on a face, slipping away before a lock of eyes could be accomplished. His hands were nervous, clenching and opening, dropping things. And he drank far more of the intoxicating liquid barley mash than he usually did; Bel was abstemious as a rule. It was almost, Lun thought uneasily, as if he had some kind of premonition . . .

The elder's nervousness, she noted with satisfaction, did not extend to his appetite. He left no meat at all on the bones littering his plate, and scraped the barley clean. As he laid the krater down, he poured himself yet another dram of the liquid mash. All to the good, she thought. When he grew drowsy, the tribe would put it down to the liquor. Lun had seen the eyes of the people take note as Bel drank.

She had not looked up at him once during the course of the meal. Yet she was highly conscious of his thoughts, of the stare of the bird who sat watchful on the roof of her hut, of Bel's eyes, slowly glazing with drugs and drink, flitting from her downcast head to the hawk and back again. She kept her face impassive, listening intently to the madness that darkened her enemy from within.

210

So absorbed was she that at Asulicca's voice in her mind she was almost unable to keep herself from jumping.

'He sinks quickly.' The colour was a deep grey, flat and broad as the sky above them. Lun sensed the questioning edge of the old woman's thoughts and immediately responded.

'No, old one, I did not disobey your wishes. I gave him enough, no more than that. If he sinks it is into the arms of the barley mash. I did not give him nearly enough to send him deep as fast as this. He is drunk, that is all.'

'If he is drunk that is no blame to you, and so much the better for us. He pays for his gluttony, as do we all.'

'I saw that you did not eat any game, Asulicca. Does meat displease you, or did you fear that my cookery would disagree with you?'

The grey eyes lightened momentarily, in silent recognition of Lun's jest. 'You use your eyes well, young one. One cannot take meat when the gods are to come. It lies heavy in the body, and interferes with the blood. If you used your eyes to their fullest, you would have seen that I drank no mash. And that is for the same reason. Remember it.'

'Oh, I will.' Lun hesitated fractionally. 'Asulicca. Is it enough, truly enough, to have him sleeping tonight?'

The old woman's certainty was enormously comforting. 'Yes, it is enough. The elders are dangerous men all, but they have no grudge against either of us. It is only Bel would stop me, and if he sleeps — why, then, all is well.'

'I am glad.' The words, formal acknowledgement, were heartfelt nonetheless. 'When must you do it?'

'Three hours past moonrise, when the night meets the horizon. Time enough and plenty. I must rest now.'

Grey, blue, gone once more. Lun finished the rest of her meat, noticing for the first time in her anxiety how well it tasted, and rose to help with the clearing. From one eyes she watched Bel as closely as the hawk behind her until he had staggered indoors and gone to his bed.

211

Lun woke, staring and terrified, into a storm of agony that burst across her brain like thunder.

The noise was intolerable. It raged in her, manic and mindless, driving her to the edge of screaming. The hut was dark, no light falling through the hide. All was oppressive, still. There was nothing to show what the hour was. She might have been sitting in a cauldron, so black was it.

She bit her lip, keeping sound and terror well back. After a moment, the noise resolved itself and she knew with dread what she was hearing. It was Asulicca, torn and wracked with a desolation of spirit impossible to bear. The noise was the very colour of grief in its purest form. Lun, feeling the raging torrent of agony pulsing like a frantic heartbeat behind her own eyes, sensed her body go cold.

Something had gone wrong. Asulicca had called the goddess, and something had gone very much amiss . . .

She climbed from her bed as quickly as she could without waking Cryth. As she stood, something moved and glimmered in the darkness only a few feet away. She bit back the cry of fear and superstition that rose in her throat, and suddenly the noise in her head stopped and the pinpoints of light flickered and she heard the soft questioning gurgle of a baby, lying wakeful in the night.

She let out her breath in a single ragged rush. Only Cel, only her darling boy, lying on his hide and watching her. She picked her way cautiously across to where he lay and took him up, nestling her face against his skin, so impossibly soft. Her naked body ran with the sweat of fear.

With Cel's solid warmth a buffer against the dark, she began slowly to calm herself. He rubbed his cheek against hers and she heard his chuckle, rich and thick. It was amazing, she thought, that she had never before realised what a comfort he was. But something had happened. Asulicca had been in mortal agony and now there was nothing, only this ominous empty place in Lun's mind. Very tentatively, she sent the beam of thought lacing its way out into the night. 'Asulicca?

212

Old one, are you with me? What has happened?'

Nothing. The dreadful shades had gone, vanished like mist into the air, leaving behind them a void that echoed with a hideous life of its own. Her knees trembling, she strained with every fibre of her conscious self to pick up something, anything, that might tell her what had happened.

The world outside was totally quiet. No footsteps, no voices; whatever had happened, it had not woken the tribe.

'Dead,' said a small voice in her ear, and this time the scream, a high husk of breath, would not be denied. Yet Cryth lay breathing evenly and she understood that the scream had been no louder than a whisper. The same small voice chuckled, the familiar fat chuckle. It was Cel.

It could not be possible. The boy could not speak. He had never managed anything more than a few disjointed sounds, certainly not clear words. She looked down at the dark eyes shining up at her, and saw the glaze of tears, brimming and silver, gathering to bead and drop on the thick lashes. No, the gods would not do this to her. It was monstrous, brutal, unthinkable. Not the boy, her boy, to be used as a weapon against her. 'Cel,' she whispered. 'Cel.'

'Dead,' she heard once more, and the baby shook with a quiet movement in her arms. The voice was small, as clear as a warning beacon. 'He is laughing,' she thought, 'this is not my child,' and the thought nearly choked her. Her body scalded with her own disbelief and the unreality of what was happening, more frightened than she had ever been in her life, she carried him out into the moonlight.

It was late, the dead hour of the night. The moon had gone down in the heavens; its upper rim was a dull silver streak where earth met sky. Yet Lun had never feared the night. She tried to still her trembling, the unaccustomed fear that the darkness had laid on her, and forced herself to look at the downy head nestled against her breast.

'Dead,' the baby chuckled, and rubbed one soft hand against her chin. His eyes were bright and wet.

213

'Be silent,' Lun whispered, and turned her face away from his questing fingers. 'Be silent.' Standing very still, she fixed her eyes on the patch of blackness that was the doorway to Asulicca's hut. As she forced herself across the clearing, the baby tightened his grasp around her neck.

Later she would remember, with a curious vividness, how her sense of touch had seemed heightened that night. She would remember the stones beneath her heels as individual sources of discomfort; remember, too, how the hide that draped Asulicca's doorway lay heavy and warm in her hand, as if it had come straight off the belly of a living goat. She shifted the baby, fighting her strange repulsion at the touch of flesh on flesh. Taking a long breath to steady herself, she pushed the hide aside and entered the hut.

And suddenly the night was alive with the flare of torches, fire and colour, voices. Blinded by the glare of the lights that surrounded her like minions of hell, she flung up one arm to protect her eyes. Through the fog of death and panic, she saw the aged body crumpled in the crudely chalked circle, saw the five men in the circle of judgement, saw her enemy not sleeping but awake and aware, heard the ugly grate of Bel's voice, weighted with a terrible, triumphant satisfaction.

'You wanted proof, my brethren,' he said. 'Proof of sacrilege, of meddling, of power taken where none was granted. I give you your proof.' In the streaming smoke from the torches, his eyes glinted like moonlight through the slits of his hood. A small dark patch appeared where his mouth must be, a betraying spot of saliva. He stood still, his hands raised, never taking his eyes from her face. Like a bird who faces the snake, her eyes were held in a lock of death and defeat that she could not break. 'Take her.'

Forsaken, she thought, forsaken and abandoned by the gods, left to die, like Asulicca's cold body lying like a rag doll on the stone floor ... The men behind her moved close. A pair of robed arms reached out and pulled the baby from her arms. The last coherent sound she could identify was Cel's wail of fright and loss, just as she started to scream.

'No,' Cryth said. His voice was numb, the voice of an old man for whom nothing remained but the grave. In truth, he felt that way. Yet there remained in him a shadow of obstinacy, a pale ghost of man's eternal belief that if you refuse to acknowledge trouble, it will fade away.

Stripped of his robes, facing the elders in the traditional nakedness of the accused, he still held a semblance of the dignity of the priest of fire. In the blaze of noonday sun, the locus showed none of the awe-inspiring holiness so vital for the trial it now hosted. Cryth, with the instinctive knowledge that even to look at his wife would break him, kept his back to Lun and his eye on Bel.

Bound in iron, dressed in the coarse plain cloth of the prisoner, Lun watched her husband. The gag that covered her mouth, to keep her from defending herself until it was her time to do so, was a bitter humiliation. Hot and unpleasantly moist from spittle, it had scraped her mouth raw. She had sat in this manner since sun up, fettered and helpless, too frightened to do anything but wait.

Now, as Cryth stood and spoke for her, the panic was beginning to fade. The first thoughts she had been able to distinguish since the horrors of the night had blanketed her perceptions began to move in her mind. She could not bring herself to listen to Bel's thoughts, spoken or unspoken. The triumph, the dark sensuality he felt, brought her gorge perilously high in her throat. She had let herself look briefly into the thoughts of the others; what she saw and heard there was not reassuring.

The deepest confusion among them was centred in Cryth. Despair, fury, a cold species of determination poured from him like sweat. So intense were the feelings that held him that Lun could gather no clue as to what, if anything, he intended to do. Would he fight for her, stand up to Bel? Could he find the courage to show the four who stood behind Bel like white shadows that the archdruid's actions stemmed from no more

215

than a thwarted and perverted lust for Cryth's wife?

Lun did not know, and the fragmented state of his thoughts would not allow her to find out. Nor did she have the courage to call to the goddess for aid. The keening of total abandonment that had dragged her from sleep into the worst moments of her life could, surely, only have come from Asulicca, and she was dead. Abandoned, betrayed . . .

Lun, without turning her head, managed to slide her eyes sideways. The wise woman, who in her day had forced the elders to do her bidding without raising a finger, lay in the posture of those damned by them. The body had been stripped of its robes and wrapped in the same coarse sacking that now enveloped Lun. Arms akimbo, head pointed to the west, what remained of Asulicca lay face down in the dust.

Lun felt rage, vital and dangerous, rising in her like sap. She savoured the anger, feeding on it. They did not know, these men, how truly great Asulicca had been. To treat her body thus, to stretch it and strip it of its dignity, was an affront to the goddess, an insult to all that was holy.

Bel's voice cut through her anger. He spoke to Cryth.

'You deny to us, Fire Priest, that you have encouraged your woman in her heresy? You deny your involvement, priest?'

'No.' Cryth's voice was thin and deliberate. Lun, her arms pinned behind her, fought back an upsurge of hope. 'I do not deny my involvement in Lun's heresy. What I deny to you, Father, is that any heresy has taken place.'

On Cryth's body, the brown skin of the Dumnonii had paled to a sickly ashen colour. He stood as tense as a boar waiting for the huntsman and stared into Bel's face. The archdruid kept his hands folded within the sleeves of his robe, but Lun sensed the tightening of his muscles, the jerk of the powerful shoulders. His voice was smooth and dangerous.

'If you can offer this circle any proof of what you say, fire priest, we are willing to hear and consider it.'

'Certainly.' Cryth lifted his head and stared straight at Bel. The contempt in his voice was now obvious. 'You have spoken

216

of heresy yet all your proof is that Lunica went, with her child in her arms, to the hut of old Asulicca in the night. You say that you raised the elders, Father, and took them to the hut, because you knew that the old woman and Lun together had tried to drug you. You have not said why you believed in this drugging, or why you thought that those who planned such an act were Asulicca and Lun. You say that you only pretended to drink overmuch last evening, that you pushed much of your mash down on the earth beside you, and dropped a stone to cover it. This is what you say.'

Bel had moved, stepping back slightly. Cryth went on doggedly, 'Yet what is your proof, Father? If you ate little and did not sleep, where is your proof of potions or poisons? You are alive and well. Here is only the old one dead, not you.' He waved a hand at the prostrate body with its face in the dust. 'And you say you found evidence that the old one, here, had tried to summon the gods to her. Perhaps that is so. Even if it is, what has that to do with Lun? I, myself, heard a cry in the night; I woke to it, and it woke Lun and young Cel too. Lun said she would see if her help was needed, and she took the boy with her so that I might sleep. Where is the heresy to help a neighbour? What sin is it to let her man sleep?'

The question and the lie alike burst from Cryth with all the force of impassioned and outraged innocence. Lun, shifting to ease the pain of her throbbing knees, could only admire him. He spoke as if he had convinced himself that every word he spoke was truth, and yet he was lying, for his life and hers. He had not woken to a cry, he had heard nothing at all, and Cel had wakened for reasons that Lun knew she might never understand. All he said was a lie, but it seemed to Lun that he had actually come to believe it.

Bel had seized on Cryth's words with the avidity of a hungry bird. Lun saw the gleam of his eyes behind the hood.

'You heard a cry, you say.' He spoke softly. 'Yet I was wakeful in my own hut and I heard nothing. What was this cry you speak of, this cry I did not hear?'

217

Cryth's face was grey but his voice never faltered. 'I do not know what you heard or did not hear, Father. For that matter, I do not know what cry we heard. It might have been a night creature on the hunt for all I know. Does this matter? What matters is the cry itself for that is what called us from sleep and sent Lun into the night.'

The archdruid's voice was a silken purr. 'And can you tell us, fire priest, if she could not say who made the cry, why she went straight to the old one's hut? What led her there, fire priest? What knowledge guided her?'

Lun, through her own fear, felt the panic strike Cryth like a hammer blow. But with the panic came his answer.

'I cannot answer that question, Bel, because I have not had the opportunity to speak with my woman, not since you took her and brought her to this place. If you will take the gag out, you may get your answer.' He stared around the circle, his voice taunting. 'Are you afraid to hear her?'

The archdruid, skin mottling, opened his mouth to sputter with rage. One of the elders cut through his protest. He spoke soberly. 'This is the truth, Bel. We know only that before the moon was down you came to each of us, saying you would show us proof of heresy. We came together to Asulicca's hut, and we all know what happened there. The girl has said nothing. This is not the law, as it is given and by which we must abide.' He waved a hand at Cryth and said, coldly and calmly, 'Take the gag from her.'

Lun stood up shakily and faced them. Her knees, with the weight of her body off them, throbbed into painful life. Around her mouth, a red mask, were the scored marks of the gag. But much of her fear had dwindled. Perhaps without knowing it, Cryth's attitude towards the men who sat in judgement over her had shown her the way.

So she ignored the needling pain and stood straight, her head thrown back. Her mind worked with unnatural clarity. No doubt, she thought coldly, Bel had the advantage in more ways than one. She must stand as a prisoner while his face was hidden

218

from her. Traditionally, she knew, a prisoner stood the best chance by a show of humility; these pigs were men like any other, after all, and they liked to see others in fear of them. But humility would avail her nothing, not after Cryth's contempt, and she had no stomach for it in any case. So she opened her yellow eyes to their widest and stared straight into the gleaming slits of Bel's hood. Behind the cloth she saw his own eyes widen, and fought to keep the hatred from her face and voice.

The four looked at Bel, waiting for his signal, his word of approval. As High Elder it was his right, and his alone, to question Lun. But he said nothing, seemingly unable to look away from the girl's eyes. When the silence had become uncomfortable, one of the four gave a small shrug and turned to face Lun.

'You have heard what has been said of you, and what you are accused of? Now, what have you to say, Lunica?'

She never took her eyes from Bel. Her voice, when she replied, was very calm. 'I have this to say, Father, and I must first thank you for giving me the chance to say it. What Cryth tells you is true. We heard a cry in the night when the moon was almost down. We woke, all of us, and the boy began to cry. Cryth was tired and wished to sleep so I took the baby with me to see if my help was needed.' She flung her arms high and spoke passionately. 'Would I have taken the boy if I had meant to do what you accuse me of? What would be the point of it?' She spoke to the elders as a group but kept her eyes on the slits in Bel's hood. 'When I came out of doors, I was confused because of the silence. But I thought I heard a noise coming from the hut of Asulicca and I went to see if the old one was taken with sickness.' Her voice was indignant. 'And for this, I am charged. How is it a crime, to offer help to the tribe?'

She shifted hers eyes finally to the others. The white hoods were blank masks, uncommunicative, giving nothing away. From deep in her belly a burning anger began to grow once more, and the anger soon became trembling that took her by the knees and shook her pitilessly.

'The High Elder has accused me of putting unwholesome herbs in his food. If I am allowed to speak in my own defence, I tell you with no disrespect to the High Elder that this is non-sense. Mydd took his spear to the hunt in the morning; the gods blessed it, it would seem, for he returned with meat for all the tribe. Meat is always given to me, since the other women do not have the way of preparing it. I did no more than season it and cook it, as usual. And why should the High Elder think that I, or any member of the tribe, would wish him ill?'

Drowning under the accumulated weight of fear, her voice had soared to the dark edge of hysteria. Cryth laid a warning hand on her shoulder. She shook it off, beyond prudence or care, and swung around to face Bel.

'You wish me to die,' she said, soft and dangerous. 'You wish me dead because you cannot have me living. All the tribe knows this, and I too. Is this your holiness, Father? Is this how you use the power given you by the gods? For your own perverted desires, for revenge on the helpless?'

Bel moved so quickly that not even Cryth had time to see what was coming. The upraised arm, the sacred blackthorn stick held tight in one hand, swept down upon her.

The blow knocked Lun to the ground. I am lost, she thought numbly, lost and it is the fault of none but myself. I let my anger out, and it has killed me, and Cryth too ...

Through the red glaze of pain she heard him cry out, and heard the scuffle as he was grasped from behind by two of the elders. She paid no attention. Her neck was stretched upward and her conscious mind was completely focused on the white-robed man who towered, a figure of doom, above her.

'We have heard enough,' Bel said. 'No woman speaks so to the elders. No woman, and no man either, can say such a thing to High Elder and live to boast of it. The matter is done with, the woman's guilt is obvious. I, High Elder, have said so. The judgement of the Circle will be rendered before sunrise tomorrow, and sentence given.'

He turned on his heel and went, stepping on one of Asulicca's outstretched palms. Above his head a dark shape dropped, lifted and was gone towards the north. The roof of the hut Lun and Cryth had shared was empty now.

Chapter 19

Marian had driven without pause since nosing the Jaguar out of its London garage, taking the roads at a fast pace but not fast enough to attract the attention of the police, or to risk damage to herself or the car. She could easily have reached the moor before sunrise, had she not taken a sudden detour and stopped in the middle of Salisbury Plain.

She could not put a name to the compulsion that had come over her; certainly she had not planned to stop. The feeling of urgency, of dangerous matters that only she could mend coming to the boil, was tangible in her blood. It was urgent, almost sentient, and pulling her towards the ancient settlement like a tide against the beach. No, she had had no intention of stopping, none at all.

And yet, when she reached the junction that led to Salisbury and the plain beyond, an even stronger need took hold of her. It was still night, though sunrise would be coming soon; there was a scarlet tint to the black sky that spoke of a summer storm on the horizon. She pulled the car to the side of the motorway and sat, smoking and wrestling with this inexplicable need. It was too strong to deny. With an abrupt push of the wheel, she turned the car back on the road and headed it towards the ancient monument that kept its timeless watch over the windy fields that sheltered it.

The slender highway dipped and rose, rose and dipped, in the usual manner of an English country road. The Jaguar moved past hedgerows that were looming masses of darkness, past houses where farmers tried to catch what last sleep they could before the sun called them to work again. She met no other cars on the road. Once, directly overhead, she heard a sudden loud hum as a small army plane circled in its night watch. Other than that, she could have been the only living thing on the vast expanse that was Salisbury Plain. Not even an animal's cry broke the silence of the beginning of the day.

It would be closed, of course. Ever since that affair with activists scribbling on the giant trilithons — some nonsense to do with ponies in the New Forest, she seemed to remember — the National Trust had firmly kept the public from venturing too close, and had kept it constantly guarded. Oh, people could still walk round it during the daylight hours but at night it was guarded by the army, fenced off from the world, and one could only look at its dangerous splendour from the distant fields. Marian remembered now that she had approved of this action when it was first taken. A national treasure must, after all, be protected from abuse by fools. But as the car came closer to its destination, and the disturbance began in her blood, she was aware of her impatience. If there was any way in she would find it, army or no army . . .

The first rays of morning touched the distance with rosy gold. Then the car had crested a gentle hill and there it was, the last of the starlight seeming to focus in a spectral dance on the trilithons that had stood there, since time out of mind. Marian pulled the car off the road and got out, leaving the door open wide behind her. Then, as though drawn, her yellow eyes never blinking, she began to walk towards Stonehenge.

The sudden touch on her shoulder was so unexpected, so shocking, that she had to bite back a scream. The flesh on her neck rose, chilled, and settled once again.

'Sorry, ma'am, didn't mean to give you a fright.' The little man wore the uniform of a British Army sergeant. He seemed genuinely sorry to have startled her. 'Afraid the monument's closed during the night. If you were wanting to see it, you'd have to come back during business hours.'

'Business hours?' The absurdity of the phrase was laughable. 'I'm afraid I don't understand. What business?'

He twinkled up at her. The air around them was now an intense, saturated pink; with the blinding edge of the rising sun lying against the horizon. 'Suppose it does sound silly when you're talking about this.' One sweep of his arm encompassed the plain, the stones, the sunrise itself. 'Fact is, we're not supposed to let people in after hours – or before either, if it comes to that.' Her voice, with its educated English tones, appeared to have had a reassuring effect on him. He asked pleasantly, 'You from around these parts?'

'I beg your pardon? Oh. Yes and no. I live near Okehampton, on the northern edge of Dartmoor. Do you know that part of the world at all?'

'Do I! The real West Country. I'm from near Taunton, myself.' He suddenly recalled his curiosity. 'We don't get many people out here before the cows come to milk. What brings you out here so early in the day?'

It sounded like a folk song dimly remembered from her youth. Surely she had heard someone singing a folk song at a church picnic or some such thing, not too long ago. How had it gone? 'Oh lady, oh lady, oh my lady gay, what bring you out a-walking, so early in the day . . .' She shook her head and smiled down at him. There was something about his face, so kind and shrewd . . . She felt an inclination to trust him and told him a bit of the truth.

'I was driving back home from London, and I suddenly knew I had to stop and see it. I hadn't seen it in years, but I simply had to stop off here. I know it sounds mad.'

He justified her intuition by immediately shaking his head. 'Not to me, ma'am. I've been stationed here for nine years now, looking after it every night, and nothing about this pile here would sound mad to me.' They both turned and regarded the bluestones, five thousand years old. 'You know, it's supposed to be a – a kind of focal point for magic. Lines of energy under the ground, or somesuch. Ley lines, they call them, and they're supposed all to meet here.'

'And do they?' Marian was experiencing an odd and disturbing sense of déjà vu, a dislocation of spirit utterly different from the shifts in time she had been undergoing since the first wisps of ancient smoke had invaded her life. For a moment she stared down at the sergeant, her brows knitted. Then she knew why this conversation seemed so familiar and pain took her tightly around the heart. The library at Okehampton. A sunlit table, cups of tea cooling to the sound of Roger Dawkins and his theories ...

The sergeant seemed unaware of any undertones. 'I wouldn't know. Geomancy, we're talking about, and I've never looked too closely at it. But Lord knows, people love to read mystery into anything, whether it's got a fancy name or not.'

He pulled off his cap and, to Marian's astonishment, pulled something out of it. It was a photograph of the standing stones, obviously taken by the first light of a new morning. The line of the sun began somewhere on the outer edge of the universe and fell, straight and clear, through the arch of the two tallest trilithons. It was a picture of the most spectacular beauty, with something unearthly about it.

'Taken at the morning of the summer solstice,' he told her, and promptly slipped it back inside his cap. 'Looks like magic, this place, when you look at that photo. Some people believe anything. I mean, I've seen some odd things out here, right enough, but not as odd as some people might make out, if they'd seen what I did.'

Marian had turned to gaze back at the stones. She had the sensation that every pock, every scar on those blue pillars was an eye, fixed on her with chilly amusement. With a sudden shudder, she forced her gaze back to her companion. Taking this as encouragement, he continued to speak.

'For example, I was out here a few years back. Night of the solstice it was, just before. Long about midnight I heard a bloody great thump and all the birds − did you know that birds

225

nest up there on the capstones? Rooks, mostly, and a hawk or raven now and again. Anyway, all the birds went up like Christmas crackers. I went running into the middle of the circle, right there, and you know what it was?' She raised an eyebrow and he continued, his voice ludicrously nonchalant, 'A meteorite. That's right, just a little meteorite, maybe two feet across. Fell right there in the middle of the circle. Now, there's nothing supernatural or magic about a meteorite, is there? But I never told anybody because some people will stick a meaning onto anything. They need to believe such things, you might say.'

'You might, indeed.' Marian's voice was very dry. Could he honestly believe what he was saying? A stone from heaven, on the night of the summer solstice, falling at the stroke of midnight into the precise heart of England's great mystery, and he truly believed there was no magic to it? How ridiculous, how credulous he was, to try and laugh such a thing away. And Marian suddenly realised that, a few short weeks ago, she would have done the same.

Yes, she thought, but I was another person then. I was another woman, gravid, tied to the dry ground and unable to smell the sky. Someone, a young girl with golden eyes, has got to me and taken me over. I've been changed. I can never be purely Marian again. The thought brought her a deep sadness and, in its wake, a strange sense of satisfaction.

The little man had been eyeing her carefully, gauging her reaction to his story. Now he made up his mind. Bending close to her, he lowered his voice and spoke confidentially.

'Listen, ma'am. It's like I said, I'm not supposed to let anyone in to see the monument, not unless its during the right times of day. But my mate's gone off duty, and I'll be going too in a bit, and where's the harm? If you'd like to go in and see it, go right in among the stones, I reckon I can take you. You're not likely to try anything, are you?'

Army or no army, if there's a way ... was this the hand of a god, watching, pushing her forward, urging her on? She turned and looked at the great stones, shimmering under their glaze of morning dew. The need to enter that circle, to be however brief a part of its reality, rose like bile in her throat. She took a deep breath and, giving a shaky smile of thanks, said to the sergeant, 'There's nothing I'd rather do. No, I won't hurt anything. Can we go now?'

She followed him in silence down the slick surface of the road, through the empty parking lot, past the refreshment stall whose corrugated iron window guards looked, in this setting, like fabulous monsters from another world. She stood beside him as he pulled open the heavy padlock, and went with him in silence through the tunnel that ran beneath the motorway. And then they emerged into the moist air and stood among the stones, and the sun, edged in blood, lifted in the sky in a blaze of amber warmth.

For Marian, the moment the sun burst into life was the culmination of everything that had happened to her since that first whiff of smoke. Ever since that day she had been changing, shifting from one time, one skin, to another. With the fall of light on her shoulders the transition was complete. She was Marian Dunne of Four Shields but she was also someone else, an entity who had known these stones, this circle and the life that breathed within it through time. Standing in the twined shadows of the stones, she lifted her arms and her face to the sky, and the sun that beat down upon her face was no brighter a gold than her eyes, slitted narrow and reflecting the shimmering light.

She had forgotten the sergeant standing a pace or so behind her. After a moment she had forgotten the fret and the worry in her head. For a few minutes she held her posture, her back straight, her hands and face lifted to absorb the meaning of the mystery that no religion, no belief in the history of her race had ever been able truly to comprehend. After a few minutes, through the golden glaze across her mind, she became aware of him once more. Turning to regard him, she found him watching her with calm compassion, and knew that in some way he had understood her. Perhaps in his blood, or perhaps because he came of this green and windswept land — the reason didn't matter. All that mattered was that this little man, who had spent the majority of his adult life guarding this spot from human harm, perfectly understood what she was and why she was doing what she now did. He had been testing her with his tale of his own disbelief; he had wanted only that she reveal herself. In some way, perhaps by her silence, she had done so. This place with its ultimate secrecy, the soul of the earth so starkly contained within it, ran in his blood, too. So he was a man in a uniform, paid by the people who owned him. But he was also a kobold; uncanny, sprung from the morning mist.

He stood perfectly at ease, regarding her calmly. She saw him only through the dazzle of these new feelings, and let herself stare blindly down into his eyes. They were nice eyes, she noted vaguely, crinkled and generous, surrounded by laugh lines. In the light of her new self-knowledge his question, when he asked it, came as no surprise to her.

'And will you be getting whatever it is you needed?'

'I think so.' Why, she wondered, did this conversation not seem completely insane? 'I'm needed somewhere else and I must get there, but I had to stop here. I told you that.'

'And stopping here, being here, has that helped?' He was fishing in his pockets. After a moment of rummaging, he pulled out a worn briarwood pipe and a pouch of tobacco. This homely touch surprised Marian as his questions had not.

'Yes, it has.' He tamped the tobacco down with one calloused forefinger and managed to light it in the teeth of the wind that never ceased blowing across this odd corner of the earth. The aroma of pipe tobacco, scented with vanilla, wafted across the clearing and disappeared among the stones. She watched him, her own features relaxing into a smile. He felt her eye on him and looked up.

'Well, then, perhaps you'd best be going to where you think you'll do the most good.' He underscored the simple words with a beautiful gesture, a sweep of the arm that seemed to encompass the bluestones, the road to the west, the entire universe. 'Take some of the power that lives here with you, lady. It can't hurt any

228

if you do, and the stones can spare it to you. They won't mind, I promise you.'

As she started the car once more, she glanced into the rear view mirror. The stones hung silent between the great plain and the heavens and, among them, a small figure stood quietly looking after her. She backed the car out of the culvert and onto the road. As she passed him he lifted a hand, perhaps in salute, perhaps in simple farewell. She put her foot to the accelerator, suddenly very aware of the time she had lost, of the fact that even now Julian might be entering the darkened bedroom in London and discovering that she had gone. The car raced to the southwest, the dust on its windscreen showing in sharp relief through the sunlight. The memory of the little sergeant remained with her like a benediction, and she held it fast in her mind.

The second stop she made was one of necessity. As she pulled the car out of Okehampton towards the moor, the engine stuttered slightly. Marian glanced down at the dashboard and swore under her breath. She was almost out of petrol.

The Jag had an emergency reserve of one gallon; not enough, she decided, to get her to the moor and back again. The quiet voice in her head, which whispered that she might not be coming back, she pushed away from her. Muttering under her breath, impatient of the delay, she drove the car rapidly to Four Shields and let herself in at the front gates.

The house, shuttered and silent, had a watchful air. There would be a fine patina of dust on the furniture, she knew. As she climbed quickly out of the car and wrestled the garage doors open, she suddenly felt a flux in herself, a feeling she had last felt the night she had called the hawk to sacrifice. With the rising of this feeling she looked up at the house she had loved so much and, without effort, could see it, hear it. There were two white china cups in the sink, the morning teacups that Julian had not given her time to wash that last morning; she had forgotten them then but she saw them now. She saw, too, the fine strand of spider's webbing running from one corner of her bathroom

229

window to the other. On the floor beneath the coffee table a butterfly lay dead, its wings crumpled, its vivid colours fading to brown.

She got back into the car and drove it into the garage, fighting back a sudden rush of claustrophobia as the walls surrounded her. It came to her, as she filled the Jaguar's tank, that this was an excellent idea in more ways than one. If her car was low on petrol, it was a fair bet that Julian's vehicle — and she did not doubt that he would find one, any way he could — would be the same. She had had just enough to get her here. If she filled the Jaguar and took the emergency can with her, Julian would not be able to fill his tank. He would be stuck at Four Shields until the people from the station in Dowbridge could get here with a spare can. She would gain an hour or two . . .

The scream across time, the red wall of purest panic, hit her with the force of a blow. The garage disappeared in a flood of terror and agony. The petrol can jerked in her hand and fell, sending a thin stream across the floor. She reeled across the room and hit the wall behind her with a hard thump that brought her, trembling and shaken, back to the present.

The screaming, the sensation of fear, was gone with the same unexpectedness as it had come. It left Marian weak, with her knees trembling uncontrollably. The smell of petrol, the sense of claustrophobia she had felt earlier, combined with the after-shock. She barely managed to reach the door before she doubled over, retching into the grass, the tears falling fast and gathering in the corners of her distorted mouth. For a few minutes she was violently ill.

When she was finally able to draw a clear breath and climb shakily to her feet, she found that the tears would not stop falling. Leaning against the side of the garage, the clean fresh air of the country moving in its healing patterns across her wet face, she was seized with a sense of loss and sorrow. Something had happened. In that hinterland of life and death she was trying to reach, something was very wrong.

Under the spur of her intuition, she managed to recover

herself in a relatively short time. She could not dawdle here, shivering in the morning sun; she must move, must get herself to the settlement somehow. She wiped the cold sweat from her face and forced her weak legs to carry her to the Jaguar.

She coasted the car down the drive, unwilling to turn on the engine in the confines of the garage. The petrol had sunk into the unfinished floorboards, and the room was filled with fumes. Carefully padlocking the front gates behind her, she slid into the driver's seat and turned the key.

A shadow, sweeping and impressive, fell across the hood. It lay there, whatever was casting it not moving, hovering in the sky directly above her. Then it streaked forward towards Dartmoor, circling and waiting.

She turned the car south and followed the hawk.

If Marian had known nothing of the roads she drove down now, if her only guide had been the bright talons of the great raptor shining like steel in the sun, she would still have ended up where she did. The bird's shadow led her past the artillery range, past Tawsand Beacon and past Beacon Tor, a solitary pile casting a long shadow of its own. The morning mist came up, as it had come when the moor was still a vast primordial swamp, and triumphed over the sunlight. You may have the sky and the upper air, it seemed to say, but the ground is mine. It curled around the tyres and slid across the windscreen in thin plumes. The creatures who lived on the moor stayed hidden; no fox or grouse ventured from its hiding place to claim her attention. And the hawk, unwavering, rode the wind that carried it to the settlement.

She got out of the car and stood beside it, staring with a sense of finality at the stone huts on the ridge. The bird crested, soaring, and came to rest on a roof she knew.

The music of the spheres . . . the phrase, heard in her school days and long forgotten, came unbidden to her mind now. Was it something she had read or had she simply thought it for herself, in the way any imaginative child might do? No matter. It was appropriate. Her own breathing was loud against the deep

231

silence that was almost a hum. She seemed to hear the rustle of the rich grasses, the gentle brush as the hawk folded its wings, the very movement of the earth itself as it turned inexorably under her. She listened, wondering, enthralled, in the grip of a strange delight that was new to her.

Without realising it, she had begun to walk, and as she walked she began to sing below her breath. It was a melody, no more than that, formless and without words. She came to the top of the rise and went straight to the stream. For a few minutes she simply stood beside it, staring at the empty village that seemed, in the clear morning light, to have a haze of yellow over it. The air was dense and hard to breathe.

A feeling of helplessness, unexpected and debilitating, washed over her. The air was thick, too thick; it held her here, held her in the present while something too dreadful for imagining was happening in the past. Her gaze shifted from doorway to doorway and then to the bird. It stared back at her, watchful, expectant. The stream babbled behind her.

The stream . . . The idea came to her gradually and, as it did so, the helplessness faded. She had come here before and, each time she had done so, she had come to the stream, to the cool laughing water. She turned her back on the huts and the hawk and stared speculatively at the water.

Could it be? Water, lifegiving and potent; water from which all life had first come and which would strip the flesh from the bones easily and cleanly. Water, which ran through myth and magic as it ran through the gullies, through outstretched fingers . . . Yes, it must be. Obeying the pull of her senses, not stopping to think, she quickly kicked off her shoes and walked to the edge of the flat rock. As she stepped off the edge and felt the shock of the chilly current, the hawk left its perch and floated across the clearing to hover far above her. She closed her eyes and heard it scream, but whether in fear or triumph she could not tell. Eyes closed, head flung back to face the sky, she answered its call as she had done once before. Her guide, her shadow, her guard of honour . . .

Through the blinding darkness of her closed lids, she smelled the first curl of the smoke and heard the voices, and the walls of time dissolved around her.

Chapter 20

As the elders gathered at the locus for the burning, as the hysteria mounted among the tribe, Lun in her basket could hear the first rumbles of distant thunder heralding the night.

She was conscious not of the fear she should have felt but of a vast desolation and confusion. As the gods, as her own luck, had abandoned her, so had she abandoned the physical world around her. In the two days of waiting after the elders had passed their sentence, the world seemed to have fallen away from her. Cryth, Cel, the very staples of everyday life, had faded until they seemed no more than a distant memory. In the extremity of approaching death, the entity that had once been the girl called Lun had contracted into a small tight knot of passionless waiting.

The externals had been stripped away, leaving her bare to what must come. Behind the rough cloth and the wicker, her outer senses had dulled while the inner ones had sharpened. The memory of Asulicca's body, face down in the dust, palms opened to vengeance, was more real to her than the bite of the hemp ropes against her bare skin. She had lain on the red earth of the holy place for two sunsets; in that time she had eaten nothing, taken no water. Her body was a shell, an empty husk both weakened and seasoned by the deprivations it had undergone. She had retreated into a dark corner of her life, awaiting death. It had not occurred to her to test her power. Was she not abandoned by her goddess?

The elders, moving about the locus gathering the hawthorn branches for the fire, were no more than distant echoes against this inner darkness. Yet as she heard the muffled chanting an old anger woke in her, resentment that was warming and very human in origin. She had lost and Bel had won. The goddess had left her servant to die in the flames. Well, she would not go easily. Bel should not have that satisfaction. If the power had gone, along with the luck, so be it. What, after all, could be lost by trying once more?

The concentration came easily; with the distractions of the body completely gone from her, the mind was that much easier to direct. She breathed deeply and evenly and gave over her spirit to the effort. Behind her eyes, the pictures came.

A woman, tall, beautiful, unlike any she had ever seen. A white cup, a white bone. A figure, indistinct and strange, walking through mist into the running water at her command. Her own hands, mixing the herbs to bring sleep. Shades of colour in the mind, blue, grey, gone . . .

'Young one. Can you hear me?'

She began to tremble. What was this come to haunt her?

'Young one. Leave your fear a moment, and listen.'

'Asulicca?' Lun did not know she had whispered aloud. She seemed to have fallen into a vast well of disbelief.

'Yes, young one. It is Asulicca.' The colours were dim and weak, but they were real; the voice flickered, fading in and out like firelight, but it, too, was real.

'I cannot help you, Lunica. I had only power enough, after Clota, to come and give you what comfort I could. But I can change nothing. Do you remember that first day of your power, when I asked you to walk with me down by the stream?' Lun had never imagined so heartbreaking a shade of blue. 'This is what I saw even then. So I came to tell you . . .'

'Yes.' Her own strength was returning. She felt it grow, and with it came a sudden, desperate desire to live. 'Tell me what happened when you called the goddess. Tell me what happened on the night you died.'

235

The air between the colours was black, rank. 'She came, young one. But she was no goddess. I do not know who she was, or where she came from, but she was no goddess.'

The enormity of Asulicca's words, of her very presence, was too great for Lun. She marshalled her thoughts. 'No goddess? I cannot understand your meaning, old one.'

The colours were dimmer now, and very muted.

'It is hard for me, too, my Lunica.' The old voice was very gentle. 'Listen, and try to understand. You believed that you had called a goddess to yourself, that she had given you power. Do you remember the night I initiated you to true power, what I told you then about its trappings? It was true then, and it is the truth now.

'She was no goddess, only a woman from somewhere else, another time perhaps. She gave you nothing, Lun. The power was within you all the time, and you used that power without ever knowing you had it to call this woman to you. Your need for a symbol you could see, for the trappings of power, transmuted her into a goddess in your eyes. Perhaps she is kin to you; perhaps she is a part of you. That is something I do not pretend to know. But I do know that she did not call you to her – you called her to you.'

The first stamping of feet, the chilling rhythm of death in the clearing beyond the wicker basket, rose like the droning of bees on the honeysuckle vine. Asulicca's voice took on an urgency it had lacked, an edge of authority.

'Quickly, young one. You know the truth now; you know what you can do. If there is to be any help, it must come from within you. You must die, nothing can change that, but you can do it yourself. It need not be a hideous death by fire. You can still thwart Bel. It will send him mad, destroy him, if you can show your power and escape his revenge. You have that power. Do you have the strength?'

Smoke, foul and tainted, seeped through the woven slats of her prison. The stamp of feet was mixed with chanting now.

'I have it, Asulicca. Tell me what I must do.'

236

'Then listen well. Forget me, and the false goddess, and the fire. Forget all the world you knew. Give yourself, body and spirit, to the power. Call the rain and the wind. Put out their fire with the thunder. Bring to their locus such a storm of lightning as will raze their holy oaks to the ground. You can do this, Lunica. But do it quickly.'

'I will.' She felt the colours fading, and knew that when they were gone she would have lost the old woman for the last time. A hatred of this second parting made her reach out desperately.

'Asulicca? Will you be here with me?'

'No, young one. I cannot stay any longer. But there is a great bird, a bird you know, in the sky above your head. It will attend the ending. Be sure, I will be watching.'

Blue to grey to gone. The night was empty, barren. The old priestess had gone from her, this time forever. But Lunica had no time to grieve for she was not alone.

The woman had filled the space left by Asulicca as quickly and easily as if she had been waiting. One moment Lun was drawing breath and trying to comprehend her loss; the next a new presence had made itself felt. It was a presence as potent and deep as Lun had ever felt. A woman, that much she could sense. And this voice, too, spoke in colours.

'Who are you, young woman? And where are we?'

On this, the last night of her life, nothing could seem strange to Lun any longer. This new intrusion had a feeling of inevitability and she answered the questions simply.

'I am Lunica. We are waiting to die. Who are you?'

'My name is Marian. Lunica, you said. A very pretty name. But where are we, and why are we waiting to die?'

'You are with me, waiting in the wicker cage,' Lun said patiently. 'I know who you are, I think. You are the woman I saw with the white cup of sacrifice, the woman who stood in the stream. I tried to touch you, that day, but I could not.'

'Yes, that's quite right.' Why such satisfaction? Was this woman, this Marian, so pleased at what had happened?

'I thought you were a goddess,' Lun said dully. 'I thought you

237

had come with power. It is forbidden. That is why the elders are feeding the fire. I will die. But you are not a goddess. Asulicca said . . . '

'Asulicca.' Something in her voice sharpened. 'I know that name, I've heard it. That's the old woman, isn't it? Where is she, Lunica? Why isn't she here, with us? I thought . . . '

'She is dead, Marian. She called to her goddess, she of the night, but you came instead. The elders found her, and she died. I heard her calling in my mind and I went to help her. But I was too late, and the elders took me.'

'The elders.' Everything was hotter now. Smoke had filled the wicker basket, leaving an ugly scent on everything it touched. The presence called Marian had darkened. 'Who are these elders, and by what right do they kill people?'

Lunica found herself puzzled by this, and aware of a growing impatience. Death must come soon and she had done nothing, nothing at all . . . 'They kill whom they choose, Marian, for they are the elders, beloved of the gods. Are there no elders where you come from?'

'Oh, yes, we have elders of a sort. But they have far less control, and they don't pretend to represent heaven.'

A crackle, a lull in the chanting. Lun froze for a moment and then spoke with fury and frustration.

'I cannot speak any longer. Asulicca came back to me, she told me what I must do. Give me room to do it.'

'Whatever you need.' In this grey witch's limbo Marian was decisive. She felt love for this girl, this doppelganger. 'May I help?'

'No. If you do not wish to die, you must go now. For myself, there is only one end. But it will be my way, and I will not go alone. I have lost Cryth and Cel; I have lost Asulicca; I have even lost my life. I have my pride still.'

'Yes, you do.' Marian was calm and still. Death was as close as the girl's yellow eyes, and she waited for it in the same way as did Lun. She had no fear. If there was to be no tomorrow, if she and this girl were one woman now, fear was pointless, shameful and a waste of time. Some vestige of the modern woman, the product of the twentieth century that had been Marian Dunne, came briefly to the surface. For a moment she thought of Julian, remembering his features like a well-known map. She thought of Gemma, of the child she had been and the woman she would become now. Then their faces were gone and she could not recall them. They were as lost to her as Cryth and Cel were to Lunica.

'You sounded as though you thought I'd be afraid to die. I'm not, you know. I'm part of you, or you're part of me, I don't know which. If you die, I die with you. That's why I came tonight. I have no place else to go now.'

A moment's incredulous silence, then Lun spoke.

'Yes, I see now. I understand things that were hidden from me before tonight. Asulicca said to me that you were kin to me, or even part of me. She said I called you, and I did.' The girl's voice was full of wonder. 'And you came. You came tonight to help me, did you not?'

'Yes.' The guilt that had haunted Marian since waking on the sofa in Julian's flat settled on her like cold ashes. She swallowed and continued, her voice hard. 'The old woman called me. She thought I was a god, too, the goddess of the night. She begged me for help. I would have helped her, but I wasn't able to stay. I came to make it up to her but she's dead. It's you and I now, Lunica, and I won't abandon you, no matter what happens.' Smoke climbed in hot wreaths until the air in the basket was useless. There were men's voices, growing louder, and a sense of imminent peril. 'Lunica, whatever you mean to do, do it now.' As the girl seemed to hesitate, Marian added desperately; 'Quickly!'

There were men's hands reaching for the basket, and a sharp cry of command and victory. Marian was suddenly flooded with panic, a sensation that had nothing to do with dying. In her mind's eye she saw the body of Roger Dawkins, and saw how it had happened. He had died at Lun's bequest, at Marian's bequest. Between them they had summoned the storm and sent Roger to his death in the water.

What a waste, she thought, what a bloody awful waste. Panic overcame atavistic instinct and she twisted and writhed in a prison of woven bars.

'Lunica, for the love of god, get on with it!'

Lun reached for the universe and the universe went mad.

'I don't believe it. I simply don't bloody believe it!'

Julian, standing with his hands on his hips in the narrow lane, turned and regarded the mud-spattered Mercedes with frustrated despair. As Gemma spun the window down with an impatient twist of the hand, Julian suddenly gave vent to his feelings and gave the side of the car a resounding kick.

'Out of petrol? Daddy, how can we be? The gauge says we've got about half a tank, for God's sake!'

'The gauge says, the gauge says ... The bloody gauge is obviously broken. And we, my love, are definitely out of petrol.' He kicked the car again. Gemma climbed out.

'How far are we from Okehampton, Daddy? Not very far, surely? There's a petrol station just outside the town.'

'Yes, love, I know.' Julian was sweating profusely, something he rarely did. Gemma watched him for a moment in silence, noting the way his hands opened and shut, shut and opened, like a man grasping for a life raft. She had never seen him this upset. He seemed almost frenzied.

She spoke soothingly. 'Look, Daddy, we can't be more than a mile from the station. I'll jog in and get petrol, and the man will drive me back. It won't take long.'

'All right. I suppose it's all we can do, really.'

Julian wiped a trembling hand across his face; it came away wet. He sounded despairing. 'Get on with it, darling, will you? I have a feeling, a bad feeling ... we're almost out of time.'

She grabbed her purse from the seat of the car and, without another word, turned and began to sprint up the road. In a few moments she disappeared from his view.

Julian lit a cigarette, the last in a continuous line of chain-smoking since pulling out of London. He sat in the passenger

240

seat, letting his legs dangle out into the road. Please, God, don't let them be too late . . .

His thoughts ran in circles, dark tortured things that spiralled round and round in his mind. So engrossed was he in his own consuming panic that he didn't hear the hum of a powerful engine. Nor did he hear that engine stop, or hear the man's voice address him the first time. The second time, however, he did hear it. It was a kindly voice, with a soft West Country drawl. A voice he knew.

'Good morning, Mr. Dunne. You're just the man I was hoping I'd see. Some trouble with the car, is it?'

For a moment Julian, dazzled by the sun and by his own exhaustion, simply stared into the weather-beaten face. His gaze travelled past the man to the vehicle that sat, motor idling, in the shade. The twin of his own sleek Range Rover, the standard issue to the police of Dartmoor. The vehicle that could travel like lightning and take whatever the moor could offer to easily in its powerful trajectory . . .

He found his voice. 'Sergeant Wilking, God, am I glad to see you.' His voice slid up the register, and he fought it back down. 'Sergeant, I need your help.'

'Seems so.' Wilking had noted the hysteria that bubbled below the surface. 'You look fair worried, Mr. Dunne. Is there something wrong, besides the car?' He glanced at the Mercedes and his brows went up. 'That's not yours, surely?'

'No, it's a rental, and it's out of petrol. Sergeant, I must get out to the moor immediately. I think my wife is out there, right now, and I think — I know — she's in trouble.'

Wilking watched him impassively. 'Well, now, Mr. Dunne, I don't know how you'd know that, but I'll help you, certainly. Where on the moor d'ye think she is?' He waved an arm to the south and added, 'It's a big moor.'

Julian, the Mercedes already forgotten, was climbing into the Range Rover. 'At the settlement, you know which one. She has my Jaguar. She took it at about midnight last night. She's — ill, Wilking. I have to get there.' As the policeman made no move,

241

Julian's voice soared. 'For the love of God, man, can't you hurry! I tell you, she's in danger.'

Wilking cocked an eyebrow. Climbing into the car, he turned the key. The Rover's engine gave a shattering roar and the car leaped forward as though kicked. Julian let out his breath raggedly, and slumped against the seat.

Wilking, without losing any of his calm, edged the Rover up to eighty. His voice was almost hypnotically soft.

'Well, Mr. Dunne, we're off. Now, can you tell me what this is all about? I might have to explain it later.'

'Explain it?' Julian gave a harsh snort of laughter. 'I've been — we've been — trying to explain it since it first started, and we haven't yet succeeded. Why should you where we've failed?' He turned in his seat and stared at the policeman.

'You didn't believe us, did you, Sergeant? It sounded so incredible: smoke, and gods, and sacrifices. But it was all true, you know. We told you the precise truth.' Julian laughed again, the laughter of a man who sees a grim joke and knows it is on him. 'Yellow eyes. After the inquest my wife had a fit, a seizure of some sort. She said something about a girl, a girl with yellow eyes, who was waiting for her at the settlement. A few other things, nasty things, happened after that. I took her to London with me.'

They might have been discussing the weather, so casual was Wilking's voice. 'And what happened there?'

Julian turned and stared blindly at the hedgerows glittering in the sunlight as they flashed by. 'Her eyes — her eyes turned yellow. It frightened us, my daughter and I. Marian stole my car last night. She left me a note asking me to sleep on the sofa. When I went in to check on her this morning, she'd gone. She's gone to that bloody settlement; there's no other place she'd go.' Tears welled in his eyes and spilled down his face. He did not seem to notice. 'Won't this thing go any faster?'

'We're doing eighty, Mr. Dunne.' Wilking turned the wheel and the car swung left. 'We'll be there in maybe ten minutes, weather permitting. There's a storm coming up fast.'

Julian jerked his head back. The Range Rover was moving quickly over the outskirts of the moor. To the southwest, a bank of purple and black cloud seemed to be gathering with uncanny speed. In the distance thunder rumbled twice.

'God,' he said, and his face was chalky white. 'Oh, God. Marian, no, not this. Not a storm, not now.'

'We'll get there,' Wilking said, and something in his voice made Julian turn to stare at him, his eyes wide.

'You believed me,' he said slowly. 'You believed us, both of us, all the time. Didn't you? *Didn't you?*'

'Yes.' How could he sound so casual? 'I saw Roger Dawkins' body, Mr. Dunne. He died of fear, plain and simple.'

Julian shook his head. 'Then why didn't you say so? With your help we might have avoided this. Why did you go to the inquest and cover everything up?'

They were passing Beacon Tor, and the air was growing darker by the moment. As the shadow of the mound fell across their hood, a streak of white light split the sky directly over them. Wilking swore, and wrenched the car sideways. On the road beside the tor, a charred and smoking patch of earth showed where the lightning had struck. Julian, watching Wilking, was perversely glad to see that there was, after all, something that could shake even the phlegmatic sergeant.

'That was too close for comfort,' Wilking said, and put his foot down hard. The car surged forward, and Wilking spoke without taking his eyes from the road. In the gathering darkness he looked reassuringly solid.

'Why didn't I get up and tell a room full of nice, middle-class Church of Englanders that the local librarian had been killed by supernatural means? Come now, Mr. Dunne, you're not a fool. Do you think that one single person at that inquest would have understood, or believed, a word of it? It would have caused talk of the worst kind. D'ye think I wanted to put the boy's mother through that? Wasn't her son's death enough for her?'

'No, they wouldn't have believed you. So what? What in hell does their belief matter?' Julian was shaking with anger and

243

reaction. 'But you might have got back to us, to tell us that you believed us. You might have given us some support, damn you! You were in charge, you saw Marian, the night it happened. You knew, you bloody knew, that she hadn't got into that state for no reason. You had only to ring us up, tell us you believed us, tell us you thought we hadn't run mad. It would have given us a weapon, Wilking, something to fight this thing with.'

He was crying now, his balled fists pummelling ceaselessly against his own knees. 'Damn you. Would that have cost you so much, to do that?'

'I did try to call you.' Mist had surrounded them now, eddying violently, obscuring the dangerous patches in the road. The sky outside was almost black, and the first hard drops of rain splashed against the windscreen. 'I tried to call you three days ago, at Four Shields. I got no reply. Where do you think I was going when I found you on the road back there? To get your London number from the town office.'

'Jesus,' said Julian. A large shape swept screaming before them and disappeared into the roiling clouds. In the short time since they had come to the moor, the wind had risen. It was now a steady howl, the sound of nature gone mad or an animal in pain. The car was buffetted, and Wilking's hands seemed to be fighting the wheel.

'I didn't try to call you earlier because I had some research of my own to do. After what your wife told me, after what I'd seen myself, I sat down and read through those books, the ones Roger Dawkins had with him when he died.'

'Timing is everything, Sergeant.' Julian spoke softly, and wondered where the words had come from but there was no time to wonder. As Wilking turned the corner that led to the settlement path, a large object loomed up out of the rain.

Had Wilking been a less experienced driver on this stark terrain they might both have been killed. The Range Rover was heavier than the Jaguar, but the Jag had been left directly across the middle of the road, blocking it. On the blind curve, it was a potentially lethal trap. The brakes screamed like a wounded creature as Wilking, shouting something incomprehensible, fought to keep the Range Rover under control. Then the tyres slipped on the wet surface, locked and skidded. There was a shriek of metal tearing like paper as the two cars hit, and a roar that deadened even the thunder. A pillar of light lit the clouds from below as the Jaguar's petrol tank exploded into flame.

Julian found himself standing in the road, his knees shaking. What was left of the inferno that had been the Jaguar was surrounded by a spreading puddle that might have been water; so hard was the driving rain that the earth was soaked black. But the smell was not water, it was petrol, and it was running, in a small burning river, straight towards the Range Rover where the unconscious Wilking lay slumped against his seat, unaware of his danger.

'Wilking!' Julian splashed through the petrol, running only a few feet from the Range Rover now, and moving fast. He wrenched the driver's door open and pulled with his full strength. The man's body, a thin line of scarlet trickling down one cheek, was a dead weight against him.

More petrol, drops of it at first and now a gush poured from the Rover's ruptured tank. Julian pulled as hard as he could and staggered back as Wilking's limp body came free of the car. With one arm clenched under the policeman's armpits, Julian began to drag him clear.

Then the world exploded and the ground beneath his feet was gone. The line of burning petrol reached the tangled mass of metal that had been the Range Rover's front end. The sound of their meeting was so cataclysmic that it could hardly be described as sound at all. Rather, it was a lunatic vibration, an earthquake, a sonic boom of unknown proportion. It lifted the two men, so oddly entwined, like a pair of leaves and hurled them into the soft grass of the hillside some twenty feet away.

To Julian, his mouth full of earth, time seemed to have suspended its rules. He did not know whether he had remained conscious after the impact but found himself lying a few feet from Wilking. He checked that the policeman was breathing,

245

and dragged himself to his feet. His right collar bone throbbed with pain. 'Broken,' he thought hazily, 'fractured, but at least Wilking is alive. But let him tend to himself, I have no time left, no time.' He promptly forgot the other man and his own pain, and began to climb the steep hillside to the village.

The storm was like nothing he had ever seen. Colours that were running sores of purple and red shot through the clouds and melted to hellish blotches in the pulse of the winds. The sky gave him no help, no light; only the two cars, burning in tandem, showed him the way. He almost lost his footing and slid down the hill as a fresh explosion shook the ground. The fire had found the emergency petrol cans that had been stored in the rear of Wilking's car and was feeding on them, expanding, a greedy, all-consuming demon.

He was exhausted, his energy almost spent. He dropped to his knees, gritting his teeth against the pain this motion sent rocketing through his shoulder, and grasped the tufts of wet grass for anchorage. The wind was gleeful, mindless, ultimately and purely violent. It seemed to Julian that it blew straight into his face, trying to keep him from reaching the top of the hill. But the summit was in sight . . .

He pulled himself over the edge, his cry of agony at the grinding of his collar bone swept away into the throat of the storm, and turned, standing, to face the clearing.

'I've gone mad,' he thought, 'I've lost my mind, I'm raving, dying. I'm not seeing this. I am not seeing this . . .'

Male bodies, five of them, brown and hooded. Four lay dying, fists clenched, muscles contorted. They were shades, only shades, incorporeal. Through the lashing rain Julian saw the pebbles on the ground beneath them. An oak tree – surely there had not been an oak tree here before? And where were the huts, the empty doorways gaping like black holes?

The fifth man, though fading as Julian watched, was still alive. He was moving, struggling with something. It was a basket woven of blackthorn wicker. He seemed to be dragging it towards a spectral fire in the heart of the clearing. And the basket was rocking. There was something inside . . .

'Marian,' Julian whispered. 'Marian?' The scene was fading, dissolving before his eyes. One robed body on the ground twitched, shuddered, and was gone; a second, curled into a foetal ball, shook and faded. The oak was swaying wildly in the wind; in the sky above this scene from hell, a hawk spiralled wildly, its beak open. He thought he heard it shrieking, then realised it was his own cry.

'Move,' he thought, 'I must move. Why can't I move?' With the thought, his feet were at last stumbling across the clearing. Something caught the edge of his vision; a pair of women's shoes, beige high heels. He knew them well; lying discarded on the rock that jutted from earth to water, they looked both pathetic and terrifying.

There were shapes surfacing in the maelstrom that had not been here a moment ago. That dark shadow was a hut and, yes, there was another. The fire, the oak, the man in the robe, were translucent ghosts. The bird was real, and the shoes, and the basket. He could be sure of nothing else. But Marian was here; he could sense her, feel her. And he knew where she was.

'In the basket,' he whispered, and the sky above him cracked open in a roll of thunder. The world and the sky rocked and fragmented. 'Basket,' he said aloud, and then his hands were on it, the woven branches rough and tangible against his palms. He looked across it at the phantom on the other side. With one swift gesture his good arm shot forward and wrenched away the concealing hood.

They stared at one another, in the long moment before the world ended, stared into each other's eyes. Grey met black, and saw the madness there. The eyes locked, mirrors out of time. Julian, staring into the face of desire and insanity, still potent across two thousand years, did not hear the sound of the car screaming to a halt at the foot of the hill. He heard nothing of the footsteps scrabbling up the hill, of the girl's voice screaming at him. He was lost in time.

His hands steady, his eyes never moving, he reached for the

thick hemp bands that held the basket closed and ripped them free. The top rolled to one side. A small brown hand shot triumphantly skyward. The hand was fisted in a parody of a military salute. The bird screamed.

Light, an intolerable firestorm of light. As far away as Plymouth, the sky went up in a pyrotechnic display the like of which even the residents of that stormy country had never seen before. It was as though, the local papers said, every crackling shaft of electricity that the cosmos could hold had gathered in the sky above the moor and unleashed itself in one blinding bolt, straight at the Iron Age village that had once stood there. Closer to home, in Dowbridge and Okehampton, some people thought the bomb had been dropped.

It struck the clearing without a sound. It took the basket and the men locked in their eternal struggle, and reduced them to ash. Nothing could withstand that heat; stone crumbled, the huts toppled into grey ash. In the stream that ran along the northern edge of the settlement, the water began to bubble and then to evaporate. The great flat rock split with a deafening crack, sliding into the stream bed.

There was silence, deep and empty. Earth and sky took stock of each other and breathed again.

After a while, the girl who had been thrown down the side of the hill when the sky lit up, got slowly to her feet. She had a burn on one hand, the one she had been using to pull herself up to her father when the lightning struck, and her face was filthy, car oil and soot mixed with tears to leave lines of grime from cheek to chin. She dashed a hand across her eyes and looked up at the sky.

It was clearing already, as she had guessed it might. And the air was full of smoke, the dark smell that no one who has been where lightning strikes can ever forget. The smoke was threaded with something even uglier.

As she stood staring at the hill above her, something floated through the ash and the now gentle rain and landed at her feet: a buff-coloured feather, charred at the edges.

'Daddy? Mum?' Gemma's voice was soft. There could be no

answer, she knew that. Yet she climbed the hill, her bent shoulders washed by the returning sunlight. In the road below her, two burned-out shells that had been automobiles lay like fossils dredged up from the swamp. The man she had stumbled over still lay there, breathing with the slow, thin rale of concussion.

She stood at the edge of the clearing, gazing with unseeing eyes at the blackened and empty place before her.

The devastation was absolute. Where short tufts of grass and gorse had forced their way through the hard and rocky soil, there were great oily streaks. Where the huts had stood, silent and watchful, there were heaps of ugly, unidentifiable rock, piled in a crazy jumble, one upon the other. In the heart of the destruction lay a small, charred corpse, all that remained of some bird, a hawk perhaps. Gemma looked down at the feather she clutched in one fist, holding the burnt trophy like a talisman against evil.

She turned her back on the settlement and went, slowly and carefully, back down the hill to where the unconscious man and the Mercedes waited. In the distance, a siren began to wail, the sound of modern man keening for the dead.

Gemma sat in the car, not hearing, thinking of nothing at all, and all around her the afternoon began its slow descent towards night.

Epilogue

In the house called Four Shields all was quiet. A spider, its senses tuned to the slight vibration along the slim strands of its web, moved cautiously towards the moth that struggled hopelessly in the web's heart. Dust settled on the tables and along the floor boards. Two white cups lay in the sink, the orange detritus of tea a week old hardening in their bottoms.

In the long building that had once held horses, a small flicker of smoke rose in a lazy spiral from floor to roof. The dark line of petrol soaked a little further towards the building's foundations, and met some inner heat. From that meeting came the first wisp of flame, the smallest tongue of it, eating its slow way through the wood of the garage to catch and dance along the walls, and then reaching the house itself, the spider, the cups, the half-eaten moth.

The sirens laughed in the distance, as time held steady and the taste of hot ash was carried south on the summer wind, settling at last like dust on the great moor.